Revenge in the Rogue's Hideaway

THE KIER AND LEVETT MYSTERY SERIES
BOOK 4

DEB MARLOWE

ARE YOU SIGNED UP FOR DRAGONBLADE'S BLOG?

You'll get the latest news and information on exclusive giveaways, exclusive excerpts, coming releases, sales, free books, cover reveals and more.

Check out our complete list of authors, too!

No spam, no junk. That's a promise!

Sign Up Here

www.dragonbladepublishing.com

Dearest Reader;

Thank you for your support of a small press. At Dragonblade Publishing, we strive to bring you the highest quality Historical Romance from some of the best authors in the business. Without your support, there is no 'us', so we sincerely hope you adore these stories and find some new favorite authors along the way.

Happy Reading!

CEO, Dragonblade Publishing

For all the readers who have taken
Kara and Niall into their hearts.
Thank you!

Prologue

Lambeth, London 1852
The Rogue's Hideaway

THE ROGUE'S HIDEAWAY was packed to the rafters. The stage lights prevented Miss Josie Lowe from seeing all seven hundred of the music hall's patrons, but she felt the weight of their gazes—and she knew she had them all in the palm of her hand.

Tonight she was debuting a new song, one she'd written herself, with help from Old Tom Barrett, the musical director hired to make the Hideaway's performances the best and most talked about in London. It was a heartfelt ballad, and Josie knew she was taking a risk, allowing so much raw emotion and vulnerability to come through her vocals. But she felt this anthem, deep in her soul. It was a plea, a wish made out loud in song, a longing to find a love worthy of surrender, one of shared intensity and intimacy.

There had been a dimming of the noise in the hall when she took the stage. She hadn't wanted to leave her acting career at the Adelphi Theatre, where she'd been becoming known for her ability to swing between comedic and dramatic skills and her ability to summon tears exactly when called for. But her patron, her *keeper*, for want of a better word, had wished it, and he had set about making it happen. She didn't know exactly how Frederick Cole had done it, but he had the money and influence to move governments and industries. The manager of the Adelphi hadn't had a chance.

So, here she stood, on the stage before the smoke-fogged rows of tables, a shining bar below and packed galleries above. The Hideaway's Winsome Warbler, they had billed her, but she had insisted her name be included, and she had decided to approach this new career in her own way.

Thus, the new song. Her truest wish sung out loud. And it had not been a mistake. She could feel it. The ever-present, low hum of conversation had stopped. Every eye was upon her. Every ear strained to hear the pleading emotion of her song. When she drew out the last, heart-wrenching line, there was a moment of utter silence. Unnerved, she straightened from her curtsy. As she looked out, the applause began and the shouting rang out. The audience surged to their feet. They called out her name and screamed their demand to hear the song again.

The stage manager beckoned her. She made another curtsy and ran off stage to the gathering of the grinning, congratulatory stage crew.

"Listen to 'em!" one of the light men said. "She'll have to give them an encore."

Josie looked to the stage manager. He gave her a nod. "A different one. Lighter. Make them come back tomorrow to hear it again."

Nodding, she straightened her green silk skirts and strode back out to the approving roar of the crowd.

Her jaunty, slightly naughty tune was nearly as well received. Blowing a kiss to the orchestra, she left the stage and took a moment to enjoy the quiet celebration in the wings before she headed to her dressing room. Dropping into her chair, she grinned at the mirror and tossed back a glass of chilled wine. She was just pouring another when her door opened and Elias Wade slipped in.

Josie raised a brow and the bottle, inviting the slim young man to have a drink, but he shook his head. "He's asking for you." His thin face looked starkly worried. "I don't think he's doing well. I encouraged him to go home early." He pressed his lips together. "He was not pleased with the suggestion."

She sighed. She was not going to be allowed to enjoy her triumph, then. "Very well. Let me powder my nose and I'll go out to him."

The boy slipped out. Josie finished her wine, touched up her makeup, set a smile on her face, and went out to dance attendance on her patron.

It took her a few moments to work her way through the crowd to Frederick's favorite table. She nodded and smiled and offered thanks for the audience's praise, but at last she reached the table midway between the stage and the bar, tucked into the shadows. Frederick Cole sat alone there, staring into the candle flame at the center of the table. He had his hands wrapped around one of the special goblets Robert West, the owner of the Rogue's Hideaway, had presented to him.

Kissing his temple, she took the seat next to him. "Well, Freddie, it galls me to say it, but I think you might have been right. Did you feel that? That was theater *magic*. I do believe that song just might make me famous."

He continued to frown into the flame. At first, she thought it might be because of the overfamiliar nickname. She was the only one allowed to use it, and he didn't care for her to abuse the privilege. But then she noted the sheen of sweat on his brow.

"Frederick? Are you well?" She clutched his wrist. "Are you feverish?"

"What? No," he said with an irritated wave of his hand that shook off her grip. "It's chilly in here. Isn't it?"

"No," she said flatly. It was overwarm with the heat of so many bodies.

"I've a headache," he said with a groan. "I swear, I can feel my heartbeat bouncing around like a child's ball in my brain."

"Perhaps we should call a doctor," Josie said, concerned.

"No, no." He clutched his fist to his chest. "My heart is racing like a thoroughbred, but it will settle down in a moment." He looked up suddenly. "That's a bilious color, Susanna," he said harshly. "You shouldn't wear that shade of yellow."

"Susanna?" She frowned. "Frederick, it's me, Josie."

He shook his head, dismissing her. "No one should wear that shade. I can't imagine anyone looking good in it." He frowned down at the table. "And what is Robert doing, using the same ugly color for the table linen?" He made a face at her. "You should go and change. That yellow is vile."

Puzzled, she glanced down at her green gown.

"That song..." His words trailed away. He glanced about, looking over both shoulders, his frown deepening.

"It was well received, wasn't it?" she asked gently.

He looked at her again, and she frowned at the blank look on his face. He stared, almost as if he didn't recognize her. "It reminded me of my mother."

"The song?"

"Aye. She had that tone, that reverence, when she spoke of my father."

"I see."

His gaze grew distant. "Fanny's grandam was a seer, you see. On her fifth birthday, the old woman grabbed Fanny's hands. She stared at her with only the whites of her eyes and told her she was meant for a prince. *He will carry you off in a gilded carriage and give you a child—a rogue with the pocketbook of a prince, if not the name of one.*"

"Goodness, that's quite a heavy prediction to burden a five-year-old with," Josie protested.

"Fanny knew it was her fate. She went on stage for her life's work. One day, in the green room, she caught sight of Prince Frederick, the Duke of York. They locked gazes, and she went silently across the room to take his hand and sit in his lap. She was a pretty girl. He was young and used to attention, but he was much struck by her simple assumption that she was his. He did sweep her off to a lovely set of rooms, where she stayed until he tired of her—but by then, she had her babe in her belly."

"You," she said quietly. She had heard the story before, but not in such detail, nor in this sentimental tone. "You were the babe in her belly."

"Yes. I was her rogue." He laughed suddenly and looked himself again. "And I did work my way to possess the purse of a prince, did I not?"

Smiling, Josie reached for his hand, but he surged suddenly to his feet, knocking over his goblet of wine. He staggered a step away, then another. He made a choking sound, then vomited.

"Frederick!"

Ladies shrieked and men protested. Frederick looked toward the ceiling and fell. He landed on his side, curled up, his face stretched into a grimace.

"Frederick!" Josie looked up into the crowd of rapt faces. "Hurry! A doctor! Someone fetch a doctor!"

She knelt down and took his hand. He clutched his chest and curled tightly into a ball. Then, abruptly, he relaxed. He sucked in a breath. His head turned and he looked at her with fondness. With a last sigh, he was gone.

"No! Frederick! No!"

"All the saints preserve us!" a woman said loudly into the shocked silence around them. She pointed to the table, where the goblet had spilled. Red wine stained the tablecloth. Mixed in with it was a plethora of green flecks.

"Poisoned!" the woman cried. She looked aghast at Josie. "Murdered!"

Chapter One

MISS KARA LEVETT turned the last screw on her specially shaped gear. Carefully, she connected the rod for this last leg to the stylus that would provide the motion. Holding her breath, she started the clockwork motor.

The cams began to turn. The stylus began to move, driving the rods. The open channels she'd drilled into the gear allowed for the correct movements. Yes. Everything fell into place, and the clockwork legs began to take on the sequence of a horse's gallop. Left hind foot. Right hind. Left front. Right front. Suspension. She sighed in relief.

"It worked, then?"

She grinned at Harold, who sat at the other end of the table with a less complicated mechanism before him. The boy's blond hair shone in the bright light of the laboratory, but it was not quite as luminous as his happy smile. "It did. I think I have the timing done right, at last."

"I knew you would."

Her heart twisted a little. The boy, rapidly turning into a young man, had been a street urchin last year, when she'd met him during the Great Exhibition. He'd witnessed a murder in a courtyard outside the Crystal Palace and was instrumental in helping her to prove that she had not been the culprit. With the benefits of shelter, food, and care, he'd grown several inches since then. He'd also made a heroic effort to learn to speak without his street cadence and habits.

"You see so many horses in a day's time," he pondered. "Who woulda thought their gait could be so complicated, it would force you to split your project in two?"

Kara grinned at his careful pronunciation of the letter H. "The client's original vision was lovely, but the clockwork needed to re-create all the different gaits of a horse would prove to be too bulky for a good, realistic design." She smiled back. "In any case, crafting both the racehorse and the clock gives you a chance to learn some basics."

"Aye, and I think I got this to rights." He gestured toward the small, roughly human-shaped clockwork figure before him.

"Let's see."

Harold checked a fitting, then reached below to turn a larger gear. The little figure lifted its arm as the tiny metal hand rotated to face upward.

"Well done, indeed."

The boy beamed. She'd first found him a place with her friend Maisie and her son, who ran a bake shop. Harold had been happy there, and enjoyed helping in the shop as well as carrying baskets of baked goods into the streets to sell. But the addition of Maisie's new man had rendered the household a bit crowded. Kara had seized the opportunity to offer the boy a room here at her estate in Bluefield Park—along with an opportunity to do some apprentice work in her laboratory. Harold had eagerly accepted—after bargaining for some lessons from her betrothed, Mr. Niall Kier, as well.

"Now that this is sorted, may I go to the forge?" Harold stood. "I'm to learn how to put a fuller into a blade next."

Kara smiled at his eagerness. "Of course. We'll start on your smaller, walking horse next time, and perhaps we'll start working on finishing your clockwork man, so that he resembles the client's husband."

"I spoke to Turner about it," he replied, standing to remove his apron. "He said he could sew some boots from leather scraps."

"A grand idea. Turner is endlessly useful." And thankfully, her butler, friend, and lab assistant had not objected to her teaching Harold to help out with her projects.

The lad bent over to spin the gear again and observe his work. He grinned in satisfaction at her before heading for the door at a clip.

It opened just as he reached it. Gyda Winther yelped in surprise and pressed back against the door as Harold surged past her. "Whoa, boy!"

"Sorry, Gyda!" The lad kept going.

"Is he heading for the forge?" Gyda asked as she came in. "Niall's expecting him."

"Of course. Didn't you see the smile on his face?" Kara gave her friend a grin and a shrug. "Gears and gadgets cannot compete with fire, flame, and the pounding of iron."

"No, it cannot," Gyda said, wiggling her own soot-stained fingers. "Harold is enamored of all of that, of course, but he also loves Niall's attention." Her mouth twisted. "And that of the steady parade of maids who still find an excuse to pass by."

Kara laughed. "Do I need to give him the same talk I gave you about sparing the maids?"

"Oh, he's not progressed past staring out of the corner of his eye and flushing yet. But I'll keep an eye on him."

"Thank you." Kara sighed in satisfaction. "He does seem to have settled in. He absorbs knowledge and direction like a sponge."

"He wants to please you both," Gyda noted. "But I've also seen that he enjoys the days when he goes back to help Maisie out." She nodded as she took a seat at the worktable. "You are doing a good job, giving the boy options and allowing him to explore them." She raised her brows. "In any case, it's not him I'm worried about. I've come to ask you a question."

Kara waited expectantly.

"Why in seven hells is Niall so damned jumpy? Do you know?"

Kara's smile faded. "You've just sat down, but do you mind walking with me while we talk?"

Gyda took up her coat again. "Grab a cloak. There's a chill in the air."

They made their way out into the winter sunshine. Kara glanced askance at her friend. "It's only been a short while, Gyda. For his entire life, only Niall and Lord Stayme have known who he is, who his mother and grandsire were. Now the truth has been exposed. You and I and Rob and our friends know, as do several villains and assorted policemen and government officials. Word is bound to spread, both at his home in Scotland and here in London."

"But why does that make him flinch at every unexpected sound, watch faces in the street, and frown at his work all day long?"

Kara pulled her wrap closer. "He feels vulnerable, I suspect." She sighed. "Stayme has put him further on edge. The viscount feels that the queen and those around her will now have learned of his existence—and they will not be happy about it."

Gyda looked offended. "They should be *grateful* to him! To all of us, for that matter. We averted a crisis that might have caused great harm to them—and to England."

"We did. And Stayme says that gratitude is not a comfortable emotion for the queen, or for anyone in power. He says their response will depend on which of her vanities and advisors will hold sway."

"Their response? There has not even been an acknowledgment, not in all of these weeks. Not even a card of thanks. I daresay there never will be."

"Perhaps not. Or perhaps Niall will find himself at the mercy of a press gang. Or knocked about and sent off halfway across the world to the colony in New South Wales."

"They wouldn't dare!"

Kara lifted a shoulder. "Stayme has convinced Niall it is a possibility. He says there will be a reaction, eventually. They are both holding their breath and waiting to see what it will be."

Gyda looked thoughtful. "I suppose that is why Niall's schedule has been so erratic lately? He says that we must work hard to get to as many commissions on our list as possible, and yet I never know if I will find him here or at the White Hart. He even spent a night at the club at Lake Nemi."

"He's spent a few nights at the Druid's Grove, as well." They had approached the outbuilding that housed Niall's forge, where two of the walls had been pushed back to leave the place open to the air. Kara paused to take in the scene. The forge was lit, shining bright and so hot she could feel it from here. Harold already had iron in the fire. Niall stood near, watching closely as the boy removed his piece to the anvil. Niall had his dark hair tied back and wore his old kilt and worn linen shirt—a comfortable ensemble that showed off his wide chest and muscled legs, making it a favorite with Kara, as well.

Niall handed the boy a chisel and corrected the angle of it before Harold began to strike. He allowed pride and approval to show in his face when the boy glanced up from his blows.

Heat, pleasure, and contentment warmed Kara from the inside out. Niall had a giving heart to go with those broad shoulders and powerful limbs. He was a good man as well as a strong one. Not the sort that Society expected a baron's daughter to accept, but Kara was thrilled to know that he was hers and she was his.

Gyda gave her a knowing look. "And how has all of this waiting and breath-holding affected the pair of you?"

Kara sighed and lifted a brow at her friend. "He's withdrawn a bit," she admitted. "After everything that happened with the League, we had a couple of blissful weeks just resting, talking—"

"And cuddling," Gyda interrupted. "It was both lovely and revolting."

Kara laughed. "It was *only* lovely," she countered with a sigh of remembrance. "He's being careful now. I think he fears that I will get caught up in whatever comes his way. He's been a bit ridiculous, trying not to travel with me or be seen with me outside of Bluefield."

"Well, where is the fun in that?" Gyda demanded. "You are betrothed now. If the government knows enough to understand his background, then they will also know of you and your relationship."

"Exactly as I have said! Now repeat that to Niall and perhaps he will listen to you."

Gyda snorted. "You know him well enough to know he will not listen to me—or to anyone—once he's got a maggot in that brain of his."

"I know." Kara sighed with resignation.

"And what about the banns?" Gyda asked. "Not that I've set foot in your village church, but surely I would have heard, had they been read. When are we going to have a wedding?"

"When Niall is ready to commit to one, I should think," answered Kara. "I am trying to step back and allow him the freedom to work through it all." She gave a little laugh. "But you are not the only one to ask. The vicar has called twice."

Gyda laughed. "Shall I speak to Niall for you?"

"No." Kara shook her head. "He feels vulnerable in a way that he never has before. He will adjust."

Gyda looked as if she might argue, but suddenly Turner was approaching, looking upset and sounding out of breath.

And Niall was there, right at her side, before Turner could even speak. "What is it?" he demanded.

"A message," Turner gasped, holding out a folded and sealed missive. "The boy says it is from Miss Lowe. He says there has been a murder! And Josie Lowe has been taken up by the coroner's officer."

≫≫≪≪

NIALL HANDED KARA up into the carriage. "Perhaps it would be better if I took the train."

"Don't be ridiculous, Niall," she responded lightly. "Gyda has already taken that route. She left early enough, and she'll likely arrive in time to make the change to the next train. We'd never make the connection, and then we'd have to wait. We'll do better to take the carriage to Lambeth."

Still, he hesitated.

Kara leaned toward him. "I think it must be urgent. Josie seems to me to be the sort who protects her privacy. It seems she never likes to present anything but the image of a woman of success and potential. She would not have easily asked for help. I think we should hurry, if we can."

Sighing in resignation, he climbed in and settled opposite her, in the middle of the bench and sitting all the way back. It was his best chance of being unobserved from the outside.

The carriage started off, and he stared out the window. "Perhaps it would be better if I do not get involved."

Kara's head reared back. "Of course you should," she said sharply. "Josie helped us get you out of that warehouse, simply because Gyda requested it of her. She helped us all to bring down the League of Dissolution. We owe her whatever aid we can provide."

"I don't wish to make matters worse," he said quietly.

His betrothed's expression softened. "You could not."

"Couldn't I?" He raised a brow. "If I am marked for suspicion and disfavor, Josie might look the worse for being associated with me."

Pausing, Kara acknowledged the truth of that with a nod. "We don't yet know that any such attitudes have been assigned to you. We don't know what will come to pass." Reaching over, she squeezed his hand. "Whatever comes, though, Niall—we will face it together."

The carriage approached the end of Bluefield's long drive. He leaned back further as they approached the gates. "Move over to the window and look outside," he told her. "Do you see a man on the road? He will be walking, or perhaps leading a mount. He'll have a long woolen overcoat with one cape and a bulb of a nose that he cannot hide, even if he casts his face down as we pass. Do you see him?"

Niall saw her stiffen.

"Yes. He's there. He looks as if he is just walking by." She turned back to him, worry in her lovely, dark eyes. "Who is he?"

"I don't know. I found him in the same spot two days ago. Last night, he spent hours in the taproom of the White Hart."

Kara cursed softly. "Did he, now?"

"We cannot interfere with him." Niall could not hide his resentment. "Stayme has forbidden it." He had argued with his oldest friend and mentor, but the viscount had won. "He says there is too great a risk that we will make matters even worse."

She looked as frustrated as he felt.

"*Something* is coming," he said through a clenched jaw. "And it appears I can only sit and wait for it."

"Let it come."

Moving across to his bench, Kara pressed close to his side. Relenting, he lifted an arm and put it around her, breathing her in. As always, she smelled of floral, frilly, feminine soap—sharpened by the tang of metal filings.

"Whatever it is, you won't face it alone," she vowed.

He wouldn't *suffer* it alone—that was the fear that haunted him. Kara had been patient, waiting for him to admit he carried secrets. She'd never asked for more than he'd been able to give. And when it had all finally come out, she'd handled the discovery of his background with aplomb. She'd accepted and loved him both before and after—and he could not repay her with pain and upheaval.

"Whatever has happened with Josie, I cannot believe she is

involved in any murder," Kara continued with a sigh. "Let us see what the situation is. If she needs assistance in proving her innocence, then perhaps it will keep us occupied while we wait."

Niall pulled her closer and took comfort in her soft warmth as they made their way into London and toward Lambeth. Kara straightened as they rolled down Kennington Lane, toward the police court.

"There is a crowd outside," she said in surprise.

"Attracted to a possible murder?" Niall surmised. "Or perhaps they've come for Josie? The Rogue's Hideaway has been wildly successful. Gyda mentioned her popularity has been growing there."

The coachman pulled up away from the crowd. Niall gave Kara his hand as she descended, then kept her behind him as they pushed their way through. The crush of people was indeed debating a murder. Some appeared incensed that Miss Josie Lowe was being held inside.

"I heard her sing, just moments before that bloke died," one young man announced. "I tell you, that voice is a gift straight from on high. And there is no possible way that angel's voice belongs to someone who could kill a man in cold blood."

"Who knows what folks is capable of," a dour woman intoned. "And slipping a dose of poison in a cup is not the same as stabbing them outright."

"Who is it who has died, though?" Kara whispered to Niall as they broke through and entered the court building.

Gyda was there. She was arguing with a constable guarding a door leading to the right wing of the building. "Niall! Kara! Thank the gods you are here. This idiot will not allow me to see Josie."

"We are also here to see Miss Lowe, sir," Kara said politely. "Please, let us through."

The constable lifted his chin. "The officer who brought her in is out conducting interviews. He bade me keep the riffraff outside."

"Riffraff?" Niall, his patience already strained, growled at the man. "I am Mr. Niall Kier. These are Miss Kara Levett and Miss Gyda Winther. We are friends of Miss Lowe and here at her request. I assure you, we are not strangers. Not to Miss Lowe and not to the workings of the justice system."

"Kier? Levett?" The officer's eyes rounded. "Them what's solved those murders?" He drew himself up straighter. "His nibs is already worked up over the crowd outside. He won't want you mucking about in his enquiry."

Kara stiffened. "I doubt he'd want me going outside and riling that crowd up with talk of Miss Lowe being kept alone and isolated without cause."

The constable sneered. "You wouldn't."

"Has the lady seen anyone at all?" Gyda demanded.

"No one!"

"Has she been arrested or charged with a crime?" asked Niall.

The constable started to look uncomfortable. "No. Not yet."

Niall stared down at the man. "So you are holding a young lady without charge, and without allowing her counsel or solace? You've taken up a girl without cause and treated her like a criminal?" He glanced down at Kara. "I think Inspector Wooten should hear of this. He'll take it straight to the commissioner."

"She's a witness," the constable began.

Kara sniffed. "And thus she should be treated as your *ally*."

Niall fought with a smile as she turned to look at him. "You tell Wooten," she said with determination as she turned on her heel. "I will tell the crowd outside just how the Lambeth Police Court treats a witness to a crime."

Niall cast the constable a sympathetic look. "Good luck to you. I hope you can solve crimes without witnesses. I doubt you'll see much cooperation once word of this travesty gets out." He turned to follow Kara.

The constable shifted, clearly in the throes of indecision.

They reached the door.

"Wait!" The officer's shoulders slumped. "You can see her. But you'd best make it quick and be gone before the coroner's officer returns."

Chapter Two

I T WAS NOT a cell they'd kept Josie in, Kara was glad to see. The door opened onto a small room with a long window close to the ceiling. It held a decently plush chair with a table next to it. The floor was covered with a colorful, only slightly shabby carpet.

The cot in the corner gave her pause, though.

"Oh, Gyda!" The actress had been sitting in the chair, looking composed. She allowed Gyda to sweep her into an embrace, but promptly gave way to tears that were swiftly accompanied by a round of deep, racking sobs.

"Oh, my dear," Gyda crooned. She held Josie tight as she cried, only loosening her grip when the young lady began to regain control. "What is it?" she asked gently. "What's happened?"

"Frederick is dead!" Josie said in an agonized whisper. She began to cry again.

Kara exchanged a glance with Niall, who shook his head. Neither of them, then, had met Mr. Frederick Cole, but they knew of the notoriously wealthy industrialist and financier who acted as Josie's patron—among other roles, it was widely assumed.

The girl took a deep breath and stepped back, wiping her

eyes. She still wore last evening's gown, a green, textured silk nipped in at her tiny waist with lovely full skirts adorned with matching dyed lace. Kara watched as the young lady sought calm. She was surely drawing on the discipline that must have helped her succeed in the competitive world of London's theaters. "I'm afraid they mean to accuse me," she said in a wavering voice. "But I did not kill him!"

"Of course you didn't," Kara said, stepping forward. "Come, sit down." She cast Niall a grateful look as he pulled the cot nearer. Josie took the chair, and she and Gyda sat on the cot, within reach. Niall went to prop himself up in a corner.

"Tell us what happened, Josie, and we will do all we can to help you." Kara stopped, waiting out a delicate beat. "Someone in the crowd outside mentioned poison?"

"Yes, I think it must have been poison," Josie said with a nod. "Frederick was acting so oddly. And he stumbled a little when he stood, spilling his wine. He vomited and collapsed. He went into a fit and then just...died." She swallowed hard. "A woman from a table nearby started to scream. She pointed at the spilled wine, and we all saw the green flakes mixed in, spread across the tablecloth."

"Green flakes? Do you remember anything else about them?"

"They were flat. There were a lot of them."

"How big?" Kara asked.

Josie made a face. "I only caught a glimpse." She held up her index finger. "But you could likely fit five of them on the tip of my finger."

"Big enough to notice, then," Kara mused. "Wouldn't Frederick have seen them through his wineglass?"

Josie's eyes widened. "No. At the Hideaway, he drinks from special metal goblets. They were a gift from Robert, the owner of the club."

"So, unless he looked directly down into his drink, he might not have noticed anything," Kara said, thinking out loud.

"You said Frederick was acting oddly?" Niall said from his

corner. "Can you tell us how?"

The actress drew a breath and frowned. "He was scowling down at the candle on the table. I thought he was angry at first, but instead he seemed...confused. Addled. He called me by the wrong name. And he kept looking around as if he didn't recognize his surroundings."

"But he spent most of his evenings there, didn't he?" Gyda asked.

"He did."

"Anything else?" Niall asked.

"He's not a man to speak of his past, but he seemed to be dwelling on thoughts of his mother. He spoke of the circumstances of his birth."

"He was the natural son of Prince Frederick, Duke of York," Kara recalled. She did not look in Niall's direction. "He was acknowledged, though, was he not? Before the duke died?"

"He was acknowledged, yes. But everyone knew not to mention it or make too much of it. Frederick would launch into a tirade, and he made sure everyone understood that he never received anything from the prince. Not money, placement, or any sort of help. Everything he accomplished came from his own hard work and effort."

"Commendable," Niall said flatly.

"His family connections would not have had any bearing on his killing, then." Kara raised a brow at her betrothed before she went on. "Do you know of any enemies Frederick might have had?"

Josie made a face. "He had business rivals, to be sure. But enemies? Someone who might wish him dead and take action on it?" She shook her head. "I don't think so, and I think he would have told me of it, at some time or other."

"Has he had any disagreements lately?" Niall asked. "Any that he has mentioned to you?"

"That's just it," Josie said helplessly. "Frederick has not been himself these last weeks. He's been irritable. Short tempered.

Impatient and pushing, as if everything must be accomplished now, immediately." She held up her hands. "We have been together this last year and a half, and we never had a disagreement. But last month, we had a terrible row. People knew of it," she said with a sigh. "Perhaps that is why I am here."

"Why did you argue?"

Josie dropped her head into her hands. "I've been at the Adelphi for nearly two years, but Frederick has been after me to leave it behind. He feels..." She stopped and drew a quavering breath. "He *felt* that the time has come when music halls are going to undergo a huge success. He would talk on and on about the mingling of the classes being a great draw. He foresaw the need for different sorts of entertainment—acts that everyone could enjoy." She straightened, a helpless look on her face. "He's likely right. But theater—*real* theater—it's in my veins. I love it all. Comedy, farce, drama. All of life is reflected in London's theaters. You lose yourself there. To be a successful actress on the stage is all I ever wanted."

"Then why did you make the switch?" Gyda demanded.

"Frederick became more insistent lately. He said he knew I would stand out with my own act in the music hall. I would become wildly popular more quickly than I ever could working my way up through the ranks at the Adelphi. It just wasn't what I wished for." She paused. "Somehow, Frederick forced the issue. I don't know how, but he must have brought pressure on the manager at the Adelphi. He let me go."

"*Fired* you?" Gyda gasped.

"He didn't want to. I could see that much. Frederick must have forced it on him."

"It's a good thing you didn't tell me," Gyda declared. "I might have killed the old windbag myself."

"You must have been very angry," Kara said gently.

"Of course I was. We had a great, loud, unfettered lightning storm of a fight. In the end, Frederick apologized, and yet he was still convinced he'd done the right thing. He begged me to give his notion a try." Josie sighed again. "And so I did. I insisted on taking the reins of this new career myself, though. I threw myself into it, and last night...I began to see the results. The Hideaway was full to the rafters, and I had them all under my spell. Everyone, from tables to galleries." Her lip quivered. "It was the first thing I said when I sat down next to him last night. That he just may have been right..." Tears welled again. "But now it's over before it's scarcely begun. I can't believe he's gone! I've lost my place in the theater, and no one is going to want to hire an accused murderess." She began to look panicked. "I didn't hurt Frederick! But the coroner's office and the police—I think they feel as if they have found an easy solution in me."

"We will not allow them to falsely accuse you," Kara declared. She knew the pain, bewilderment, and fear of such a thing. "You can help us, though. Think back. You said Frederick had become irritable. Did he grow angry or argue with anyone else that you know of?"

Josie frowned. "I—Yes. He and Robert erupted at each other last week. At the club. It was in the afternoon, before opening. The musicians and I were practicing. I was on stage and they were in the pit. Frederick and Robert were upstairs in one of the offices, but we could hear them shouting. Things have been tense between them since."

"Robert, the man who owns the Hideaway?"

"Yes. Robert West. But no one would suspect him of killing Frederick."

"Why not?"

"Because Frederick is—was—Robert's father."

Gyda frowned. "I thought Cole had only a daughter?"

"Another natural son?" Niall asked, his tone a bit rough.

"Yes. It's not a secret," Josie replied. "There have been whispers about it for years. Robert actually goes on about it when he's had too many pints. Frederick approved of him, because he never approached him until after he'd become a success. He's a self-made man, too."

"Then why did they argue?" asked Kara.

"Oh, yes." Josie blinked. "I suppose I would not be surprised to find their fight was over money. A loan, perhaps? I know Robert has been making plans to open another club in Leicester Square. He's been seeking investors."

"You don't think Frederick would have invested in the growth of his son's business interests?" Kara was surprised.

Josie made a face. "Normally, I think he would have. But Frederick has been acting so...put upon. I suppose that is the phrase that comes to mind. He's been so touchy and mostly unwilling to discuss it, but he began to spend more time with me. He would wish to relax in my rooms or come to listen to rehearsal. He told me once that I was the only one not constantly demanding something from him."

The door opened and the constable peered in, looking alarmed. "You must go, now! His nibs is on his way back." He waved an arm, beckoning. "Come. You must be out before he returns!"

Kara stood. "We'll talk to Inspector Wooten and see if he can have you interviewed and released. In the meantime, Turner is waiting for word of what he can bring to make you more comfortable."

"Oh, thank you. I hope I won't be here much longer. I feel like I've answered all of their questions twice over already." Josie paused. "But in all honesty, your questions felt more thought out." She hugged Gyda again. "Thank you," she whispered. "It's a relief to feel that I'm not alone in this."

The constable beckoned again, and Kara had made it to the door when Josie suddenly stood. "Oh, wait! One more thing! You asked about Frederick's odd behavior. I don't know if it is important, but it was the oddest thing—he scolded me for wearing this gown." She swept her hand along the green silk skirts. "He kept commenting on the ugly shade of yellow."

"*That* gown?" Kara asked.

"Yes. And he made the same comment about the white linen

on the table."

"He called it an ugly shade of yellow?"

"Bilious, I think he said," Josie confirmed.

Kara and Niall exchanged a glance. "We don't know if it is important, either, but we'll find out what we can," she said.

"Thank you," Josie repeated.

"But first, we'll have a word with Robert West," Niall said darkly.

Chapter Three

T HE ROGUE'S HIDEAWAY was also located in Lambeth, not far from the police court building. Niall and Kara had only been in the carriage for a few minutes when he caught a glimpse of the place from down the street. He knocked on the ceiling and called out for the coachman to stop.

He helped Kara down and then stood still as the carriage moved on. He wanted to take in the whole scope of the place.

The building stood taller than its neighbors. The ground floor featured alcoves surrounded by blocked stone, one of which held the entrance. The next two floors were lined with Doric columns, and the final floor showcased arched windows, all in a row. A large, domed roof supported a huge sign. *Rogue's Hideaway* was carved in sweeping wooden letters above a jungle of lush foliage, hiding a glimpse of a timbered, thatched-roof cottage.

"It's beautiful," Kara said, standing beside him. "But…"

"Different," Niall finished as she hesitated. "Bigger, grander, bolder than its neighbors. It stands out from nearly every building in the city. It's a message," he concluded. "This club is an extension of West himself."

She frowned at it. "Do you really think so?"

"He's the bastard son of a bastard son of a royal prince." Niall shrugged. "My background is not exactly the same, but close enough that I can understand the temptation to make your own mark on the world." He held out an arm. "Let's go and see if I've got it right, shall we?"

They had just reached the corner of the building when a young boy ran up, stopping before Kara and bending over to catch his breath.

"Good morning," she said, as if she'd been expecting him. "Well done, young man. You got here just in time."

He held out a sealed note and wheezed his thanks.

Kara broke the seal and read the note. She gave the lad a coin. "Tell Miss Harriet that I will indeed join her for tea tomorrow afternoon."

The boy nodded as the coin disappeared into the folds of his clothing and he melted away into the flow of passersby on the street.

Niall gave her a questioning look.

"I sent a note to Mr. Moseman this morning," she said in response.

"Ah." Moseman was her man of business, the one who worked with her in the running of the family businesses and manufactories that she had inherited from her father. "It does seem likely that he would know something of Mr. Frederick Cole."

"I thought so, too. So I sent around an inquiry this morning."

Niall stopped in his tracks. "Wait. We didn't even know who had died before we talked to Josie."

Kara lifted a shoulder. "Well, I reviewed those of Josie's acquaintances whom I knew about, and I thought the wealthy, older man who acted as her protector might be a candidate." She raised a brow. "And if it wasn't him, then we might possibly interact with him—and it doesn't hurt to go into a situation knowing all you can."

"You have a devious mind, Kara Levett," Niall said with a grin.

"It takes one to know one."

"Well, I am glad to have yours on my side of things," he said, lowering his tone.

"Always."

She smiled up at him, and his heart thumped with gratitude for fate or providence or chance—whatever or whoever had allowed him to find this woman. "And what does Moseman have to say about Cole?"

"He says the man started out in banking, in the north. He started investing in smelting factories and got his first big payoff with fire clay manufactories."

"Fire clay?" Niall frowned. "The stuff they line furnaces with?" He nodded. "Genius. Every railcar, railroad, iron works, and other sort of industry and factory needs furnaces. I think it might even line my forge. All of those industries in need of his product? He must be richer than Croesus."

"Rich enough that Moseman warns me not to annoy him," Kara said sadly. "What an interesting life he must have led. It makes me wish I had met him."

"Well, let's go and meet his son," Niall said, urging her toward the entrance to the club.

"Elegant," Kara whispered as they made their way inside. They were in a long, narrow room. Everything was done in dark wood, shining glass, and greenery. Arched doors marched across the next wall. The two on either end led to staircases. The middle two gave entrance to an expanse of tables set before the stage.

Niall led Kara through one of the middle doors. The tables all sat as empty as the stage. At the other end of the room, facing the stage, a large bar occupied the whole of the back wall. Its fixtures shone even in the dim light. Two men lingered there. One sat on a stool, bent over stacks of papers. The other stood behind the bar, holding a mug and dipping a baguette into it, chewing as he listened to the other.

"They will require a statement of debt before they even begin to consider—"

"Hold a moment, Benton." The tall man behind the bar set

down his breakfast. "It appears we have company."

Niall drew closer, Kara on his arm. "Mr. Robert West?"

"Yes, indeed." The tall man came down the bar as they approached. He was slender, but looked resiliently strong at the same time. Dark blond hair and blue eyes made him look younger than his years, but Niall guessed he was probably ten years older than himself. Certainly West's eyes carried the weight of experience behind an openly curious gaze. "I am he." He ran that avid gaze over the two of them. "I'm afraid you have me at a disadvantage..." He stopped, his eyes fixed on Niall's face. "But no! I do know who you are! Mr...." He cast about, clearly searching for a name. "Kirk? No." He frowned.

"Kier. I am Mr. Niall Kier. This is Miss Kara Levett."

"Of course, of course! It took me a moment, but I should have known you anywhere. We are family, after all. Of a sort." West gestured to the other man. "You can take all of this upstairs, Benton. I'll come and find you when I've finished with our guests."

The man gave them a nod, gathered his papers, and left in a hurry.

"Can I offer you coffee?" West asked. He gestured toward a nearby steaming pot. "I spent time abroad as a young man, and I'm afraid the habit of strong coffee and good bread in the morning has stuck." He lifted a shoulder. "Too much time in Paris, I imagine."

"Thank you, but no," Niall answered with a nod. "We don't mean to take up much of your time, but we do have a few questions we'd like to ask you."

"Of course. I was wondering if we would meet, now that your story is out. And here you are, come to join our club."

"Your club?" Niall glanced around.

"Oh, not *this* club," West answered. "Although, of course, we would be happy to offer you membership to the Hideaway. All are welcome, should they be able to pay the fee. Different prices for floor and gallery, but stunning entertainment and refreshments for all. No, but I meant the other club—uniquely suited for men like us, the bastard branch of the royal tree." He grinned. "There is no denying your claim to belong, is there?" He gestured between them. "Look at us. We both have the family nose."

Kara glanced back and forth. "He's right. It is the same nose."

West shot her a brilliant smile. "And I have been very much looking forward to meeting you, Miss Levett. I have heard of you and your famous creations." He leaned in, and the smile widened.

She smiled back. "Good things only, I hope."

"Oh, not at all!" He laughed. "But how boring that would be. I doubt anyone has ever accused you of being boring."

"Not to my face, in any case," she said.

"Of course not. Nor behind your back. It would be utter nonsense." He raised a brow. "A beauty of a baron's daughter who shuns Society to pursue her own interests in art and science? Who ignores the *beau monde*, but keeps company with the famous forge artist? You, I think, will fit in very well with us at the Rogue's Hideaway."

She returned his smile. "I thank you for the compliment."

"I assure you, it was meant as one." He took another drink of coffee, then waved a hand toward Niall. "No one could blame you, of course. Our old King George was so swollen and vile at the end, it is hard to recall that he was once slim, tall, and handsome, and a favorite with the ladies. But here stands Mr. Kier, a living reminder."

West tilted his head and gazed at Niall. "I've seen the portraits of Mrs. Fitzherbert. You have her eyebrows. And something of her chin." He heaved out a sigh. "Ten years younger, looking like that, and a woman like this at your side? What is it you mean to accomplish, I wonder? Whatever it is, I'll wager you'll make it happen."

The man shook his head and gestured toward a portrait on a perpendicular wall at the end of the bar. "There is my grandsire. Prince Frederick, Duke of York and Albany. Brother to your own grandsire. I share the nose, as noted. If you look close, you'll see I have his dimpled chin. Unfortunately, I also got the sloping forehead. Mine is not so noticeable, thank goodness—and I was lucky to keep my hair, which helps to disguise it." He shrugged good-naturedly. "There are a number of us on the rogue branch of the family tree. We are all loosely connected, of course, but some of us have formed an alliance. We do what we can to help each other. We would be glad to welcome you."

Niall was surprised to find himself touched. "That is generous of you, Mr. West. I appreciate the kind offer." He gestured toward the black armband nearly invisible against the man's dark coat. "I understand you have just lost a member of your alliance—and your close family. We offer our condolences on the loss of Mr. Cole."

Something in West's face changed. "You knew Frederick?"

"No. I'm afraid I never had the pleasure of his acquaintance. Of course, we have heard of him and his impressive successes. But we count Miss Josie Lowe as a friend of ours, and we heard the news from her."

The ease returned to the man's manner. "Ah, Josie. Yes. I didn't realize you were acquainted, or I would have pressed her to introduce us sooner." He nodded. "Thank you for your kind words. Frederick was a complicated man, but we managed to muddle through and become close. I will miss him. In fact, he will be missed by a great many people here at the Rogue's Hideaway."

Niall felt Kara reach back and give his leg a nudge, but he shared no reaction.

"It must be difficult for you, Mr. West," she said quietly. "Josie said you only forged a relationship with your father in the last few years. To then lose him so early…" She shook her head.

"I've heard you were extraordinarily fond of your father, and he of you." West ran an assessing—and appreciative—eye over Kara and her close-fitting woolen day dress. "And you lost him early, as well. We've had opposite timelines with our paternal figures, Miss Levett. We should get together and discuss them. I'll wager we would discover some interesting similarities—and differences."

Niall might have objected to the man flirting with his fiancée, but he was distracted by the sudden, strong feeling that someone was watching him. All the hairs on the nape of his neck shivered to attention. Slowly, surreptitiously, he shifted his weight so that he stood perpendicular to the bar and had a peripheral view of the room.

There. Had someone just ducked behind the curtain on stage?

"I'm sure we would." Kara was responding to West's flirtation with a tiny, tart bit of her own. "Niall and I would love to spend an evening here at some point, but I assume you will be closed for a time?" When West raised a questioning brow, she continued, "Due to your loss and the unfortunate manner and place of Mr. Cole's death?"

"We will be closed tonight, to be sure, but we are planning a memorial performance in Frederick's honor for tomorrow evening."

There was no one on the stage now. Niall turned back in time to see Kara's surprise, and West must have noted it as well. "I'm afraid it is the nature of our business. To stand still means certain decline." He straightened. "In fact, I need to speak with Josie about our plans for the evening. I know she must be devastated, but it might help her to keep busy. Do you know if she means to come to the club today?"

Niall raised a brow. "Josie Lowe is still currently being held at the Lambeth Police Court."

He judged the surprise on West's face to be genuine.

"Why is that? I know they wished to ask her about Frederick's demeanor just before he died, but you cannot mean... They cannot think that Josie had anything to do with his death? He was an old man, for heaven's sake!"

"You thought he died of natural causes?" Kara asked in surprise.

"Of course he did!" West frowned. "I heard the whispers last night, but they cannot be anything more than hysteria." He waved a hand. "Drama. A place like this practically courts such rumors, but the policemen did not seem overexcited." He shook his head. "Josie would never harm the old man. She cared for him. In truth! I saw it myself."

"Perhaps you might inform the coroner of your opinion," Niall said wryly.

"Did you not see the wine he spilled?" Kara asked.

"No, of course not. My staff is impeccably trained. A mess like that would have been whisked away and cleaned up in moments."

"Even Josie saw that something had been added to it."

"To his wine?" West still appeared shocked at the news. "Perhaps that's why they questioned the barkeep."

Niall glanced at Kara, but held to the subject. "Green flecks were noted in the wine. Do you have any idea what they might be?"

West blinked. He looked to be absorbing the news. Or was he a skilled actor in his own right? He certainly must have been in company with his fair share of them.

"No. No idea." He frowned. "I don't believe Josie could have had anything to do with such a thing."

"Nor do we, Mr. West," Kara said firmly. "Which is why we are trying to provide some alternate theories."

"Where were you when Mr. Cole collapsed?" asked Niall.

"I was in the private box." He gestured toward a spot in the gallery, right next to the stage. "I invited several special guests last night." His gaze went unfocused. "And Josie certainly did her bit to impress them. She was magnificent."

"Investors? Is that who you were entertaining?"

West jerked his gaze around to stare at him. "You are well informed, Mr. Kier." He sighed. "Yes, I was hosting several men, all potential investors in my new club."

"Josie also told us that you had a rather serious argument with Frederick Cole last week—likely over investment in your new club."

West's mouth dropped. "Alternate theories? Is that what I am? Are you actually insinuating that I might have killed my own father?"

"What did you argue about?" asked Kara. "Did Mr. Cole decline to invest in your new venture?"

West's face closed. "We did have words over my plans. Things got heated. We are both men of passion. But in the end, it all worked out. The Sock and Buskin Partnership has committed to a large investment in my project."

"Sock and Buskin?" asked Niall.

"Oh, yes," Kara chimed in. "I learned of them when I once took an extensive tour of a playhouse. They are the names of the masques that represent the theater, are they not? The comic and tragic masques?"

"Yes. Frederick named his investment company after them. So, you see, I had no reason to kill him," West said, still prickly. "In fact, his death complicates things for me."

"Didn't get the money in hand yet?" Niall asked with a bit of sympathy.

"No, I haven't, since you are bold enough to ask." West looked troubled. "But I am sure the agreement will hold up."

"I hope so, for your sake." Niall drew a breath. "Very well, then. Tell us about the special glasses that Cole drank from."

"Goblets," West corrected him. "And there is nothing suspicious about them," he said defensively. He turned to walk to the center of the bar. In the middle, among the mirrors and the shining glasses and bottles, a framed shelf acted as a display for two metal cups. He brought them down and set them in front of Niall. "I had them made to my own design. To honor my father."

Kara took one up and looked inside. "Clean," she murmured.

Niall took the other. "The Duke of York Column," he said, running a finger along the raised representation of the monolith that stood at the end of Regent Street.

"For obvious reasons," West said. He turned the cup. "And

there. The sock and buskin, the age-old symbol of the theater. Frederick has always been a great lover of the stage. He grew up in a theater, did you know?"

"No. I recall only that his mother was an opera dancer when she met the prince?"

"She was. She was well known and lovely. He was young and still unattached. They were together for nearly a year, and when they parted, she took the jewels he gave her as a parting gift, cashed them in, and bought a theater in York."

"Frederick grew up there?"

West nodded.

"He must have known the place from the top to the bottom," Kara mused.

West sighed. "No matter how many businesses he owned or how much money he made, he never got the theater out of his blood. It called to him."

"Are these the only two goblets?"

"They are."

"And only Mr. Cole drank from them?"

"Yes. They were reserved for his use."

"And who poured Mr. Cole's drink last night?"

West's eyes widened. "Oh, no. Do not even think it. My servers and tapsters are all good employees. Good people. Jimmy was behind the bar last night, and he would not harm a flea. Even less of a chance that he would harm Frederick. My father was notoriously generous with his vails, especially if he liked the server. He and Jimmy got on well."

"What is Jimmy's surname?" Kara asked.

"Oh, no. Jimmy answered all the police's questions to their satisfaction. Leave him alone."

"He might have seen something—"

"Then he would have mentioned it last night," West insisted.

Kara glanced back at Niall. "Perhaps you are right."

Niall was surprised when she pushed away from the bar.

"Thank you for speaking with us, Mr. West. Forgive us if we

have been too zealous. I'm sure you can appreciate our eagerness to see Josie set free."

"Yes, of course."

"If you think of anything that could help, do let us know." Kara handed him a card. "You can get word to one or both of us at Bluefield Park."

"We would appreciate hearing from you if you think of anyone who might have wished to harm Mr. Cole," Niall added.

"Poisoned." West shook his head. "I just cannot fathom it."

"Well, I suppose the coroner will give us the final word." Niall nodded. "Good day."

"Yes," West said vaguely. "Good day." He visibly collected himself. "Do come back so that we might get to know each other better."

"Oh, we will definitely be back," Niall assured him.

Kara gave the man a nod and a smile. She laid her arm in Niall's, and they turned to go.

"We need to speak to that barkeep." She pulled her coat closer as they stepped out of the building.

"We do. Perhaps Josie might know his full name and where he lives."

"I'll wager the police know."

There it was again, the feeling that someone was watching. Niall shifted his gaze about, but couldn't see anyone who looked out of place. "I doubt they will share that information with us. In fact, we should probably wait to go back until the constables change shifts."

Her mouth twitched. "Good idea." She stumbled suddenly and lost her grip on his arm.

"Kara?"

"Oh, dear."

A young man had bumped into her. He appeared mortified. "Oh, do excuse me. I am sorry. I wasn't looking, wasn't thinking…"

"I'm fine. Fine," she repeated as Niall gave her a questioning look. She shook her head as the young man hunched thin shoulders and stepped around her. His hat was pulled low and his chin was buried in his chest as he walked on and went around the corner.

"He didn't pick my pocket, if that's what you are thinking. I think he just wasn't paying attention," Kara reassured him.

Or perhaps he'd moved too close so that he could hear their conversation? *Bah.* Niall shook his head. Stayme was making him grow paranoid. "Very well, then." He glanced up at the sky, which was unusually clear. "We've most of the afternoon before the constables change shifts, I would imagine. I think I'll go to ask Stayme what he knows about Cole—and West." He tilted his head. "Care to come along?"

"No," Kara replied. "I think I'll see what I can find out about medications that make one see yellow."

"Ah." Niall thought a moment. "Jenny?"

"Jenny's *sister*," she corrected him.

"Oh, yes. Married to the apothecary." He grinned at her. "Good thinking. Give them my regards. You take the carriage," he said as he spotted it heading in their direction. "I'll get a hack."

"Shall we meet at Bluefield later to compare notes?"

"No, let's meet at the Lambeth Police Court this evening and talk it all out with Josie."

She smiled up at him and gave his arm a squeeze. "I will see you then."

Chapter Four

KARA STEPPED INTO the White Hart and breathed in the familiar, comforting fragrance of the place. Niall still kept rooms here. This was the place he had brought her, months ago, when they had teamed up to try to clear her name of the suspicion of murder. So many significant firsts had occurred here, in fact. She'd first met Gyda here. She'd first seen Niall in his formal dress kilt, right there on that landing. Twice she'd convalesced here—once from a fall and a blow to her head and later from a stabbing to her shoulder. Most importantly, it had been right upstairs in the Woodland Room that she and Niall first confessed their feelings for one another. She pulled in a breath, reliving the memory and enjoying the comingled scents of hops, yeast, and lemon wood polish.

The door to the taproom opened and Kara's friend, the maid Jenny Green, came backing out. The White Hart's owner, Mr. Hywel, followed, flapping his hands in agitation.

"I don't care if he has as much money as the queen," Jenny declared. "He pinches the maids' bottoms, and he's gone and stepped right over the chamber pot to piss in the corner again! He's worse than my mother's territorial tomcat! I won't be cleaning it up again, d'ye hear? I warned you not to give him a room."

"Jenny, Hoardman pays his shot, tips well, has a scholarly interest in Boudicca, and plays the bodhrán! I've talked to Mr. Towland about him, and I'm coaxing the man along, hoping to interest him in becoming a member of the Druidic Order of Bards."

"Then you tell Mr. Towland to put him up at the Druid's Grove," Jenny snapped. "For I've had enough of him, and so have the other maids!"

"Erm…good afternoon," Kara interjected.

Jenny spun around. Her expression quickly changed from frustration to delight. "Kara!" She rushed over to take her hand. "How lovely!"

"Miss Levett," Hywel said stiffly. "Welcome." He glanced toward the stairs. "I'm afraid Mr. Kier is not here at present."

Kara nodded. "Yes, I've just left him."

"We're that glad to see you," Jenny said with a grin. "We've had nary a peep at you since you told us of your betrothal. Niall, man that he is, only mumbles when I ask him when the wedding is to take place."

"Oh, don't be too hard on him. We've both been very busy. We are still filling commissions and orders placed at the Great Exhibition, and that is no bad thing. Neither of us is in a hurry." Kara gave her friend a small smile. "We've just been enjoying the glow and basking in the warmth of our promises."

Jenny sighed. "How lovely that sounds."

It *had* been lovely—until Niall's worries dimmed his happiness. But Kara was a patient woman. She could wait. Turning to Hywel, she gave him a look of apology. "I'm afraid it's Jenny I'm after. I know it would be a great favor, but I could very much use her help." As the innkeeper hesitated, she rushed on. "I would be happy to pay her wages for the day, as well as enough extra that you could send down to the staffing agency for a replacement."

"No need for that." Jenny was already removing her apron. "Flora is not working today, and she is looking for extra hours, so that she might send her little one to have his weak eyes examined."

"Very well," Hywel said. "Since it is for you, Miss Levett."

Kara thanked him as Jenny snorted.

The innkeeper gave the maid a sharp look. "I could use a rest from nagging, in any case."

Jenny pointed her finger at him. "Ha! Flora will be no happier than I am about that man and his messes." Tossing him her apron, she turned to Kara. "I am at your service. What can I do?"

"When we last took tea with your sisters, Mrs. Canham invited me to visit her husband's apothecary shop. Would you take me there? If you think she wouldn't mind us dropping in?"

"Goodness, no. Ellie won't mind. She'll think it a high treat."

"Excellent. Niall and I are looking into a situation for a friend. Your sister and her husband's expertise might help."

Jenny's eyes widened. "Never say you've got in the middle of another murder enquiry?"

Kara paused. "Well. Yes, I suppose we have."

"Ooh! And we get to put a hand in?" Jenny squealed in delight. "Ellie will be chuffed, and all my other sisters will be green with envy!"

Kara laughed. "Well, then. Good. My carriage is outside. We can catch up on the way."

A BELL RANG over the door as they entered Canham's Apothecary, in a winding lane off the Strand. Kara's eyes widened in surprise. She'd been in shops like this before. Most were dim, slightly dusty, and busy with customers who kept their heads down, as if they had no wish to admit a need or an ailment to their fellow men. One notable place had been shrouded in dark shadows, the walls marked with mysterious runes, and featured shelves lined in animal bones, hides, and murky containers of morbid curiosities next to the medicinal products on offer.

But this... The shop was brightly lit and spotlessly clean. Every surface gleamed, from wooden counters to glass vials and jars and mirrored shelves. A group of ladies surrounded a separate counter where a young lady showed them cold creams and cosmetics. Mrs. Canham was on the other side of the room, weighing out a powder for a waiting gentleman.

"Good afternoon," she called, concentrating on her measurements. "I will assist you in a moment."

"We'll wait," Jenny said cheekily.

Her sister looked up, smiling in surprise. "Jenny! What are you doing—Oh! Miss Levett!" She blinked rapidly and glanced about as if to make sure all was in order in the tidy shop. "Welcome!"

"Thank you, Mrs. Canham." Kara smiled reassuringly. "I've been wanting to visit your shop. Today I have an excuse, and Jenny was kind enough to bring me."

"We'll wait over here until you are freed up," Jenny called. She pulled Kara over to a corner where labeled jars lined shelves nearly to the ceiling. "Do you see any with green flakes?"

They scanned them all, moving down the counter.

"I don't see any," Kara said, disappointed. "These all seem to be fine powders or tinctures."

The customer took his package, and Jenny's sister approached. "The pair of you look like you are up to something," she said, brows raised. "Why aren't you at work, Jenny?"

"I stole her away," Kara confessed.

"She's looking into another murder," Jenny said with excitement. "And she needs our help!"

"Oh, my. Well then, let's go through to the back and have a cup of tea, shall we? We can talk privately back there."

Mrs. Canham spoke quietly to the girl at the other counter, then beckoned them through, leading them into a small workroom that contained a stove and a small table amongst the counters and worktables. "Come and sit. I'll put the kettle on." She glanced at Jenny. "Mama knew I would be busy this week, with my Edward gone. She sent a spice cake over. It will be just the thing."

"Mama's special spice cake? This *is* turning out to be a good day," Jenny said, going to a cupboard to fetch small plates.

"Oh, your husband is away?" Kara asked. "I'd hoped to ask him some questions."

"He will return next week, and I'm sure he'll be happy to speak with you." Mrs. Canham hesitated as she turned up the flame on the small stove. "I will do all I can to help, in the meantime."

"If you've questions about ailments, Ellie can help," said Jenny. "We spent our summers in Dorset as young girls. We stayed with our Aunt Gilly. She's the local witch, and Ellie was her prize pupil."

"She's not a witch." Mrs. Canham looked uncomfortable. "She's an herb woman, a healer. The teachings of it have been passed down among the women of our family. The locals know to come to her, and she helps where she can. She does no harm."

Jenny waggled her eyebrows at her sister as she set out teacups. "We always said Ellie caught Edward Canham because she could talk for hours about the preparation of willow bark tea and the steeping of nettles."

"As I've been the beneficiary of your work, I would never disparage it," Kara told Mrs. Canham. "And you might, indeed, have an inkling about what I've come to discuss." She explained about Cole's death and Josie's situation.

"Flat green flakes?" Mrs. Canham scowled. "It doesn't sound like a proper medicine. Not something you'd find in an apothecary. We grind our substances finely, in most cases. Perhaps it was the work of an amateur, or an herbal woman like my aunt?" She held up the box she was taking from a cupboard. "Although, in London, I'd say it was more likely to be a tea."

"A tea?" Kara considered the notion. "That is an idea. It makes me wonder. Perhaps it was a case of longer exposure, rather than just one dose?"

"With a poisoning, I believe that is often the case. It's why we are careful with our instructions when we sell medicines with harmful effects." Mrs. Canham frowned, thinking. "Did the gentleman show any symptoms before he passed, do you know?"

"Indeed, yes. Josie said he had a headache and seemed confused. He didn't seem to recognize her or his surroundings. He seemed fixated on the past. He said his pulse was bouncing, and then racing, before he vomited and collapsed."

"Was he being treated by a doctor? Taking any medicines?"

"Josie didn't mention it. And I think she would have, given the green flakes in the wine."

"It sounds like it might have been something that affects the heart. My aunt knew of several plants that she gave to those with heart ailments." Mrs. Canham frowned. "He did not happen to mention seeing everything in a yellow hue, did he?"

Kara straightened. "He did! Does that tell you something?"

"Yes, indeed. Foxglove. That's what he was likely given."

"Foxglove? The tall, spiky plant? With the purple flowers?"

"Yes. It grows in many places. My aunt warned me specifically about it. Seeing strange colors, especially yellow, is a sure giveaway that a patient has had too much. If they do, it adversely affects the heart and causes such symptoms as you mentioned." Mrs. Canham grew sober. "Too much and..."

"They could die?"

She nodded. "They could."

"Foxglove," Kara mused.

"Digitalis is the scientific name. We have it stocked here. Powdered, in a jar. Doctors use it to scatter dropsy in their patients, or for swelling of the liver or fluid in the lungs. Sometimes for childhood seizures. My aunt used it for dropsy as well, and also for those who suffered from headaches or a weak heart."

"Dropsy—that's when there is swelling in the lower limbs?"

"Among other symptoms. The swelling can occur elsewhere, as well. Someone suffering from dropsy might also grow weak with fatigue. They might wheeze with each breath or have a cough. Sometimes, a bloody cough."

"Thank you, Mrs. Canham. You've given me the answer I needed, and perhaps a way to help Josie."

"I am happy to help."

"The other girls will be that jealous," Jenny announced. "Now, the water is ready. Let's have tea and cake and talk of pleasanter things, shall we?"

"That sounds delightful," Kara answered. "And I'd like to ask you about Flora's child, Jenny. You mentioned he needs a doctor who specializes in the eyes? I don't know of any, but I do know some fine doctors. I'm sure I could get a recommendation on who would be best to see."

"Flora would be grateful, I'm sure. Thank you, Kara." Jenny sat down with a flounce. "Now, tea, please, before I have to go back to work." She shook her head. "I only hope Flora has dealt with that mess before I return." She snorted. "Tomcats and men! Both are a bother."

Chapter Five

NIALL KEPT AN eye out as he made his way to Berkeley Square, but he saw no sign that he was being followed. But did that meant that the man outside Bluefield was the only one watching? Or that the others were more skilled at it?

He moved quickly over the wide pavement, just in case, but truly, anyone who knew anything about him would know where he was headed in this area. In fact, it appeared his arrival was anticipated. As he approached Viscount Stayme's elaborately carved door, it opened even before he could reach for the slightly naughty knocker.

"Do come in, Mr. Kier." Watts, Stayme's butler, held the door wide. "We were all vastly relieved when you were seen approaching."

Niall shot him a questioning look.

"He's in a bad way," the butler said in a whisper.

"Ill?" Niall stopped in alarm.

His oldest friend and mentor had been kidnapped during the adventures that led to the exposure of Niall's secrets. While the viscount had not appeared to suffer any negative health consequences, he was still an elderly man.

"Not ill. Not exactly." Watts beckoned and headed for the stairs. "Come up, please. You will see what I mean."

Niall followed the servant upstairs to the viscount's private parlor. He entered to find it dimmer than usual, with none of the many lights burning. The large window was half covered with heavy drapes. Books were strewn about, but the massive desk stood empty. Peering about, Niall finally spotted the viscount seated in a corner, idly spinning the large globe.

As Niall approached, Stayme rolled his head to look up at him with empty eyes. "I'm shut out," he said hoarsely.

Niall studied the old man. He'd never seen him look less than dapper and immaculate, but today his cravat was askew and his waistcoat was unbuttoned. Niall pressed his lips together and exhaled heavily. "Come on, old man."

Stayme protested, but Niall was ruthless. He asked Watts to fetch the viscount's coat and call for the carriage. Watts obeyed with obvious relief and approval.

There was a bit of grumbling, but Stayme did not put up a real fight. He let Niall bundle him into the coach and scowled out at the passing city. He held his peace until they turned into Hyde Park.

"The place will be empty," Stayme groused. "The nannies will have taken all their charges home for their luncheon, and it's far too early for the fashionable set to promenade."

"That's why we are here," Niall replied casually. They drove along, passing the Serpentine and a stray rider or two. He waited until they'd reached a deserted, wooded section at the edge of the park before he thumped for the driver to stop. "Come. Let's walk."

Stayme sighed, but he clambered down and set off at Niall's side. The air was crisp, but the day was clear, and thanks to a brisk wind aloft, there was plenty of blue sky to see above. They walked slowly, still silent. Gradually, though, Stayme straightened and began to breathe deeper. When he finally spoke, he sounded sour. "It's a fitting setting, I suppose. The hinterlands of the park. An accurate representation of where I stand now."

"I know you are used to being in the thick of things," Niall began.

"I am used to being in the *center* of things," Stayme corrected him. "I take part in the important discussions. Damn it, my sources provide much of the information that drives the important discussions. But now? Decisions are being made and I am pushed out. And the hell of it is, it's the first time the outcome truly matters to me." He didn't look over, but Niall knew it for the declaration of care and support that it was meant to be.

"Perhaps that's why they excluded you from this issue," he said with a sigh. "You'll likely be back in the midst of it all, once they've got me sorted."

"I might be, boy, but where will you be?"

"Hopefully not bound in the belly of a ship headed for the Indian Ocean."

"There will be hell to pay, if that ever becomes the case," Stayme spat. "Everyone has secrets, even those in power. *Especially* those in power. And I'm the one who knows all the secrets."

"All?" Niall asked doubtfully.

"*All.* Those with bloodlines, money, and power like to put forth a lily-white image, but I know what they get up to behind doors. Peccadillos, plots, even treasonous thoughts. They all come to me, eventually."

"Perhaps that's why you were pushed out, then," Niall said lightly. "Be careful, or you'll end up in that sailor's berth beside me."

"They wouldn't dare," Stayme growled.

They walked a little further while the viscount seethed. Niall spotted a bench ahead, under a pair of trees. In the summer it would provide a shady spot. Now, with the branches still bare, it was a sun-dappled place to rest.

"Let's sit a while, if you'd care to rest."

They'd just settled in when hoofbeats sounded and two horses came around a corner to pass in front of them. Niall whistled as they went by.

"Would you look at that bay?" he said reverently. Both horses were obviously expensive bloodstock being exercised by proud grooms.

"Plain-headed, if you ask me."

"Perhaps, but look at that chest. He's likely got a pair of lungs that would make him all but inexhaustible. Perfect for distances."

The viscount didn't reply, but Niall watched the pair until they were gone before he turned back to find Stayme staring at him with a strange look on his face.

"That may be the first time in all of your years that you've reminded me of your grandsire." He turned away.

Niall looked away as well. He was uncomfortable with the comparison. Few enough people knew that his mother had been a secret child of the invalid marriage between King George IV and Maria Fitzherbert. Stayme himself had insisted he keep the fact utterly secret. To hear him speak of it out loud… It gave Niall a shiver.

"The man loved his horses," Stayme said in a tone of reminiscence. "He created one of the best studs in England, at one time."

"Until he was forced out of racing because of a cheating scandal. He sold it then, didn't he?"

Stayme sat back. "I do not believe that George knew of the scheme involving Escape. He was proud of that horse. He didn't believe the jockey had done anything questionable. And he stood by Chifney. He retired from the turf rather than dishonor the man, and he gifted him an annuity of two hundred guineas a year, despite the furor." The viscount shrugged. "George was no leader. I'll admit it. He could be frivolous and petulant. But was a true friend. Loyal and steadfast."

Niall stared, incredulous. "It's too bad, then, that he did not extend such loyalty to the women in his bed."

"No. It's true. He was not happy unless there was an element of drama in his love affairs. But don't mistake drama for lack of feeling. He loved Maria. I was there, through all the turmoil. I know he cared for her more deeply than any of his other women.

And she loved him as well."

"But he was no good for her in the end, was he? All she got for her trouble was heartache, scandal, and the notoriety of being left behind. She would have had a better life had she never met him."

Stayme stared. "Is that what this is about? Are you imagining your woman in place of his and worrying over Kara? Well, I cannot advise you on your own love affair. I never had the patience or the talent for it, myself. But I will say, if you are worried that your uncertain fate might adversely affect Kara Levett, then you should tell her so, and allow her to make her own choices. Maria certainly did."

"Well, I've no plans to marry her, get her with a secret child, then abandon her to marry someone else, in any case." Niall's shoulders slumped. "I want nothing more than to spend the rest of my days with Kara, but what if we do marry, and then I end up press-ganged one night, never to be seen again?"

"Then Kara will likely hire a crew of marauders to intercept your ship, board it, and take you back in a bloodthirsty, daring rescue."

"For pity's sake, never say anything like that in her hearing! You don't need to be giving her any wild ideas. She has plenty of her own."

"What she has is courage, backbone, and a real love for you, boy. Maria loved you and your mother, but she was forced to do so from afar. It was one of the most difficult things for her to endure, in a lifetime of trouble. Don't push away the opportunity to enjoy what you and Kara have found between you. Not everyone gets a chance at such a thing."

"You are right, I know." Niall stood. "Come on. Let's walk back and meet your carriage. You can share some of your vaunted knowledge on the way, for I also came with another reason to see you."

"Did you?" Stayme cocked a brow in surprise. "What is it you wish to know?"

"Tell me what you know of Frederick Cole, if you will."

Stayme stopped walking. "Cole? Why? Has he approached you?"

"No. He's dead."

"Dead?" The viscount gaped. "As in, *died*? Or as in—"

"Murdered, it appears."

"Hell and damnation."

"See? Occasionally I know things, too."

Stayme grunted.

"Poisoned, it appears. A friend of mine is under suspicion for it. I see the question in your eye, and the answer is no. No, I don't believe she did it. Which is why I came to ask you if you might have an idea of who might want him dead?"

"Who *wouldn't*, is the likelier question. A man doesn't grow from poverty to vast riches without making enemies along the way."

"The sort of enemies who might wish him dead?"

"The sort who might pray for it every night."

"But would they put it in motion?"

"Some might. The man was ruthless. In business and in general. He'd eye up a competitor and do all he could to drive them to the brink of collapse. Steal customers, undermine contracts... There were whispers of sabotage and other chicanery."

Niall made a face.

"Once he had them in a weakened position, he'd buy them for pennies. Ruthlessly dismantle everything and feed it like scraps to his own concerns."

"Difficult to endure."

"Without a doubt. I once saw a man fight his way into a club and fall at Cole's knees, begging for a price that would allow him to see his children taken care of. Cole just gave him a cold stare and had him thrown out." Stayme was warming to his subject. "Hell, he made the board members of his companies as rich as lords, but still, many of them hate him."

"That sounds...unusual."

"Cole is abrupt in manner and just as quick to move in business. Makes decisions in an instant and acts right then. No time for parlaying around a board table. He stirred up plenty of bad blood, but most everyone swallowed their anger and their pride and followed where he led, for he always found them money in the end."

"A difficult man, then."

"Complicated, I would say." Stayme gave him a side-eyed look. "Like his own father, the Duke of York, brother to your grandsire."

Niall hesitated before taking up the new topic. "They were close, I've heard."

"Indeed. They had a difficult childhood. Demanding and harsh at times. Strictly 'spare the rod and spoil the child' thinking. And often administered by their father, the king." He sighed. "They got through it together."

Niall's skepticism must have been apparent, as Stayme shook a finger. "Royalty comes with its own drawbacks, boy. It's not all crowns and feasts and roses. And in this particular family line, it seems to come with a great deal of trouble between fathers and sons."

"I had a lucky escape, then, didn't I?"

"You think you are being facetious, but you were better off out of all that. You did all right," Stayme finished gruffly.

"Largely thanks to you." Niall thought a moment. "And what of Cole's son? How did he fare? I've heard rumors of tensions between them. Perhaps they did not escape the curse."

Stayme shrugged. "I have almost no information on the lad."

"Lad?" Niall repeated with a laugh. "The man has a good ten years on me."

"As I said." Stayme glowered. "When you grow as old as I have, you all look like striplings." He thought a moment. "He runs a music hall, does he not?"

Niall nodded. "It's a cross between a music hall and a private club. And it appears to be doing very well."

"Then you know more about than I." Stayme dismissed the topic as his carriage came around a bend. "Are you coming back to Berkeley Square?"

Niall eyed the sun lowering in the sky. "No. I'll walk back to the corner and catch a hack to Lambeth."

Stayme reached out and grabbed his arm. "You be careful. Keep that lucky streak going, for my sake."

Niall nodded. "I'll do my best, sir."

⊱⊰

WHATEVER BREEZES HAD blessed them with blue skies earlier had blown off again by the time Kara returned to Lambeth. And even as the clouds and ever-present smoke thickened overhead, so did the crowd gathered outside the police court building. Traffic had become congested as vehicles slowly took turns swerving around the people who had begun to spill into the street. Kara's coach was forced to pull over a good distance away.

"Please, do not worry," she told John Coachman, who was trying to apologize. "Just wait here, rather than trying to get closer to that mess. I doubt it will be long before Mr. Kier and I are ready to return to Bluefield."

She set off, walking briskly. She wanted to gauge the mood of the crowd, but she found both her view and the acoustics blocked by a large, clumsy stack of boxes and wooden crates outside a cobbler's shop. They took up nearly the width of the pavement, and she found herself steering to the edge of the street to get by. Stepping carefully, she was held up as she encountered a small girl blocking the way. Tears tracked down her dirty cheeks as she stood stock-still, sobbing as though her heart was breaking.

Kara was a lady, born and bred. The daughter of a baron with deep pockets and a business empire, she'd had a privileged upbringing—until fate and unscrupulous kidnappers intervened. Afterward, her father had seen to it that she took the sort of lessons no peeress would learn. The sort that taught her to think, to react, to fight, to escape—and to survive in the streets.

It meant she knew enough not to carry an easily cut reticule or anything of value in her vulnerable outer garments. It also meant she knew to reach back and down to catch the thin wrist of the boy who had taken advantage of her hesitation to pick her pocket.

"Oi!" She'd caught him by surprise when she grabbed him. He fought to get away. "Le'go!"

"Come now," Kara said to the still-sobbing girl. "That is enough of that. Although you *are* quite good. I'll give you that."

The tears dried as the girl gaped at her.

"Le'go! Le'go!" The boy struggled to pull away.

Kara held on. "I would advise you to find a new occupation, young man, before you lose a hand or find yourself transported to Botany Bay."

"Le'go, ye mad old sow!" he spat.

"Can you read?" she asked him.

"I can," the girl said eagerly. "Me mum taught me my letters, afore she fell down drunk afore a carriage in the road."

"I don't need ter read," the boy said with a sneer. He pointed to his waist, where a ragged length of rope substituted as a belt. A length of leather hung there, and when he gestured to it, Kara realized it was a sling. "I can hit a bloke bigger'n me from twenty paces, right in the eye."

"A useful skill," she admitted. The boy's struggles were growing frantic, but Kara bent down to him. "Would you like to learn to read?" she asked him quietly. "Two useful skills are better than one."

He stopped fighting her, for just the briefest moment. She was wise to his tricks, however, and tightened her grip. She wasn't prepared for the kick the girl aimed at her shin, though. She stumbled, and the boy wrenched away. He stood for an instant, grinning in triumph and contempt. "Now!" he shouted as both children stepped back. "Do it now!"

The tower of boxes beside her began to tremble. The sharp-edged crates at the top rolled off first, cascading in her direction. Kara leapt forward, but she moved an instant too late. A good-sized box clipped her shoulder just as one of the crates landed at her feet. She tripped and went down, covering her head as the rest of the pile fell in a jumble atop her.

"Kara!" The call came from a little distance away.

Niall. She groaned and pushed away a box whose corner was poking her in the neck. "Niall!" she called.

She froze as a voice answered, very quiet and very close. "Best to keep your mind on yer own business, missus." It was the girl. "Dangerous to poke around where ye're not wanted." Kara heard the distinct slap of her feet as she ran away, a counterpoint to Niall's louder footsteps approaching from the opposite direction.

"Kara! Are you all right?" He was tossing boxes in every direction, from the sound of it.

"Yes. I think so," she said, trying to get to her hands and knees.

It took only a moment before he'd cleared the wreckage and helped her stand. "Are you hurt?"

She took a moment to assess the state of things. "Only bruised, I think." She shook her arm, sure she was going to feel worse tomorrow than she did right at this moment.

"Here, now!" The cobbler had come hurrying out. He blinked at her through spectacles as he ran his hands down his stained leather apron. "What do you think you're up to? You cannot make a mess like this in front of my shop! You're blocking my customers!"

"Then perhaps don't leave a hazardous stack of crates out here, where they might fall on anyone passing by?" Niall bit out.

"Me?" The man's mouth fell open. "Not a bit of this is mine! None of it was here an hour ago!"

Kara carefully straightened her back and rolled her shoulder. "Niall, I don't think this was an accident."

"What do you mean?" He sounded outraged.

"I mean, I think this was a rather pointed warning about interfering in this murder enquiry." She told him of the street urchins and of the whisper after the fall, then she went around to the back of the pile—or to what was left standing. There was a small space back there, between the stack and the wall. "I think one of their friends was back here—waiting on the signal to push it all over."

"Blast and damnation," he cursed. Pointing at the cobbler, he barked out an order. "Leave it for just a few minutes. I want a constable down here to take a look."

"You cannot leave this—"

The cobbler stopped at the look Niall shot him. "A few minutes only, I said."

Wrapping an arm around her, Niall softened his tone. "Come along—let's get you to the court building so you can rest a moment."

"I'm fine." Kara managed to walk at a normal pace as they headed toward the shifting crowd. The daylight was nearly gone, but the crowd remained. They shifted and flowed. Some had clearly just gathered to enjoy the spectacle and the titillation of a murder enquiry. Others had come and brought strong opinions with them.

"Murdering jade!"

"Witch!"

"She's innocent, I tell ye! Too lovely to hurt a flea!"

"Aye, and always generous to those outside, who cain't afford ter get inter the Hideaway."

"Hang her!"

"Release her!"

Niall pushed through, and the crowd gave way before them. Two burly constables stood watch at the door, but they waved them through without comment. Kara exchanged a questioning glance with Niall, and he merely shrugged.

Two men waited in the entry hall. One of them caught sight

of them and waved.

"Ah, that's why," she said, but she smiled as the tall man approached. He had the look of a man who had once been powerfully built, but who had grown soft with age and care. And was happier for it. But Detective Inspector Wooten was a good man. She had better cause to know it than many. He had taken the time to look past the obvious when she had been accused of murder. His wisdom was exactly what was needed here, and she was more than a little relieved to see him.

"Inspector. I hope this means you are going to head the enquiry into Mr. Cole's death?"

"Mr. Kier. Miss Levett." He gave them each a nod. "I am. I made the request as soon as I heard Miss Lowe's name. And, of course, I was not surprised to hear your names tangled up in it when I arrived."

"Tangled? We've only come at Josie's request."

"And promptly dived in, or so I've heard." He beckoned to the man he'd been standing with.

"You are not the only one who has heard of our involvement," Niall said darkly. "And someone doesn't like it." He told Wooten of Kara's accident.

"Right here in the street? So close to the police court?" Wooten sounded surprised, but he cast a warning look at Kara.

"All we've done is ask a few questions!" she protested.

"That's where it begins, isn't it?" He frowned. "This enquiry does seem to hold a few surprises. Miss Levett, I cannot have you getting hurt. I should say you've risked enough, lately, and in any case, I doubt we'll have need of you to clear Josie's name." Wooten gestured to the gentleman who had arrived at his side. "Allow me to introduce Sergeant Landover. He works with the coroner and was one of the first to arrive at Mr. West's club after the police."

The man bowed, and Kara looked him over with interest. He appeared surprisingly young. Tall and slender, he wore a distant expression on his face, as if he was not quite planted firmly in the here and now. He was handsome, too, with a long nose and impressive blond whiskers. "Good evening." He looked them over carefully. "You are the pair that bluffed your way past my officer this morning?"

Kara greeted him with a nod. "How nice to make your acquaintance, sir. I must assure you, though," she said sweetly, "I was not bluffing."

The man's eyebrows rose in surprise.

"Surely you must have realized by now that Josie did not kill Mr. Cole."

"Actually, I believe we *have* reached that conclusion." The sergeant gestured toward the passage that led to where Josie was being held. "But I would like to discuss something with her, and she might appreciate some friendly advice, if you would like to join us?"

"Of course," answered Niall. "And I'd like to see that Miss Levett has a seat. She's just been accosted in the street."

Surprise moved across the sergeant's face again, but he merely nodded. "Of course. I'll have chairs enough for everyone brought in."

He moved away to consult an officer, and Wooten stepped closer. "Landover is meant to shadow me for this investigation," he said quietly. "He possesses some sort of talent with numbers and a connection with the commissioner. The powers that be want him sent up quickly through the ranks. I'm to show him a proper enquiry and allow him to gain a bit of experience."

Kara noticed Niall's expression go blank. She recalled what West had said this morning about making his own way in the world and how Niall had admired the notion. He'd done the same, making his reputation as an artist by the sweat of his brow, the strength of his arm, and the beauty he saw in his mind's eye. She thought he might not approve of the idea of someone using connections to move past others.

Landover called them in, and Kara moved past as he held the door open. She went straight to Josie to clasp her hands. Her friend looked a little bewildered at the crowd filing in, and Kara gave her a nod of encouragement.

"Is it true they are planning a special performance to honor Frederick at the Hideaway?" Josie asked Kara in a whisper.

At Kara's nod, her friend looked incredulous. "For *tomorrow*? Why so soon? I feel as if I have barely registered the fact that he's gone."

Kara shrugged but could not reply further as the men shuffled in. Introductions were made. Seats were taken. Kara sat next to Josie and held her hand.

Sergeant Landover cleared his throat. "You do understand, Miss Lowe, that as an accusation was leveled, we had to bring you in to ask questions and ascertain whether an inquest is warranted."

Solemn and pale, Josie nodded.

"It seems that Mr. Cole was indeed poisoned."

Josie covered her mouth with her hand. "I can scarcely believe it." She shook her head. "I did not do it, sir. I would never harm Frederick."

"I believe you, Miss Lowe."

Kara felt her friend go slack with relief.

"But who?" Josie whispered.

"You've said that you did not know of any illness Mr. Cole might have been suffering from?"

Josie shook her head. "He seemed the same, physically. He's been...agitated these last weeks, but he never complained of any physical ailments."

"Do you know what this is?" Sergeant Landover held out a hand-sized twist of paper. He opened it to show a quantity of green flakes inside. "Have you seen this before?"

"No." Josie looked perplexed. "What is it?"

"Digitalis," breathed Kara.

Landover looked sharply at her. "Indeed. The coroner believes Mr. Cole was exposed to a dangerous dose of it. That is what killed him." He raised a questioning eyebrow at Kara.

She lifted a shoulder. "Josie mentioned the way that Mr. Cole was acting last night, and the fact that he mistook her gown and the table linen for a yellow color. I visited a friend's apothecary shop to ask about it."

"Where did you find that?" asked Niall, nodding toward the drug.

"It was found on Miss Lowe's dressing table, in her backstage room at the Rogue's Hideaway," Wooten said quietly.

Looking shocked, Josie shook her head. "It's not mine," she said, dismayed. "I swear, I've never seen it before."

"I inspected your rooms myself last night, Miss Lowe." Landover sounded aggrieved. "This was not there to be found, at that time."

"This morning, when I went to the music hall, it was there," Wooten said. "Sitting in the open, right between a wineglass and your mirror."

"But that means…"

"Someone is trying to implicate you, it would appear."

"In a rather clumsy fashion," Kara said.

"But who?" Tears started to well in Josie's eyes.

"The true killer," Niall told her gently. "Whoever they are, they are willing to sacrifice you so that they might go free."

The tears fell.

"Whoever they are," Landover repeated, "they are likely someone who was close to the victim. The coroner believes it was not just one dose of the drug that killed him, but a longer exposure, perhaps topped off by a larger quantity."

"It's likely that the killer is someone you know or have encountered," Wooten said gently. "And for that and other reasons, we have an…*unusual* plan to propose."

"A plan?" Josie sounded bewildered.

"The killer is trying to manipulate us," Wooten explained. "They likely feel that the police are either easily fooled or just too eager to find a suspect to look for true justice." He glanced at Landover. "I had a notion to allow him—or her—to believe their plan is working."

Kara saw what he meant at once. "You mean to keep Josie in custody?"

"If she is amenable to the idea," Wooten said soothingly. "The killer may grow complacent if they think their plan has worked. They might make a misstep. Say or do something to alert us to their identity."

"You wish me to stay here?" Kara was surprised Josie didn't sound adamantly against the idea. "While you pretend I am still being investigated?"

"You are not obligated to go along with the idea," Wooten admitted.

"No, actually, I don't mind." Josie shivered. "You said it was someone close to Frederick? That means it might be someone I know. Or someone who resented my relationship with him. Either way, the thought that they might try again to make it look like I did it...or they might act against me directly..." She shook her head. "I wouldn't feel safe. I would be watching everyone with a suspicious eye. I believe I'd rather stay here until you know who did it." She looked to Landover. "But might I get some paper, and perhaps my guitar? I could put the time to good use. And if I'm to be allowed visitors, I could consult with our musical director?"

"Of course. Although the visits would have to be short, to keep to the illusion."

Josie nodded, but her gaze went unfocused. "You said someone might have been giving this drug to Frederick for a while? What does Elias have to say about it? If anyone would know when Frederick would have been vulnerable to such a thing, it would be him."

"Elias?" Wooten asked. He and Landover shared a look. The sergeant shook his head.

"Yes. Elias Wade."

"Who is Elias Wade, Miss Lowe?" Wooten asked.

"Oh! I just assumed you'd spoken to him already. Elias is—

was—Frederick's… I don't know what to call him. His pageboy? His assistant or personal servant, I suppose. He managed Frederick's schedule and saw to his wishes and to all the details of his life. He's very good. Extremely helpful. And I should know, for he was my servant before Frederick tempted him away from me."

"What do you know about him?" asked Wooten.

"He's a quiet young man. Shy. He sticks to the background of things, but he notices everything. He's wonderful about anticipating needs and meeting them almost before you realize it." She arched a brow. "And you needn't suspect him of harming Frederick, for the two of them got along famously. Elias idolized Frederick, and Frederick truly appreciated Elias's manner and skills. He often told Elias that if he had ten of him, he could give the queen a run at managing the country."

"Where is the young man from?" Wooten asked. "Where does he live?"

Josie frowned. "He's from Wales, originally, I believe. And I believe he lives in Frederick's household, here in Town. He had a place in my rooms when he worked for me."

"We'll speak to him," Wooten said. "Thank you." He looked to Kara. "Now, I hope you'll see that Miss Wooten is quite safe from being falsely accused—at least by us."

"I do, and I am vastly relieved." She grinned at the inspector. "So I shall do as you obviously wish and take a step back." Sobering, she pointed a finger at him. "But do not forget that there is something unusual about all of this—or you would not have found that obvious clue and I would not have been warned off asking questions."

"Warned off?" Josie repeated.

Kara told her of her encounter with the urchins and their tower of crates.

"Oh, dear. I would never have asked for your help if I thought it would place you in danger."

"You haven't, not really. In any case, we were happy to do

what we could."

"I appreciate you being sensible about this," Wooten told her.

"Actually, if I might interject," Sergeant Landover said with hesitation. "I meant to ask for Miss Levett's help."

"In what way?" Niall asked before Kara could respond.

"I was wondering if perhaps you have an acquaintance with Mrs. Cole?" Landover looked uncomfortable. "I spoke with her last night. She was understandably upset. She also appeared to have a dim view of the police in general. She's distraught, I understand, but there are questions that she must answer. If you know the lady, I thought you could, perhaps, smooth the process, maybe even accompany me while I interviewed her." He looked to Inspector Wooten. "If you've no objections, that is."

"It's not a bad idea," Wooten admitted. "I've no place to complain, as Miss Levett has done a similar service for me, and she was extremely effective."

"I would be happy to help, but unfortunately, I do not have an acquaintance with Mrs. Cole," Kara told them.

Landover was clearly disappointed. "Would she receive you, do you think? You are a member of the peerage."

Kara delicately cleared her throat. "As a woman of wealth, but not bloodlines, I doubt Mrs. Cole is invited to move in Society. She might resent that fact and those associated with it."

"Or she might crave contact with it," Landover countered.

"She likely has her own circles," Kara said, but she was struck by a sudden thought. "However, I am well acquainted with someone she just might know, and I happen to already have plans to see her tomorrow. Perhaps, through her, I might gain a letter of introduction to Mrs. Cole. I will see what might be done."

"Thank you. I'll wait to hear from you before I approach her again." Landover glanced down at his notebook. "Heaven knows I have plenty of people to question in the meantime. Hundreds of witnesses, and Cole seems to have more than a few potential enemies."

"Do you have plans to speak to the bartender who was serving at the club last night?" Niall asked.

"Oh, yes. We meant to ask where he lived," Kara said to Josie.

"Jimmy? He lives in Jeremiah Yard, down by the river. Not too far from the Rogue's Hideaway."

"Do you know his surname?" asked Niall.

Josie had to think a moment.

"It's Gibbs, and I've spoken to him already," interrupted Landover. "He claimed to know nothing of how the digitalis might have got into Cole's wineglass."

"Did he perhaps notice anyone new hanging about the bar?" Niall persisted.

The sergeant frowned. "He said he noticed nothing unusual. I believed him. I moved on."

Kara deliberately did not look at Niall. "Very well, then." She kissed Josie. "Make a list of what you need from your rooms, dear, and we will have it brought to you."

"Thank you," Josie whispered.

"We will be back, never fear," Kara said firmly. She and Niall bade farewell to the inspector and sergeant and took their leave. They were forced to push through the crowd once more, but the carriage awaited them, and had managed to move a little closer. Though she peered down the street, it seemed the crates had been removed from the pavement in front of the cobbler's shop.

Taking Niall's hand, she climbed into the coach. Once he was settled and they had begun to move, she leaned back. "Sergeant Landover seems like a decent man."

"He does."

"Wooten won't make the mistake of ignoring the barkeeper, will he?"

"No. I predict he'll send a constable around to talk to the man."

Kara sighed. "And the constable will ask the same obvious questions that Landover asked."

"Very likely."

"What the police need are some men with a bit of nuance."

"Men who can observe and use their imaginations and think," Niall agreed. "There are a rare few," he reminded her. "They've mostly been made detectives."

She leaned back and raised a brow at her betrothed. "We are going to talk to that barkeeper, are we not?"

"Oh, yes," Niall said, one side of his mouth rising. "We are. First thing in the morning."

Chapter Six

NIALL WOKE BEFORE dawn the next morning. Without striking a light, he slipped from the loft above his forge and crept out from the small building without making a sound.

Standing in the shadows, he breathed in the cool, nearly-morning air and listened to the sleepy mutterings of the birds coming awake. All sounded calm. Everything felt normal.

He went prowling about on a patrol anyway.

Everything about the house lay clear. Niall eyed it with affection, this rambling Elizabethan bastion armed with secret passages and hidey-holes, filled with a staunch community of servants who had banded together to keep Kara safe. He would be happy to live here with her, just as he would be happy to travel with her and explore the wonders and beauty of the world.

Once he knew he wouldn't be putting her back in the sort of danger that had hung over her head for so long.

Keeping to the grassy sides, Niall followed the drive down to the gate. No one lurked about. The lane looked clear. Using his key, Niall slipped out, then locked the gates again. He walked down the road, then veered off to follow the hedge that curved around the main park's perimeter. No one lurked at the secret entrance in the hedge, either. He let himself through and went to encircle Kara's lab. He encountered no one until he came back around to the front and the main door.

"Did you find anything?" Kara, bundled in a heavy cloak over her robe and fur-lined boots, waited for him.

Niall shook his head.

"I checked the post. Nothing there. I spoke to Turner about the fellow in the lane, too. He and the groundskeepers are going to keep watch. No one had noticed him yet."

"Perhaps he followed us into Town." Niall waited as Kara unlocked the lab. He went to build up the fire, then sat down in one if the stuffed chairs. She fussed with her latest project a moment, then approached. Reaching out, he pulled her into his lap. They sat in silence for a while, just enjoying the warmth and comfort of being together.

"It's been long enough, surely." Her head rested against his shoulder, and he could feel the warmth of her breath on his neck. "I think they are going to ignore you, as they have done all along."

"They might." He didn't believe it, but if it gave her comfort to think so…

"It couldn't have been such a shock. Surely someone must have known about your mother, about you, despite what Stayme thinks. He's the one who knows all the secrets. They must keep a watch on him."

"He believes he covered his tracks all of these years, both with secrecy and with false rumors. He's convinced I am a nasty surprise, especially to those around the Crown."

"Even if you are, they must understand that you are loyal, or else why would you not have thrown in with Petra Scot's plans?"

"Because I might have disruptive plans of my own."

"What would make them think so? You've given them no reason to believe such a thing."

"They believe it because that's what they would do, according to Stayme."

She sighed. After a moment, she tensed in his arms. "If they are watching so closely, what will they make of you meeting with

West?"

"I suppose it will depend on how well they are paying attention. If they are truly acquainted with everything going on, they will see it for what it is—an attempt to help Josie."

"But wouldn't they find your talk with him reassuring? After all, he and his confederates on the rogue branch of the royal family tree are resigned to their status and have only pledged to aid one another. They are not making demands or causing trouble."

"Perhaps. Or perhaps they will wonder if I plan to stir them up to some discontent? Likely they—whoever they are—are merely waiting and watching." He sighed and buried his face in her dark, fragrant hair. For several moments, he just breathed her in. "Something's coming," he whispered. "I feel it in my bones."

Sitting up, she took his face in her hands. Smiling at him, she leaned in to kiss him. "You have a beautiful, superstitious Scots soul."

"It's true—"

"Let it come." Her expression grew fierce. "I won't let them harm you. Nothing they throw at you will come between us."

He wanted to believe it—that they could withstand anything. So he wrapped his arms around her and let himself do so.

After a while, she sat up and changed the subject. "I feel guilty, going back on my word to Inspector Wooten. I told him I would take a step back, away from his enquiry."

"I made no promise," he returned. "And in any case, the circumstances of your promise changed when Landover requested your help."

"What we are planning this morning has little to do with his request."

"It does have much to do with our promise to help Josie, which came first." Niall was feeling stubborn about it. After his initial reluctance, he found himself wanting to grab a hold of the puzzle, to help Josie, to distract himself from his own worries, and to protect Kara, who was going to end up entangled, one way or another. "We need to get a clear picture of the club that evening. And one of Cole's life in general."

"The barkeeper should be able to fill in a few gaps. If he didn't do it himself," she added darkly.

"I doubt it. Too obvious," Niall said, thinking. "But I shall be interested in his theories. Tapsters see all sorts of people. They tend to understand them, their follies—and perhaps their motives."

"I asked for breakfast to be sent out here," she said. "We can eat and then get ready to set out. I'll need the carriage later, too, when I go to tea at the Mosemans'. I'll send—"

She was interrupted by a knock on the door. Turner pushed in, bringing their breakfast on a cart covered in trays and dishes. Kara made to stand, but Niall held on for a moment.

"Thank you for a lovely start to the day," he whispered.

"Every morning is lovely when I start it with you." She buried her hands in his hair and kissed him again. "I cannot wait to be married, so our nights will be as wonderful."

The thought galvanized him, making him wild to be done with this endless waiting—and it also haunted him with the possibility that something, anything, could occur and snatch their chance of happiness away.

KARA WATCHED DISPASSIONATELY out the window as the carriage moved slowly down Fort Street in Lambeth. The Thames rolled by, just on the other side of a row of houses and businesses. The stink of the river hung in the air, and rubbish blew in the street. This section was not nearly so nice as the area around the Rogue's Hideaway, but it was close enough to make it feasible to work there.

The coach slowed as the driver began to scan for their destination. A girl, on the cusp of womanhood, her hair brushed, wearing a dress that was only slightly shabby, saw them coming and stopped to stare. The coachman slowed and called out to her, asking for directions.

The girl spoke and pointed. Kara could not hear her words, but the girl turned and followed, keeping pace with them as they turned a corner and pulled up before a run-down building of crumbling brick. Kara stared up at the place, which stood three stories high. She could see cracked tiles on the roof and broken panes in windows. The building stood in three sections. The two ends each contained a shop in the bottom—a barber and a locksmith, respectively—with rooms above. The middle section had the rooms above, but instead of a shop, a causeway had been cut through, leading to an enclosed space on the other side. As Kara descended, she could see cobblestones and a couple of ladies standing together in there.

"Jeremiah Yard is through there, according to the girl," her coachman said.

"Of course it is," answered Niall, making Kara laugh.

"Thank you for your aid," Kara told the girl.

Gawking, she merely curtsied in answer.

"Do you know where Jimmy Gibbs lives?" Kara asked her.

The girl nodded. "Right through here. I'll show you."

Kara and Niall followed her. Kara choked a little when she stepped through the causeway and found the river stench replaced with something worse in the small and dirty space of the yard.

"That's just Night-fingered Nel's dyes," the girl said as Kara began to breathe through her mouth.

She saw several lines had been stretched across a corner of the yard. They were hung with freshly dyed lengths of cotton and silk, left to dry in the air. They emanated scents of wet dog, sulfur, and old urine.

"Sorry, missus!" The woman hanging the cloths waved a hand, and her fingers had indeed been marked by what looked like indigo dye. "It do stink, but it's only a couple o' days o' the week! The stink fades as the fabric dries."

"And leaves such wonderful colors behind," Kara said, admiring the vivid display. "My old French nanny used to say that we all must suffer to find beauty—and your work is beautiful indeed."

"Eh, what do the Frenchies know?" the old woman said with a shake of her head. "But I do thank ye, just the same."

"Jimmy lives over here, in the corner," the girl said, beckoning.

"Jimmy don't mind the smell none!" the older woman called as they moved on.

"Or so he says," Kara muttered as Niall knocked on the door.

The only answer was a clanging noise. Niall knocked again, and a male voice yelled in answer. "Yes! What is it? Come in, if you must!"

Niall held the door for her, and Kara stepped in. He crowded in after her, making a noise of protest as she stopped—frozen in surprise.

It was all one room. Mostly bare, save for a table and chair, a narrow bed along one wall, and a long counter running the length of the back wall. It was also astonishingly clean, with every surface polished and gleaming. It was a shock to the senses, after the run-down dirt of the neighborhood. And the bad smells had been banished by the sweet scent of something fresh—and sugary?

"Yes? What is it?" Mr. Gibbs stood tall and handsome, young and clean-shaven. He hovered over what looked like a handmade, portable gas burner. It glowed with heat, and the barkeeper stirred something in a pot over it. He didn't stop, even as he looked over his shoulder at them.

Niall closed the door. "Good day, Mr. Gibbs. I am Mr. Niall Kier. This is my betrothed, Miss Kara Levett. We are friends of Josie Lowe. She gave us your address."

"Ah, do come in, then. And call me Jimmy. Everyone does. Is Josie preparing for tonight's wake? Robert means to give the old man a proper send-off. I am trying to make ready the ingredients for a special punch, to be served in his honor."

"One hopes the ingredients do not include foxglove," Kara said wryly, approaching and nodding toward a pile of greens, freshly washed and waiting on the counter.

"No, this is basil. I am infusing it in a syrup I mean to add to a punch for the ladies attending this evening." He paused, his stirring slowing as he processed her words. "Foxglove?" he asked. "Is that what the leafy bits were, in the spilled wine?" He shook his head. "What foolishness. Even my old grandmother knew to be careful with the stuff."

"The coroner says a dangerous dose of it is indeed what killed Mr. Cole," Niall said.

"Poor old codger. He were a right one." Jimmy Gibbs gave a sigh, then suddenly stiffened. "Wait a second, now. Is that why you've come? You cannot think that I had anything to do with that. I do come up with an odd recipe, now and then. Mr. West encourages me, especially, to create drinks to tempt the ladies. But I would never use ingredients that would harm anyone. Especially not old Mr. Cole."

"No one accuses you of any foul play," Niall assured him. "In fact, Josie is still being held by the police and the coroner's office, in association with Frederick Cole's death."

"What?" The young man appeared genuinely shocked. "That cannot be. I won't believe it. They must be mistaken. Josie would never harm the old man."

"We don't believe so either," Kara said. "That's why we wished to talk to you."

"I already told the constables last night—there is no way Josie had anything to do with anything shady. Mr. Cole had that goblet of wine at least an hour before she finished her performance and came out to join him. And before you ask—I poured that wine myself. No, I did not add anything to it. Couldn't have been anything in the bottle, either, as I poured from it for several customers afterward." He shook his head. "It had to have been spiked while he was at the table, but I was too busy to have seen everyone over there with him."

"Can you recall anyone specifically who stopped to talk with him?"

"At least a dozen other guests," Jimmy said helplessly. "Everyone wants to shake his hand, exchange a word of business or gossip. Even just to say good evening, for the thrill of telling people they've talked with the great man."

Kara, imagining the scene in her mind's eye, had a sudden notion. "Could the foxglove have already been in the goblet before you poured the wine?"

Jimmy stopped stirring, frowning. He yelped when a drop of the syrup jumped up to burn his hand. "Let me get this basil started steeping, aye?" With the ease of practice, he tied the stems of the herbs, removed the syrup from the heat, and hung the basil from a makeshift rack above it, allowing the leaves to stay suspended in the sugar solution. "There now, I'll let this cool, strain it, and I'll have the makings of a grand punch that will keep the ladies coming back."

"What will you mix it with, out of curiosity?" Kara asked.

"Lemonade, ice, and a shot of gin," he said proudly.

"Gin?" she repeated, surprised.

"Aye. It's titillating, isn't it, for the ladies to have a tipple of something low like gin. Adds to the adventure." He lifted his chin. "I concocted it myself. Come around tonight, Miss Levett, and you'll have one, on me." He winked at her, then grew serious. "Now, that was a good notion you had. Let me think back, exactly to when I poured that goblet of wine."

"Are you sure you poured it?" asked Niall. "Would anyone else have been behind the bar with you?"

"No," Jimmy answered decisively. "I don't let anyone back behind the bar with me. It causes confusion and sets my nerves off something fierce. It's my domain, you see? My workshop. A lot of it is just pouring, talking, and listening. But Mr. West gives me room to explore with new breweries and with imported wines and brandies so we can serve the best and the most unusual. And, of course, he encourages me to create new mixes that will keep the customers coming back to get something they can't find anywhere else." He smiled, his gaze far away for a moment. "Ah, there's nothing like seeing that moment of surprise and pleasure on someone's face, when you've given them a taste of something entirely new. Something they couldn't have imagined for themselves."

Kara found herself liking the young man, both for his defense of Josie and for his obvious passion for his work.

"So you must have poured it," Niall said, going back to the timeline of Mr. Cole's death. "And you didn't notice anything in the goblet before you poured the wine?"

"No, but I'm not sure I would have noticed, nor looked. Those goblets are metal. Dark. And I was likely doing three other things at the same time. We stay busy, and I have to be quick."

Niall nodded. "This was about an hour before Josie's set, you said?"

"A little less, perhaps." Kara could see the man thinking back, even as he tidied his counter. "Yes. I recall old Mr. Cole looking like thunder when he entered. Then the magician came on stage and he looked even more put out." He lifted a shoulder. "He never did like that act."

"Who served the wine to Mr. Cole?" asked Kara. "You wouldn't have left the bar?"

"No. Elias took it over to him. He nearly always did. I remember, that night, he gave me a shock. I turned away to some gent at the end of the bar, and when I looked back, there he was, as if he'd appeared out of thin air. He looked low, too, and I thought the old man might be taking his temper out on him."

"Elias Wade, you mean?" asked Niall.

"Yes, and don't go suspecting that boy, either," Jimmy said with a sigh. "I used to tease the lad about their mutual admiration society. He and Mr. Cole got on famously."

Kara quirked a smile at him. "That's exactly what someone

said about you and Mr. Cole."

Jimmy flushed with pleasure. "We did get on. He would sit at the bar, at the end of the night, when everyone had gone. He'd be waiting for Josie and I'd be straightening up, counting my bottles. He weren't a high and mighty sort, for all of his money. He talked to you like a regular chap. Always asked after my mam, and after the young women I was chasin' after."

"Did he talk to you about his life?"

"Oh, yes. He weren't too high to tell me about his own troubles. He would speak of his highs and lows."

"Did he tell you about anyone he might have had difficulties with? Anyone you can think of who might have wanted him dead?"

Jimmy made a face. "The man made enemies. In business like that, with so many thousands of pounds on the line every day, he couldn't avoid it, but honestly? He mostly complained about his wife."

"His wife?" asked Kara, surprised.

"Aye. He were that bitter about her. They never got on, it seemed, but it seemed to grow worse these last months. *Jimmy,* he'd say. *Never get a leg shackle. It's always more trouble than it's worth.*"

"Did he say what they argued about?" Kara was reluctant to let the man continue to disparage marriage.

"All manner of things. The prospects of their daughter. Josie and the time he spent with her," he said, flushing a little. "And money. His wife was a spender. She wouldn't curb it, no matter how often he told her. Said his money was all she got out of him, and she'd be damned before she gave it up." His mouth dropped open. "You don't think she could have done it?"

"Did she ever come to the Rogue's Hideaway?" Kara asked.

"No. She'd never set foot in the place. Not in a hundred years. But she could have hired some lowlife to do her dirty work." Jimmy was clearly warming to his theory.

"Did you see any lowlife of that sort that evening? Anyone

new or suspicious?"

"No. I don't recall anyone who stood out. I told the police so."

"If the police come back, tell them the bit about his wife, will you?" asked Niall.

"And so I will. They need to think about someone besides Josie for doing this to Mr. Cole."

"Our thoughts exactly. Thank you for your help, Jimmy," Kara said.

"Wasn't nothing, Miss Levett. Happy to do what I can. I'll miss the old bloke. Now, you come and try one of my special creations, eh? You won't be served no bland negus at my bar."

"We will indeed visit, someday soon. Good day to you."

"Good day, and good luck, too. Whoever it was who done Mr. Cole, he should pay for the deed."

"We'll do our best. Thank you."

Niall ushered her to the door. Stepping out, Kara paused to look around for the girl who had helped them earlier. "Do you see our young guide?"

"No. She's gone on, it seems." He accompanied her through the yard to the waiting carriage.

"Goodness," Kara said as she settled in. "I think the stink has taken lodging in my nose. I'm glad I thought to send a change of clothes on to the rooms on Adams Road. Will you accompany me to tea with the Mosemans? Harriet will be thrilled to see you."

"No. I think I will see what I can discover about Elias Wade."

"Ah. A good idea."

He kissed her hand, and even that small, tender gesture caused a stir in her belly. She gazed at him in the open doorway, so tall and broad and with a light of appreciation in his eyes. Good heavens, but she hoped he got over his uncertainties soon. She was very much looking forward to being married.

Sooner, rather than later.

Chapter Seven

NIALL WATCHED THE carriage head north toward Westminster Bridge while his brain replayed everything Jimmy Gibbs had told them. He set out in the same direction, on foot. He wanted to head back to the Rogue's Hideaway and find out what he could about Elias Wade, Frederick Cole's personal servant.

Several minutes walking had him nearly to the intersection with Broad Street. His mind was still grappling with the pieces of the murderous puzzle when he spotted the girl from this morning. She peered around the corner of a narrow lane between two houses ahead. Meeting his gaze directly, she very deliberately shook her head.

It gave him pause. What did she mean by it? Did she not want him to continue to travel in that direction? Why? He stepped up his pace, meaning to ask her what she was about, but suddenly her eyes widened and she disappeared, snatched into the shadows of the alley.

Stunned, Niall broke into a run. Skidding around the corner of the lane, he saw a man halfway down the length of it, holding the struggling girl and attempting to drag her along with him.

"Hold there!" Niall shouted, running faster. "Take your hands off her! What in blazes do you think you are—"

Oof. The second man caught him completely unaware, stepping out of a recessed doorway and striking him hard across the abdomen with a long plank.

The impact sent him sprawling backward into the filth lining the lane. He scrambled away as the man stalked toward him. The miscreant behind him let go of the girl and marched into step as well, even as a third man rose out of the shadows to join them.

Niall saw the girl scrambling on, safely away. He weighed the odds, taking the murderous looks on the men's faces into account, rose to his feet, turned—and sprinted away.

With a chorus of shouts, they were after him. Niall pounded around the corner onto the larger avenue of Broad Street, hoping that the increased foot traffic would slow them. People gave way before him as he ran full tilt, but judging by the cries of anger and dismay rising behind him, the trio was still in pursuit.

He ran on. Up ahead stood the gated entrance to a mustard manufactory. The gate stood half open as a pair of men carried a stack of crates inside. Niall slipped through and rammed the gate shut as the porters yelled and the three men came up to slam against it.

He turned and ran. One of his pursuers climbed the gate while the others rattled it and shouted orders at the porters. Niall skirted a building that emanated wafts of vinegar and garlic. Beyond it lay a drive occupied by two delivery wagons.

He spent a second deliberating whether to hide in one, but they were shallow and he would be easy to spot if they paused to look. Going past them, he found a warehouse only half full of hogsheads and massive packing crates.

With relief, he slipped among them. Ducking down and moving as soundlessly as he could among the goods, he headed for the wide, open doors on the other side. When he reached the end, he paused. Ten feet of empty space lay between his cover and the door. Crouching, he waited a moment, listening. No footsteps, calls, or other signs of pursuit. Taking a deep breath, he stood and dashed for the door.

A shout came from the other side of the warehouse. Cursing, Niall kept going. The high fence of a burial ground lay beyond the warehouse. He pelted east along a footpath running beside the fence. When it ended, he turned north.

He ran smack into a construction site. Something had recently been demolished here. Rubble and dirt lay about in piles. Wide planks formed walkways through the mess. One side showed signs of clearing. He headed in that direction.

He heard the call just as he reached a complete section of wall that had been knocked down. The shouter was giving directions, instructions to surround him. He started out over the walkway laid over the wall, moving quickly, heading for the row of back gardens and larger houses just beyond.

He was halfway across when he realized his mistake. This board was not meant as a walkway. It had been tossed on as a throwaway. He felt the soft wood give way beneath his boot just before the board cracked and his foot went through it and the damp, crumbling plaster beneath. He froze, but a creaking sound emanated around him. The wall was groaning in protest of his weight. A great crack sounded, echoed, and he went down with the decorated wall, plunging into darkness below.

Niall struck hard, and the impact had his head bouncing off something solid. His vision grew blurry—then dark. He came back to himself gradually, with his ears buzzing and his eyes blinking furiously to focus. He must have been completely knocked out for a moment. He groaned and rubbed his eyes. It took a few moments for his senses to clear.

He found himself surrounded by flocked wallpaper, chunks of plaster, wood debris, and a great cloud of dust. Moving carefully, he checked his limbs, making sure all were intact and functioning. He stopped suddenly as his gaze turned upward, and through the dust he saw his three pursuers standing at the edge, staring down.

No one said a word. They all stared at each other, then the three men above exchanged a speaking glance, turned, and left.

Well, then. At least they had not shot him like a fish in a

barrel. Slowly, carefully, Niall climbed to his feet. It must be a cellar he'd fallen into. He was twelve feet down, give or take. He was lucky he hadn't snapped his neck. A few bruises and a sore back felt like a small price to pay for his foolishness.

He began to pick through the debris, looking for anything sound enough to help him get out. There was not much that might be useful. Most everything was cracked or rotting. He'd collected several possible pieces and was bent over, examining another, when the back of his neck began to prickle.

He looked up again.

A different man peered over the edge of the cellar at him. He wore a voluminous dark coat with the collar pulled high, but the bulbous nose was familiar. It was the man who had been watching the road outside Bluefield Park.

They stared at each other. Niall cursed under his breath. After a moment, the man disappeared.

Niall sat abruptly down. What in the blazes? Who in seven hells was that man? Was he connected to the ones who ambushed him? Was all of this about his background? Or was it about their continued interest in Frederick Cole's murder?

A whisper of a sound had him flinching and looking up again. The watcher was back. He shook his head, then tossed down a knotted rope. Once it had reached Niall, he stepped away again.

Niall hesitated. He gave the rope a tug, and it appeared to be well anchored. Was this a trick? Were they waiting for him above?

He couldn't stay where he was. With resignation, he took hold and began to climb.

It was slow going. His body protested and his back made its grievances known, but he made it up on his own. When he crawled over the edge, he saw no one waited for him. None of the men were in sight, nor anyone else. The rope was tied to the burial ground fence, but the demolition site was deserted.

With a sigh, Niall climbed to his feet and began to pick his slow way back toward the main streets.

※≫≫≪≪

"Good afternoon, Creech," Kara said as she entered the Mosemans' home on Red Lion Street.

"Good afternoon, Miss Levett." The butler took her bonnet with a smile. "We are all glad to have you back. May I ask after Mr. Turner?"

"You may. He is doing well and has bade me to give you his regards and an invitation to visit him at Bluefield Park, when next you have a free afternoon."

Creech nodded, his face flushed with pleasure. "I shall happily accept. Now, if you will follow me? Mrs. Moseman means to serve tea in the south parlor."

She trailed after him and smiled broadly when Mrs. Moseman stood as she entered the parlor.

"There you are." The older woman greeted her with a kiss on both cheeks.

"It's so lovely to see you, Joanna. Thank you for the invitation."

"We are thrilled to have you. Creech, will you send upstairs for Miss Harriet?"

"Of course. Tea will be served shortly, madam." The butler bowed out of the room.

"Now, come and sit." Mrs. Moseman gestured toward the chairs gathered around a table. "Where is that grand, hulking fiancé of yours? You didn't bring him?"

"No. He had enquiries of his own to make."

Joanna paused in the act of sitting. "Enquiries? Never tell me the pair of you are mixed up in another investigation?" She saw the answer on Kara's face. "Not Frederick Cole?" she asked.

"Yes, indeed. He was...patron to a friend of ours. A woman who helped save Niall's skin when he was captured by those League men, weeks ago. Now she's asked for our help, and we are glad to give it."

Mrs. Moseman glanced toward the open door and lowered her tone. "But I heard—through unofficial channels, of course—that the young woman in his keeping is being held, awaiting an inquest."

"She did not murder him," Kara said firmly. "We are bound to help her prove her innocence."

"By finding the real killer, I presume? Kara, how do you manage to get involved in these affairs?"

"I don't know!" she answered truthfully. "Strange situations seem to be coming at me lately." She raised a brow. "I would blame my circle of friends, did it not also number such eminently respectable people as you."

"Flattery? Oh, dear." Joanna tried and failed to suppress a grin. "This smacks of an impending request."

"I am ashamed to say you are correct, but—"

"Kara!" Miss Harriet Moseman rushed in. Bright with excitement, she embraced Kara before looking around with a pout. "Niall did not accompany you?"

"No, but he bade me send his regards, as well as his thanks again for your gift. He said it was a lovely surprise, and a flattering one."

Harriet, nearly sixteen and just starting to look at gentlemen with a woman's eye, had formed a slight *tendre* for Niall. When she had encountered a lovely gate of Niall's design in a friend's garden, she insisted on painting a watercolor of the scene. She'd written a sentimental verse on the back of the framed image and sent it to Niall as a gift.

"So he said in his note." Harriet was not one to give up easily. "How I should love to see it hanging at Bluefield."

"Harriet, you should know better than to angle for an invitation," her mother admonished her.

"You are welcome at any time, of course," Kara said with a laugh. "Why do we not plan for you to spend a day with us next week?"

"May I help in your lab?" the girl said, flushing with pleasure.

"Of course."

"Will you ask your cook to make her fig and apple tart?"

Doubtless, the girl had somehow heard that the tart was Niall's favorite. "If you wish."

"Speaking of tarts, will you run downstairs to ask if Cook has any of those lemon curd pastries left from last night's desserts?" Joanna asked. "I seem to recall Kara's fondness for lemon."

"Oh, my. Yes. My favorite," Kara agreed.

Harriet sprang out of her seat, as spry as a monkey, and went on her way.

"Now, it won't take her long," her mother said as the door closed behind her. "Why don't you tell me about the favor you meant to ask?"

"Honestly, I had no notion of it when I accepted your invitation," Kara assured her old friend. "But last night, a coroner's officer asked if I had any sway with Mrs. Frederick Cole. It seems that she is not inclined to cooperate with the authorities, nor answer their questions. I told him I did not know the woman, but afterward, I thought you might perhaps have an acquaintance with her, and if so, you might speak with her."

"Oh, dear. Well, I would help if I could, but I am afraid I am not accepted into Mrs. Cole's social circles."

Kara's back went up at the phrasing. "Not *accepted*?"

"Indeed, no." Her hostess looked uncomfortable. "I am afraid Mrs. Cole does not deem us as worthy."

Kara blinked. "Why on earth not?"

Joanna cleared her throat. "Mrs. Cole's grandfather made his fortune in shipping—and in privateering, if you believe the whispers—but both Mrs. Cole and her mother were raised in very fine circumstances. In contradiction, my husband started his career as a clerk."

Kara straightened. "Moseman has not been a clerk for a very long time. He is my right hand in business. He oversees my largest manufactories and interests. I pay his substantial and well-earned salary, and I thank God for him every day. Together with the sound investments we have both made, I know that your husband is a very rich man, indeed."

"So he is, but that does not stop Mrs. Cole from viewing him as your lackey."

"Lackey?" Kara repeated, incredulous. "Has the daft woman met your husband?"

"No, indeed. As proud as she is of her wealthy family, as the mere daughter of a rich merchant, she finds herself shut out of the highest, blue-blooded circles of Society. To compensate, she's created her own social circle. She takes great delight in making it exclusive, mostly according to her whims. She is queen of a certain set of wealthy cits, industrialists, and business families, and she is very particular as to whom she admits into it."

"Is she, indeed?"

"Mr. Moseman and I are not invited to their events. We do manage to bear up," she said with a wry smile. "However, our Harriet has had cause to interact with the young people, the children of many of their set. As she has proved quite popular with both the young ladies and the young gentlemen, she has been allowed to form a friendship with Miss Charlotte Cole, who is just a year older than she."

"Has Mrs. Cole been so condescendingly gracious?" Kara asked with irony. "Heavens, but the woman sounds appalling."

"Who is appalling?" Harriet flounced back in. "Mrs. Pritchett has added the pastries to the tea tray, Mama," she reported dutifully. "But who is appalling?"

"No one you need worry over, dear," her mother assured her. "Oh, look. Here is Creech with the tea."

The talk grew general as the ladies partook of the excellent offerings. Harriet was full of questions about the betrothal and especially about the wedding.

"We've not really started planning," Kara admitted. "We've both been busy, and there are still a few matters that need working out. But we've discussed it, and Niall and I have agreed that we would like it to be a small affair, with just our nearest and dearest in attendance."

Harriet looked anxious.

"Don't worry. You will all be invited, of course." Kara leaned forward. "In fact, you know how I adore your poetry, Harriet. I should love it if you would agree to do a reading, perhaps before the ceremony?" She looked to Mrs. Moseman. "If your mother approves, that is."

Joanna smiled as Harriet gazed imploringly her way. "Your mother approves. You've worked hard, darling, and I know you will make us proud." She turned to Kara. "Thank you."

"I would be *honored* to read something," Harriet said breathlessly. She clasped her hands together. "Oh, I cannot *wait* to go to balls and get engaged and get married." Her eyes were shining. "Just wait until I tell Charlotte!" Her expression dimmed. "Oh, but perhaps now is not the time to share such news with her."

"Your instincts are correct," her mother said with approval. "Charlotte will be thrilled for you, eventually, but you should wait a few weeks, at least, before you tell her. She needs time to grieve."

"The poor thing," Harriet said. "She was meant to come out this Season—in just a matter of weeks. She has the most beautiful collection of gowns being made. But that will all have to wait until next year." She brightened. "But the good news is that we will come out together. What fun it will be, but it feels very long to wait. Poor Charlotte." Harriet looked beseechingly at her mother once more. "Are you *very* sure that I cannot go to her this afternoon? Her note sounded so sad."

"I'm sorry, my dear, but my charity event is next week. I simply must attend this afternoon's meeting. As it is Miss Miller's half-day off, you must stay home." At Harriet's mutinous look, her tone hardened a little. "If you started running about unaccompanied, Mrs. Cole would be quick to cut your friendship with her daughter."

Harriet sighed.

Kara straightened. "If all she needs is an escort, I should be glad to go along with her. I'm sure I can sit with the governess or the staff as easily as Harriet's governess does."

"Oh, Kara, would you? May she, Mother? May I? Charlotte did write and ask me to come. I'd like to comfort her, if I can."

Kara gazed at Mrs. Moseman with a raised brow. She knew the older woman would understand her eagerness to get inside the Cole household.

"Very well," Joanna said after a moment. Kara saw her press her lips against a likely wave of comments. "But keep it a short visit only."

"Yes, Mama! Thank you!" Harriet was already heading for the door. "I shall fetch my coat and hat and have Creech send for the carriage." She looked back. "I'll return in a moment!"

Her mother looked sternly at Kara. "I trust you will not do anything to harm our standing with Mrs. Cole further?"

Kara laughed. "I promise. On the contrary, I just might manage to help in that direction."

Chapter Eight

T HE COLES' HOME was a three-storied affair that could have rivaled a palace. It looked like the sort of home that had its own moniker. Cole House or Cole Hall, perhaps. It sat in the section of Mayfair near Hyde Park, taking up a great deal of space. It was also one of the few homes in London with enough land for an actual garden with a tall fence surrounding it. Now, the wide street before the place had been laid with rushes.

"It's meant to deaden the noise of the traffic, so as not to disturb the mourners inside," Kara explained to Harriet.

A footman gave them entrance through the gate and another let them into the house. Both wore black neckcloths and armbands. Kara looked around the wide entry hall as they handed over their outerwear. The grand central staircase was empty. The mirror over a marble table had been covered with black cloth.

Harriet seemed to shrink a little. "It's so quiet," she whispered.

The hush was indeed oppressive. "The people here are in mourning, dear," Kara told her quietly.

She waited for the footman to lead them into the house, but he was young, and perhaps new? He stood still, staring at Kara. She was suddenly glad she'd had the foresight to send a change of clothes to her London rooms and had no cause to worry about carrying the stink of Jeremiah Yard. Surreptitiously, she checked the lay of the crossed front of her gown. It was an elegant day gown of deepest maroon, with black trim at the wrists and swooping across the skirts. She knew she looked neat and that the tightly pulled cross panels made her waist look tiny.

Harriet shifted on her feet.

"Since Charlotte is expecting you, perhaps you could just run along up to her room?" Kara looked at the footman for confirmation, but he seemed unsure. "Go, dear, but step quietly."

Harriet moved off, sure of her destination. Kara threw the young man a look of exasperation. "I'll be happy for a visit with young Miss Charlotte's governess, or even for a spot below stairs. Wherever Miss Miller might have expected to wait."

He awakened from his daze at last. "Oh, no. I, uh… Please, just wait here a moment and I'll ask the butler what's to be done with you."

He scrambled off, and Kara was left alone to contemplate the richness of the marbled hall and the excellence of the house's design. After a moment, a door opened somewhere down a hall and a man's footsteps echoed, ever closer. Stepping out from behind the staircase, the tall man with the severe mien of a senior servant regarded her frostily.

"Miss Levett?"

Apparently, she'd been recognized. "Yes?"

"Miss Kara Levett?"

"Yes."

He looked faintly alarmed. "I am Choate, Miss Levett. I am afraid Mrs. Cole is not at home to visitors. We've had a—" He paused to clear his throat, obviously affected.

"Yes. I am very sorry. I know about your bereavement, of course, and I do not mean to be a burden. I have not come to call upon your mistress. It's just that Miss Charlotte Cole wrote to young Miss Harriet Moseman, asking her to come to her. There was no one else to bring her." She smiled in what she hoped was a comforting manner. "Please, I am happy to sit in a corner downstairs, out of the way. I'm sure I won't be here long."

"No, no. That won't do. The governess has retired with a headache, and though our housekeeper is busy with arrangements for a wake, she would keel over in a faint if she knew you'd been treated like a servant." He hesitated for only a moment. "Please, follow me. You can wait in the morning parlor and I'll have tea sent to you."

"Thank you." Kara had to hide her disappointment. She'd hoped for a comfortable bit of gossip with some of the staff. Ah, well. At least Harriet could comfort her friend.

She looked about as she followed the butler. The house was huge and very finely decorated. Creamy marble, reds, and golds dominated the decorating scheme. It was as impressive as a house of state, and she'd been in several. Choate led her to a small room on the east side of the house, with windows that must capture the morning light.

"If you will make yourself comfortable, tea will be provided in a few moments. I will fetch you when Miss Moseman's visit has concluded."

"Thank you."

The butler retreated, and Kara waited a bit before she got to her feet and began to search the room. She didn't know what she was looking for. Some clue as to the nature of the family that lived here, she supposed. What sort of family life had Frederick Cole had?

But there was no hint of it to be found here. The parlor was as lovely as the rest of the house, done in varying, light shades of blue. Though the walls were hung with fine paintings and the surfaces scattered with sure-to-be-valuable bric-a-brac, the drawers were empty. There was no clutter. No detritus of life lived in here. The only unexpected thing she found was an old embroidery set, half finished and stuffed between the cushions of a settee.

She stuffed it back when she heard the rattling of porcelain in the passage outside. When the door opened, she was back sitting sedately in the chair she'd been left in.

"Good afternoon."

The maid nodded as she came in with a tray.

"I'm very sorry for the loss your household has suffered," Kara said gently.

"Thank you, miss."

"I know it is a difficult time for all of you, but I wondered if I might speak with Elias Wade while I wait for Miss Moseman?"

The cup and saucer rattled. "I'm sure I don't know who you mean, miss."

The girl set down her burden, curtsied, and left in a hurry. Kara gazed at the single cup of tea, already poured. The staff was uncertain, then. Hedging their bets. They could not fail to offer hospitality, but neither did they wish to lavish attention on an unwelcome, unwanted visitor.

With a sigh, she lifted the cup and drank—just as the door swung open with a dramatic flair.

A woman of medium height and an angry aura stared at her before entering and shutting the door behind her. The stiff, dull black bombazine of her gown crackled with each movement. "What are you doing in my house?" she demanded.

Moving with deliberation, Kara set down her cup, stood, and gave her best meeting-the-queen curtsy. "Mrs. Cole. I did not mean to disturb you at this time of your great loss. I am Miss—"

"I know who you are. What are you doing in my house?"

"Your daughter asked for Miss Moseman. There was no one else to bring her."

"Balderdash! I know why you've come. You are friendly with that *low* woman."

Kara heard the swapped meaning in her words. "I am indeed a friend of Miss Josie Lowe, but that has no bearing—"

"Of course it does. I am not a fool." Mrs. Cole raised a haughty chin. Doubtless, she had once been pretty, but years of indulging in spite and bitterness had taken their toll. Dull gray threaded her dark hair, but it was the permanent frown lines around her mouth and on her brow that aged her. Kara could not help but wonder when the woman had last smiled.

"You are here to convince me to cooperate with the police, are you not? To name Frederick's enemies? To air our dirty laundry before a bunch of grubby constables? Why should I? Especially as the culprit has already been apprehended."

"I think we both know that it makes little sense for Josie to have killed your husband, ma'am."

"It doesn't make sense for *anyone* to have killed him," she said stiffly. "And in any case, they are still holding her, are they not?"

"They are," Kara said.

The other woman's eyes closed as she leaned back against the door. "Much as it pleases me to think of that woman in a cell, it won't last, will it? She'll be released as soon as they find someone with a better motive to harm Frederick."

Kara held her silence. She jumped when the woman thumped a hand against the door.

"Damn Frederick to hell!" she raged. "Even in death, he must be contrary and utterly inconvenient!"

"I don't think your husband intended to die, Mrs. Cole, let alone inconvenience you with his murder."

"Ha! You obviously didn't know my husband well. He might indeed have gone so far, just to spite me. He always had to have the last word."

Clearly there was no appropriate response for such a statement.

The woman straightened and sank into a chair near the door, as if she had no wish to come closer to Kara. For several long minutes, she merely stared ahead, her gaze unfocused and her thoughts turned inward. Kara waited, not moving, wondering if the woman would speak again.

When she did, Mrs. Cole's words were steeped in anger and despair. "Everything I've worked for, all the heights I have achieved—gone. I worked as hard as my husband, I tell you. And I swear, it's more difficult to climb a social ladder than it is to build a company, in my opinion." She dropped her head in her hands. "The *timing* of it all," she choked out. "I was within weeks of launching my daughter to a better, safer life. Now it is all ruined. She will carry this scandal for all of her life. Our names will be bandied about every dinner table in London and across every fence in every backwater in England."

"Surely not," Kara objected. "With a murder there will be notoriety at first, but—"

Mrs. Cole interrupted with a bitter laugh. "Oh, how rich. I should not expect you to understand. You, of all people!"

"I understand what it is like to have a false murder charge hanging over your head, just as Josie has now."

"But your good name was part and parcel of seeing you free of the charge, was it not?"

Kara rather thought the opposite was true, but Mrs. Cole was not going to allow her to say it. The woman's head came up, and she regarded Kara with incredulous ire.

"You actually, miraculously, got a second chance, didn't you, Miss Levett? You would have been welcomed back into the best Society, with open arms. A daughter of a peer. And if that social standing was not enough, you are also a *woman* in ownership of one of the greatest industrial fortunes in England. And do you appreciate your good fortune? No, here you are, throwing it away."

"I am doing no such thing," Kara said quietly.

Mrs. Cole scoffed. "Nonsense. You have the sort of acceptance that so many pine for, but do you value it? No. You are wasting your time traipsing around London without proper supervision, messing about with bits of metal, and appear set to marry a man with no money, connections, or bloodlines." The woman snapped her fingers at her. "Wake up, girl! If you were mine, I would beat you soundly! But it's not too late, you know. You could still turn it around. You could contract a marriage with one of England's grandest bachelors and catapult yourself to the top of Society." She shook her head restlessly. "But my own girl...

All of those opportunities are lost to Charlotte now."

"I know it feels like that now, ma'am, but none of this is your daughter's fault. Surely she—and you—will recover."

Mrs. Cole glared at her with a distaste bordering on hatred. "You really are so foolish as to believe that, aren't you?" She tossed her head. "And if you think that I will willingly make the scandal bigger by blackening Frederick's name or spilling his secrets, then you are more than a fool."

Drawing in a breath, Kara watched the other woman closely. "Do you not wish to see your husband's killer brought to justice, ma'am?"

Mrs. Cole glared daggers at her. "I should like to thank him," she spat. "And then I should berate him for not doing it sooner, before—" She stopped herself and burst into angry, desperate tears.

Kara took the linen napkin from her tray and went to offer it to her.

Mrs. Cole snatched it away. "For heaven's sake, do not take my words seriously. Of course I didn't want my husband dead," she said, wiping her eyes. "He enraged me. He mocked me. He occasionally tormented me. But I gave as good as I got. We knocked heads, but we respected each other, deep down. And I would never have achieved so much, nor climbed so high, without him." She heaved a sigh. "But that is over now."

Kara sat quietly, just looking at her. The woman was highly unlikeable, but still, Jimmy Gibbs's idea that Mrs. Cole might have arranged her husband's death seemed far less likely to her now. "Perhaps I can help with your recovery from this scandal."

"The scandal has barely started," the woman bit out. She stopped herself suddenly, looking terrified, as if she'd said too much.

"What will come will come," Kara said. "You will have to endure it. But perhaps a marriage invitation would help."

"What marriage?" Mrs. Cole asked. Her eyes widened. "Yours?"

"Miss Moseman will take part in the ceremony. I'm sure your Charlotte will wish to see her friend's triumph. We have not yet set a date, but I am sure a widow might safely attend a morning marriage ceremony. Especially one that is sure to be attended by many notables."

The woman's look turned crafty. "Notables? Perhaps the Viscount Stayme will attend?"

Kara grinned. "He might even worm his way into giving me away."

"And Lady Margaret Simmons?"

The woman was certainly familiar with Kara's social connections. "Oh, Lady Madge will be there." Tilting her head, she mused out loud. "I am trying to imagine her reaction to you. She has strong opinions, as you seem to do. Perhaps she might admire you? Or she might decide to despise you. I can hardly wait to see which."

Mrs. Cole looked like she'd love to be given the chance to find out. "And you'll do this for…what? I do not believe you offer this out of the kindness of your heart."

"I like to think I do indeed have a kind heart, Mrs. Cole, but I daresay you would not respect me if I did not demand payment in kind. And, in fact, I have two concessions I would like you to grant me."

"Two?" she asked scathingly.

"Yes, indeed. The first relates to your imminent period of mourning. Your carefully crafted social circle will no doubt miss you terribly these next few months. I suggest you begin to fill the hole you will leave by suggesting your cronies invite Mr. and Mrs. Moseman to an affair or two. Once they are acquainted with them, I am sure they will find what a lovely, intelligent pair they are. A fine addition to any social occasion."

Mrs. Cole's lips thinned as she considered. "Very well. And I suppose the other one relates to my agreement to speak to the police?

"I do think you would be wise to share pertinent information with them."

The woman sat a moment thinking. "Well," she said at last. "Perhaps I will talk to them. After all, if I am to crash, I needn't go down alone. The police *should* be looking at those who will benefit from Frederick's death. Or even those who are just made happy by it, yes? God knows there are plenty of them out there."

Good heavens. The woman was incorrigible. Kara kept her sigh of exasperation to herself.

Mrs. Cole was warming to her subject. "Let them look into Sock and Buskin, eh? Oh, the nerves that will jangle, having the police look into their files." She almost giggled with glee. "And they can have a nice, long talk with Randall Abbott and ask how he was getting along with Frederick lately."

"Randall Abbott?"

"One of the men on the board of the company, and one of my husband's oldest friends and business allies. But the police will be very interested in the state of their relationship recently." Her expression darkened. "And let them dig into *Robert West's* background, as well." She nearly spat the name. "*West*, indeed. I will never understand how everyone just plays along, accepting that it is his real name. The favored son, bastard though he may be. At least, that's the tale he likes to tell. Well, the man allowed Frederick to be killed in his wretched club. Let him pay the price and have the old scandal dragged up again."

Kara was listening in fascination. She wished she could take notes. But Wooten would be able to handle the woman. And she would compare notes with him, to be sure. A sudden thought struck her. "One more thing you could do for me, Mrs. Cole. Elias Wade? Might I talk to him before I leave?"

The woman's expression twisted into distaste. "Wade? Why would you wish to speak to him?"

"He might have some answers to questions we had about your husband's health."

"Well, he might at that, but you won't find him here."

"He does not live in this house?" Kara asked, surprised.

"Indeed, he does not. I kicked him out months ago."

"Why?"

"Because I could not abide the creature. No one could, not below stairs nor above. He belonged in neither world, and yet acted as if he owned both. He is a strange little man. He was always oddly defiant, and I could not tolerate it. He had to go."

"Where does he reside now, do you know?"

"No. Nor do I care." She stood, looking weary. "Charlotte and Harriet have visited long enough. Our bargain is struck. Now, I want you to go."

"You will adhere to our agreement?"

"I will if you will."

Kara nodded. "I give my word." She blanched a little, wondering about Niall's reaction to this promise.

"Good. I'll send the girl down to you. Good day."

The woman swept out of the room, and Kara was left wondering just what she had done. But there was no help for it, and several minutes later, she and Harriet were being hustled out of the gate and to their carriage.

After the coach had got underway, Kara squeezed Harriet's hand. "How was Charlotte?"

"Distraught," Harriet answered. Her lip began to tremble. "Her heart is broken." Tears welled and began to fall. "I don't know what I would do if something happened to Papa."

"Oh, my dear." Kara crossed to the other bench and pulled her close. "Your papa is hale and healthy. He is a kind man. He has not spent a lifetime collecting enemies as Mr. Cole did."

Harriet cried a little longer, then made a valiant effort to dry her tears, though she did leave her head resting on Kara's shoulder. "Charlotte says nothing will ever be the same."

"Of course it will not. She and her father were very close, by all accounts."

"They were. She is furious at him for leaving her alone with her mother."

"Well, Mr. Cole did not choose to be murdered."

"But she says the result is the same. She won't have her Season this year, of course. She and her mother will have to retreat to the country, she says, and they are not likely to come back. Not for next year's Season, nor at all. Not ever."

"Surely that will not be the case," Kara said soothingly, but hearing that made her think back to some of the things that Mrs. Cole had let slip, and she was convinced there was more going on in this case than appeared on the surface. And she wondered suddenly if this enquiry wasn't going to be far more complicated than they had expected.

NIALL TOOK ALL the anxiety and frustration that had accumulated over the afternoon and turned it into fuel, using it to pound the metal on his anvil into submission. As always, it was a relief to see it work, to take his negative feelings and use muscle and fire and sheer will to transform them into beauty.

He bent low over the surface of the anvil, ignoring the twinge in his side. He knew better than to give in to such bruises and injuries. Wait too long and he'd turn stiff and sore. Nothing happening in his life right now lent itself to difficulty in moving, reacting, or thinking. He needed to be ready.

The project he was working on was a customized standing screen. His garden-loving client had requested a design of ferns, thick with fronds. Niall was absorbed in the delicate work of creating fiddleheads in the act of unfurling when he heard voices outside. Pausing, he thrust the piece back in the fire and gazed out into the gathering dark of the late afternoon.

"Go on, now. Back to the house with you all."

It was Kara, and she sounded annoyed. He hid a grin. The maids must have snuck out to spy on him again.

"Mr. Kier deserves his privacy," she scolded, unseen. "I don't want to have to speak with you all about this again."

Niall moved his piece to a cooler area of the fire. If Kara was scolding the maids, she must be in a mood. He hoped her afternoon had not been as frustrating as his.

She came out of the shadows into the light of the forge, and Niall blinked. "Aren't you a sight?" he said admiringly. "That's a new dress, isn't it? Come here."

She drew closer, and suddenly her eyes widened in horror. "Niall!" She rushed over and touched his back with gentle hands. "What's happened to you?"

"It's nothing. I'm fine. It was a fall. I'll tell you everything, but first... Come and let me look at you."

"Well, the dress is new," she said, looking pleased. "And I am glad you like it, but it is hardly meant to tempt, and I am covered from neck to toe."

"Covered *tightly*, at least on top. It makes a man want to uncover you." He encircled her waist. "I swear, I can span your waist with my hands."

She rolled her eyes at him. "Your hands are very large."

"My hands are very talented," he countered as he pulled her in. "Let me show you." He bent to kiss her and allowed said hands to roam a bit.

After a moment, she pulled back, her dark eyes twinkling. "My hands are talented as well. You are about to find out how skillfully I can apply liniment." She made him turn so she could examine his bruises. "And you will need to learn that your talented hands are very capable of pulling on a shirt." She *tsked* at him. "Working without one? You are really not being fair to the maids. How are they to resist peeking at you?"

He laughed. "They've learned to avoid the doorways and linger out in the dark. I scarcely even know when they are there."

"Well, I really cannot blame them, but neither can I encourage them." He shivered as she ran her finger down his arm to grasp his hand. "Come. Let me get something on those that will ease the soreness."

"Nothing that smells too strongly," he cautioned. "We have

plans this evening."

She pulled back to look at him. "This evening's tribute to Frederick Cole?"

"Yes." He sighed. "I think we'd better be there. I keep finding more questions wherever I look, instead of answers."

"We'd better invite Gyda, as well. She's itching to do something concrete to help Josie."

"We could use the help."

"Did you find Elias Wade?"

"No. I went to the club, but it was nothing but chaos. Apparently, throwing together a whole new evening's entertainment on a day's notice puts everyone's back up. I asked around, but no one had seen him. Nor was anyone eager to talk to me. They were all extremely busy."

"Well, I tried to find him, too. He is apparently not living in the Coles' household." She arched a brow and gave him a grin that was only slightly triumphant. "I did speak at length with Mrs. Cole, though."

"Did you? Well done. What did you find?"

"Come, I'll tell you while I douse you. And then I will take a bath and don something that is definitely meant to tempt you."

"Wicked girl. I cannot wait. Let me shut down the forge and tidy up, and then I will put myself at your mercy."

She perched on a stool while he puttered about. Glancing up, he caught a worried look on her face. "What is it?"

She sighed. "Several things. The oddest of which is that I invited Mrs. Cole to our wedding."

His mouth slackened. "You did *what?*"

"It was a compromise, but I think you will agree it was a good one."

He considered. "You traded an invitation for her agreement to cooperate with Wooten?"

"Well, essentially." She made a face. "But I forced her to throw in social recognition of the Mosemans as well."

He shook his head. "I have no head for social maneuverings.

I'll have to trust your judgment on that one," he said, dubious.

"I sent Wooten a note, telling him she will speak with him and Mr. Landover."

"He'll be grateful, I'm sure. But come, tell me the tale. I want to hear everything." Lifting an arm, he let her slip close against him.

"You first," she insisted. "I want to hear what happened to you. And I'm afraid that, like you, I've come up with no answers, only more threads to pull."

"Fine, then. I'll start. You remember the girl, our young guide from this morning…"

Chapter Nine

KARA WORE A gown of deep violet silk that shimmered in the lights of the entry hall at the Rogue's Hideaway. It had the added attraction of making her skin glow like pearls in contrast. The dyed, lace-trimmed bodice rode low across her shoulders, baring a daring-but-decent amount of décolletage. She wore peacock feathers in her hair, and a particularly long one curled down to tickle her neck as she waited for Niall, taking in the spectacle.

Oh, and it *was* a spectacle. Clearly no one had been put off by the idea of staging a tribute to Frederick Cole even before he was safely buried. Or perhaps they were titillated at the thought of spending the night at the actual scene of his murder—before the murderer was caught.

Tables had been added to every spare foot of space on the floor. They were all filled, which left the lower level nearly as crowded as the galleries above. Spirits were high and voices rang loud.

She wondered if Frederick would have been pleased with the display, or annoyed.

"Old Mr. Cole would have loved this." Jimmy Gibbs had paused at her side, his arms filled with a crate of wine bottles. "All these people come to raise a glass to him? It would have touched his heart."

"I am glad to hear it. I had wondered."

"I didn't expect you'd come in tonight, Miss Levett, but it's glad I am to see you. Be sure and stop by the bar. I'll save you a glass of the basil punch. It's going fast."

"I'm sure it is. The flavors sound intriguing."

"It tastes nearly as good as you look," he said with a glance toward her cleavage. "But it's the naughtiness of the gin that tempts the ladies."

"I think perhaps it's the handsome tapster," Niall said, coming up on her other side. "You are not flirting with my girl, are you, Jimmy?"

He had not worn his formal kilt tonight, to her disappointment. But he still looked devastating in black tie and tails.

"No, sir. I would never poach." The bartender grinned. "But if you ever set her free, I'd take my chance." He tossed her a wink, then glanced over at the crowd at the bar. "Excuse me. I must get back. My public awaits."

"Wait, Jimmy?" Kara called. "Can you tell me if Randall Abbott is here tonight?"

"Aye." He turned his head and pointed his chin toward a table in the front, to one side of the stage. "There he is. With the crowd standing around Mr. West. Abbott is the one with the white hair."

"Thank you," she said as he turned to go.

"Don't forget," he called over his shoulder.

She turned to look up at Niall. "Well, that makes it easy, doesn't it? Two birds with one stone."

They had agreed on the way that their top priorities were to speak with Elias Wade, Randall Abbott, and Robert West.

"Gyda has headed downstairs?" she asked.

"Yes. She's convinced she can learn more about Wade if she flirts with a few footmen and befriends a maid or two. A rebellious guest? A woman, preferring to hang about with the staff? She says they'll talk, if only to impress her."

"I hope she's right." They both believed that Niall would have the best chance to get West talking about Mrs. Cole's aspersions. That left her with Randall Abbott.

"Don't change your expression," Niall told her. "But look over my shoulder to the far side of the bar."

Kara took a moment to do it, striving to make the motion look natural. "Oh! Wooten!" The inspector stood in a corner holding a notebook instead of a drink, but everyone appeared to be ignoring him.

"I'm sure there are some of his men mixed in with the crowd," Niall said.

"It cannot hurt. Let's hope we discover something of use."

Not wishing to appear obvious, they took their time meandering over to the group that stood around the table in conversation. They were easing closer when West caught sight of them. "Kier!" he exclaimed. He beckoned them over. "You came back, and so soon. Delighted to have you with us. Delighted!"

West held a glass of wine, and it was clear it was not his first. With enthusiasm, he introduced them all around. Besides Randall Abbott, it appeared the other gentlemen were all also involved in Frederick Cole's business empire. West called for wine for the both of them. He might have spoken again, but just then a loud banging sounded, along with a call to attention.

In the music hall, the chairman was the man who kept order and introduced the acts. He made his own introduction in a smooth, carrying tone. Mr. Trask stood at his table, placed on its own level between the orchestra and the stage, on the far end from where they stood. He wore tails and a top hat, and he banged a gavel on the table until everyone had quieted. Once he had everyone's attention, he called for a toast to the queen.

It was given heartily by all. Afterward, he raised his glass once more. "We at the Rogue's Hideaway welcome you all tonight to a special evening. Tonight we honor our fallen friend, Mr. Frederick Cole. A great man. A titan of business and industry. A father, a husband, a friend. We raise our glasses in his memory, with the best wishes for a speedy journey home to his spirit, and a fond farewell until we are united with him once more."

"To Frederick Cole!" The toast was repeated all throughout the place and glasses were raised high. Kara moved closer to Randall Abbott, who appeared much affected. He was tall and still quite handsome for an older gentleman. He had kept his hair and obviously decided to make the most of it—his thick white locks were pomaded and brushed to a sheen. His clothes were impeccable and obviously of the highest quality. Everything about him appeared to be meant to catch the eye. Kara sidled up to him as Mr. Trask banged his gavel once more.

"Now, we've all outdone ourselves here at the Hideaway tonight. I am not too shy to proclaim it! Each act you will see this evening has been specially prepared to glorify our lost friend. Each and every act is a one-time-only tribute to the great man. You are the only—and the most fortunate and wise—audience who will see this once-in-a-lifetime show."

The crowd cheered. Men pounded the rails upstairs and women laughed and shouted. Trask graciously allowed them to vent their excitement. "Now," he said when the applause faded. "Make ready to be enchanted! First on our stage, I give you all the marvelous musical talents of the Lively Lindells!"

Abbott clapped with enthusiasm, and Kara joined in. On the other side of the group, Niall had moved to stand next to West.

The orchestra struck up. The curtain rose. Onto the stage strolled a man and a woman. The background had been set with desks and windowed stalls where tellers counted out cash to customers. The pair began to sing a lively, catchy ditty whose chorus must reflect the title—"When Freddie Ran the Bank."

The man was meant to be Frederick Cole. With cute verses and background vignettes, he told the story of growing up in his mother's theater, of discovering a talent with numbers and with money, of how he began a bank that allowed actors and theater staff to borrow and loan and invest, to make their money work for them in ways they could not easily access before. The audience laughed at the antics on stage and applauded the success of Frederick's venture. At the end, as the applause stretched out, Abbott grew visibly emotional. "How well they portray those simpler, happier times," he said with a sigh.

He'd been speaking generally, but Kara turned as if he'd addressed her. "Did you know Mr. Cole so long, then?"

"Oh, indeed, yes." Straightening, he preened a bit. "It may be difficult to believe now, but I once trod the boards myself."

Kara let her eyes widen in surprise, but inwardly, she thought that anyone might have known it, so obviously did he still seek to be in the spotlight.

"That bit might have been written for me," he continued. "I was a star attraction at the Frisk."

"The Frisk?"

"The theater owned by Frederick's mother. Oh, what a woman Fanny was. She wore the fragile air of a woodland fairy, but possessed a mind and will like a bear trap." His expression was one of fond remembrance. "She ran that place with an iron fist. No detail overlooked. No shenanigans tolerated. She was tough but fair, and still managed to be compassionate. Frederick got all of his best qualities from her."

"How wonderful to have enjoyed such a long friendship," she said sincerely.

"Yes. We were friends. The sort that saw each other at our best and worst." He stared ahead at the lowered curtain. After a moment, he gave himself a shake. Eyeing Kara more closely, he took a step nearer. "I daresay I was one of Frederick's first clients. He was just a money lender, then, at the beginning. He made me a loan, and I quickly paid it back. I saw how well he was doing, and I quickly began to invest what I could with him. Every time I made a profit. Every time I put it back into his hands. We grew the business quickly, and Frederick eventually founded Cole's Bank. The *actor's* bank, the gentry called it, their tone of disparagement clear. But there were plenty of ordinary folks who flocked to bank with him. The snobby lot has suffered years of their estate profits falling, but Frederick's climbed higher. I quickly made enough money that I had no need to go upon the stage." He glanced over. "But, I confess, I do miss it, even now."

"Gracious," Kara said innocently. "You were a part of Mr. Cole's first venture and you stayed with him all of those years? He must have made you a very rich man indeed."

Some of the light left his face. "We made each other very rich," he corrected her.

"Oh, of course. I did not mean—"

She was interrupted when the gavel was banged again and Trask introduced the next act. It was an acrobatic troupe, awing the audience with their feats. Using twists, tumbling, and costume changes, they represented all of the varied workers employed by Cole in his financial houses, smelting companies, fire clay manufactories, and more. Their antics grew more thrilling as they went on, until they ended with a tall pyramid of bodies that exploded outward with a bang into separate vaults and rolls.

The audience shouted their appreciation, and Kara leaned in toward Abbott. "I do apologize. I didn't mean to denigrate your contributions to Mr. Cole's success."

"No, no. Do not worry over it, my dear." He waved her concern away. "It is an oft-made mistake."

"That must be hurtful," she said, all wide-eyed with sympathy.

Something hardened behind the man's eyes, altering his air of solemn affability and loss. "There's no need to fret. I have pots of money, my dear, and plenty of ways to spend it."

"Oh?" she said with a smile. "Are you a racing man? Or have you commissioned one of those private railway cars I've heard about?"

Abbott laughed. "Oh, no. I am a botanist now, and expend my energy amongst my plants when I am not working. I am known as an avid gardener and a collector. My conservatory is one of the largest in England."

"Do you grow roses? My mother loved them."

"No, no." He shook his head haughtily. "I don't bother with domestic plants at all. You won't find common hedgerow plants in my conservatory. I grow rare and exotic specimens. Unusual plants from all over the world. A visit there is akin to a tour of the world."

"Goodness. How interesting."

"I do enjoy it, but, you know, it doesn't provide the same excitement as our work does. We are creators, builders of industries and empires, my dear. Our little partnership has vast reach. And I know how valuable my work, never-ending interest, and vigilance have been to the company since the beginning. I know of the ideas and investments I proposed that have led us to marked success." He swung his glass around to indicate the other men at the table. "Even if Frederick did not, the board members of Sock and Buskin know it as well." He took a deep drink. "And that is what truly matters," he said with satisfaction.

"Even if you had your differences, I'm sure you will miss a friend of such long standing."

"Of course," he answered, but there was a smugness in Abbott's tone that sharpened Kara's curiosity.

On the other side of the table, Robert West rapped on the linen-covered surface and rocked a little on his feet. "To Frederick Cole," he proclaimed loudly. "A man of stern character and unshakable faith...in himself!" He gave a laugh and tossed back his drink. There were a few buried grins and someone snickered, but they all drank. All except for one gentleman, who contented himself with a sip and a scowl into his glass.

Abbott saw her interest in the man. "Don't mind Carver. He and Frederick got into a contretemps not long ago, and he's still not over it."

Kara nodded. "He looks perhaps a little younger than some of the other men." She'd put Carver at forty, while the others were all seemingly in their sixties or higher.

"Younger, yes, but with a brilliant mind. Unfortunately, his comparative inexperience leaves him with a need to prove himself. He and Frederick did occasionally butt heads over it."

Kara nodded as she made a show of finishing her wine.

"It seems we must find you another drink," he said, hoisting the empty bottle on the table.

"Oh, yes. Please. If you see a waiter, could you signal for his attention? The bartender promised to save me a glass of his special punch."

"Did he? How kind." He looked her over, as if speculating. "The ladies do seem to love his concoctions."

"I am eager to try his latest."

"Well, then, allow me to go the bar myself."

"Oh, no. I didn't mean—There's no need. I can wait for the server."

"Nonsense. A lovely girl like you should never have to wait. For anything." He sent a quick glance in Niall's direction, and Kara flushed, wondering, suddenly, if others beside her friends were discussing the length of her engagement.

Abbott gave her an elegant, showy bow. "I shall return."

"Thank you, sir." She bowed her head to hide her slightly embarrassed flush. When she looked up, she found Carver watching. She sent him a sheepish grin, but he looked away.

She turned her attention to Niall then. West had claimed his attention, putting a hand on his shoulder and leaning in to talk in his ear. She hoped the man was confessing something useful, but by the dull edge of Niall's gaze, she doubted it.

A bang of the gavel and the next act was announced. It was a young singer, with a halo of bright red hair and lips painted to match. She crooned a song about a marriage of convenience that turned to true love.

Just before it ended, Gyda strode up to stand at her side. "I see we are embellishing the truth with sentimental bits of fiction," she said, laughing.

Kara smiled back. Her friend looked divine, like an ice princess in slim skirts of light blue and silver. Her hair had been braided in the front and pulled back into a mass of curls in the back. She looked gorgeous, daring, and different from every other woman in the room.

"That Sergeant Landover is downstairs asking questions," she reported.

"Wooten is over on the other side of the bar."

"Landover is a clumsy oaf. He acts condescending and hostile and then wonders why no one wants to help him." She wiggled her shoulders. "I, on the other hand, have got a description of Elias Wade, if not a glimpse of him. The staff here are all wary of him."

"Wary?"

"'Off-putting,' was how several of them described him. They all said there was something odd about him. He's young, it seems, although he speaks with authority beyond his years and beyond his status as a servant."

"Mrs. Cole said something similar," mused Kara.

"He's thin. Slight of build. Short. And blond." Gyda shook her head. "But not as blonde as me." She grinned. "I asked if he would be out here, taking part in the big send-off, but everyone I spoke with agreed he would be skulking about the edges of the party, not taking part."

"Would he?" Kara took a glance around the lower level, then offered her arm. "Then perhaps we should take a turn about the room?"

Gyda laughed and entwined her arm with Kara's—and they were off.

NIALL WAS NOT going to get anything useful from Robert West. The man was three sheets past full sail, and sloppy with it. He was currently bemoaning everything he'd lost after Cole's passing—a father's care, the cachet of the great man's presence in his club, and the opportunities that might have arisen in the future. He cried real tears on Niall's shoulder and called for more wine.

Niall sighed as West dropped into a chair. Glancing over to see if Kara might be meeting more success with Abbott, he saw her and Gyda slip away from the group, heading along the edge of the floor.

"Good evening."

One of the businessmen had slipped into the spot that West had vacated. The younger one. Niall had noticed he looked to be in a mood throughout the evening. He gave him a nod. "Good evening, Mr....Curving?"

"Carver."

"Apologies. It was already loud in here when West made the introductions."

"No worries." Carver raked his gaze around the men standing in their group. "And are you a member of the Frederick Cole Admiration Society, like the rest of these sycophants?"

Interesting. Niall gave a twist of his mouth. "Actually, I'm afraid I never met the man."

He had surprised Carver, that much he could tell. But the man shrugged and nodded toward the retreating pair of Kara and Gyda. "The dark one, she's with you?"

"My fiancée."

"She seemed interested in Cole's history."

Niall made a face. "Or perhaps she was just being polite to Abbott."

"Perhaps. Though if I were you, I'd keep my betrothed away from the old man."

"From Abbott?" Niall gave an easy grin. "I have no fear of such competition."

"Nor should you, but I meant something else altogether. The old man is schemer." Carver's lip curled. "It's all a large game to him. Or perhaps a play is the better way to describe it. And Abbott likes to write and direct the play. He's also always on the lookout for someone he can turn into a player." Shaking his head, he took a long drink. "I've said too much. And I have another question entirely. Tell me, who is the blonde? The one who left with your lady?"

"Ah. That is Miss Gyda Winther."

"She is…interesting."

Niall laughed. "You have no idea."

Carver stared after the women for a moment, but when he spoke again, it wasn't to discuss Gyda. "If you didn't know Cole, why are you here tonight?" Perhaps he realized the impertinence of his sharp-toned question. "If you don't mind my asking," he said in a milder manner.

"We are friends of Josie Lowe. It seemed someone should be here to represent her." He glanced around. "Just in case."

Carver tossed back the dregs of his glass. "God, I wish she were here tonight. She's the only one worth listening to in this place." He glanced aside at Niall. "I assume she'll soon be released? Anyone who knows her knows she wouldn't do such a thing."

"You know Josie?" asked Niall.

Carver reddened. "I've heard her sing several times. She's very talented. I spoke a few words with her once, at Cole's table after a performance. Gave her a compliment on her voice." He still looked uncomfortable. "That's all. Nothing further. But she seemed genuinely fond of Cole. Solicitous of him, too."

Niall nodded. "I believe she was both. I have no doubt the true culprit will be discovered."

The man cast an uneasy glance toward the corner where Wooten was ensconced, observing all around him with a measuring eye. Niall instantly wondered, of course, what the man had to be uneasy about. He looked again. Kara and Gyda had stopped to exchange a word with the inspector, but they were already moving on, still keeping to the edges of the room.

"A pleasure to meet you, sir." Carver took up his glass and began to move away. "I see a friend I must speak with."

"Of course. Good evening." Niall looked back to Kara and Gyda. They were smiling and chatting as they strolled, and Niall was just turning his attention away again when he saw Gyda tense up and reach for Kara's arm.

His gaze snapped back. Gyda was motioning ahead of them. He turned just in time to see a dark-clad form rise from behind the chairman's desk, take the few steps up to the stage, and disappear behind the curtain.

"Excuse me." He moved past Carver, headed for his edge of the stage, and leapt up. He ducked behind the curtain just as it began to rise. A pair of dancers moved to mid-stage, ready to begin their performance. He moved forward, hoping to get across before he could disrupt the performance, but he was cut off by a stream of background dancers moving quickly to take their places.

Huffing a snort of exasperation, he headed toward the back of the theater, hoping to find a way to cross unseen.

Chapter Ten

"I DON'T SEE him," Kara said. But then, she hadn't glimpsed Wade earlier.

"I tell you, I spotted him," Gyda insisted. "And he saw me recognize him. He was half hidden behind that desk near the stage, watching all the action across the room. When he saw I had noticed him, he stood and ran up and behind the curtain, quick as Freya's cats."

They were in the way, caught in the midst of the frantic activity backstage.

"Move." A stagehand in a cap and apron growled at them as he slid along a set piece.

They stepped aside. "Did you see where he went?" Kara asked.

"I cannot see him at all now," Gyda complained. "Let's move around to the back."

They tried to stay out of the way. Circling buckets of sand and coiled ropes and busy workers, they peered into nooks and corners.

"What's he doing, playing at hide-and-seek?" Gyda asked, annoyed. "Why should he want so badly to avoid us?"

"I don't know. Maybe he's not hiding and he's just gone down to the wardrobe or dressing rooms. Let's look down there."

Kara nodded, but they both started when the wall opened up next to them and a woman emerged. She was in a hurry, carrying a costume and biting thread from it as she went.

"Excuse me," Kara said politely. "But what is that?" She pointed to the wall, which looked solid and normal again after the door had closed. "A secret staircase?"

"It's the narrow stair," the woman said impatiently. "Runs all the way from basement to attic. A quick way to get about, if you don't mind the dark and small spaces. The actors like to use it to get up here quick." She rolled her eyes. "And the dancers like to use it to get up to the offices without being seen."

"It has an exit at every floor?" Gyda asked.

"Aye, or else it wouldn't be half so useful, now would it?" The woman started to walk away, but looked over her shoulder. "Don't go tearing up there like that lunatic just did. You're like to smack your head or go tumbling down—and it's steep. You'll feel it, if you don't break your neck."

She moved on, and Kara exchanged a look with Gyda. They moved closer to the wall.

"How do you open the blasted thing?" Gyda complained. She ran her hand over the wall.

"Make way. Coming through." A man in a coat and tie and with an air of importance came up behind them, carrying a locked metal box.

"Cashbox," Kara whispered. She watched closely as he pressed a section of paneling and the door sprang open.

Gyda grabbed it before it could close again. "Up or down?" she asked.

"The woman said 'tearing up there.'"

"Up it is, then." They waited until the man had disappeared, also climbing upward, before they entered the narrow stairwell. There was only room to go single file. Kara fell in behind Gyda and stepped as quietly as she could.

The staircase turned and doubled back on itself once before they reached a tiny landing.

"Offices?" Kara asked.

"Likely. That's probably where the bloke went with his box."

"Should we look there?"

"We should likely look everywhere."

"Let's try the trigger and make sure we can get it to work before we go on." Kara searched the area on the far side of the landing, where she'd expected the door to be. It was harder in the dim light. She found the right spot. When she pressed it, she felt something give. The door opened. Gyda grabbed it and they peered through. Down a long passage lit with dimmed gaslights, they saw the clerk unlocking a door. It swung open, and he carried his box in. Despite the noise echoing from below, it was quiet up here. So quiet, they heard the turn of the lock behind him even from here.

"He'll be occupied counting his money for a while," Gyda whispered. "Let's check the other offices for Wade."

They made their way down the corridor, opening doors quietly and peering into empty offices and a storage room full of locked cabinets made to hold files. In one office they discovered a man asleep on a sofa. He wore a rumpled suit and reeked of brandy. His hair was short and chestnut colored, so they knew he wasn't Elias Wade. He never moved, even when Gyda snorted, so they closed the door and went on. All the way at the end, they found a door leading to an office several times larger than the others.

"West's?" Gyda guessed.

"Or Cole's?" Kara ventured. She tried the latch, but this one was locked. With a shrug, she knocked softly on the door.

No answer.

"There he is," Gyda whispered suddenly.

Kara turned her head and just spotted a figure slipping back into the narrow stair. "Come on!"

They raced back, struggled to get the door open, and pushed through to the tiny landing.

"Shh. Listen," Gyda ordered her.

They heard no footsteps, either above or below, just the distant beat of a song echoing through the walls from below.

Kara tried to quiet her breathing as they waited.

Very faintly, the snick of a door closing sounded from above.

"There!" Gyda was triumphant.

Kara raced up the stairs behind her. The next landing was configured in similar fashion. Gyda cracked open the door. They saw the same sort of corridor with doors marching down it, but there were no lights, and all the space between the doors appeared to be lined with trunks and boxes. The nearest one spilled over with programs and flyers. As they stared, they heard the distinct sound of a footstep, almost directly over their heads.

Gyda straightened and pointed upward. "Let's go," she whispered. She started up.

Kara's blood had frozen. She knew what must lie up there, based on the number of floors they'd explored. It must be the attics up there.

"Kara! Come on," Gyda growled.

It took an effort to force her feet to make the climb, but Kara told herself sternly to go on. With each step, the dread rose higher within her.

Breathing deeply, she took one step at a time. *One more. One more.*

The last landing was different. Bigger. There was room for one to set down a burden, likely because here, the landing featured a real door. A proper wooden door with a latch and locks.

Leading to the attics.

"He must be in there," Gyda said quietly.

"I don't think it was him."

"Of course it's him. Who else would it be?"

"He looked smaller when we spotted him on the office floor."

"He *is* small! And we were far away."

"Perhaps we shouldn't go in. I think we should wait for Niall."

"And allow Wade to give us the slip again? Look, we can handle him. Convince him to talk to us. Either he knows something or he's guilty of something," Gyda said darkly. "Why else run like that?"

"We don't have a key," Kara said, eyeing the locks.

Gyda reached out and tried the latch. The door swung open.

Kara suppressed a moan. All the short, fine hairs on the back of her neck began to prickle.

"Let's go," whispered Gyda. She pushed the door wider and slipped inside.

Kara swallowed.

Whatever, *whoever* was in there, she couldn't let Gyda face it alone. She could do this. She could. Moving woodenly, she followed, stopping just inside the door.

It wasn't as big a space as she'd expected. The attics must be divided into two or more sections.

This did not make her feel better.

The walls on one side were steeply slanted. A tall window stood at the far end of the room. Moonlight poured in, lighting a path down the center of the place. Racks of garments lined up along one wall, row after row of costumes. Many were covered in protective cotton. Others dripped feathers, trailed trains, or flowing sleeves.

Carved panels were stacked in a corner. Set pieces, brightly painted. Her mechanical brain sorted them into the correct order. Assembled, they would create a volcano, complete with a climbing spire of smoke. The other wall was lined with trunks and a collection of artificial fronds, shrubs, and trees.

The space in the middle lay bare. It was not the same place, she reminded herself firmly. It was organized. Cleaner. There was no smell of dust or mold, no stink of stale beer or old mutton. "Gyda? Where are you?"

"Here." Her friend stepped out from behind a fake carriage. Kara could see her outlined in the moonlight. With a sigh of relief, she propped the door open wide. When she was sure it would stay, she headed into the room.

She took deep breaths. Listened carefully. She was fine. *Fine.*

She'd only made it halfway to Gyda when she heard a distinct noise behind her. She froze, her hands tightening into fists.

But it was worse than someone looming behind her. No one was there. Whoever was in here with them, they were back by the entrance now. She heard the door shut, followed by the sound of the locks turning.

It echoed loudly in Kara's head. *Oh, no. No, no, no.*

"Odin's *arse!*" Gyda swore. She ran past to try the door. "The little arse wipe has locked us in!"

Fear was a sizzling tingle at the base of Kara's spine. It crawled upward to her scalp, making her hair stand on end.

"We've got to get out," she said hoarsely. She stood very still, hiding from the memories that threatened to swamp her. Was the air being pulled from the room? She couldn't breathe. Pulling the feathers from her hair and casting them away, she gasped, and gasped again.

"Kara? What is it?" Gyda sounded faintly annoyed. "What is wrong?"

"Air. I need air." Stumbling, Kara headed for the window. Her fingers fumbled as she unlocked it. She pushed, but the sash wouldn't budge. "Gyda, help! Help me!"

Her friend came out and pounded until the sash swung open. Kara leaned outside and bent over the windowsill, pulling clean, cool air into her lungs. It helped, but still, she trembled.

"Kara?" Gyda was staring down, far down into the fenced yard behind the theater. "Look! Down there!"

Kara tried to focus. It took effort. It was a large space. She could see a line of privies and stacks of empty casks and crates. At the back, a gate led out into a mews. Two men stood before it, shouting at each other. She and Gyda were too high to hear their words clearly. Or perhaps she just couldn't hear them over the pounding of her pulse in her head.

"That's Abbott. The white-haired one, yes?" Gyda asked.

"Who is he arguing with?"

Kara tried to see. It took a moment, but the moon moved out from behind a cloud and the scene grew clearer. "Carver," she said faintly.

"What's that?" Gyda said suddenly. She turned to stare back into the room. "Did you hear something?" After a moment, she relaxed. "Just rats, most likely."

Kara let out a sob.

But Gyda was staring down again. "Look! Right there! Behind the casks! Someone is spying on them. Who is it?" Leaning out, she shouted down into the yard. "I don't think they can hear me."

Kara could not make herself care. *Locked in. With rats.* She shook her head. Could not stop shaking it.

"Ha! That got his attention!" Gyda leaned further out the window. "Look at that! He's blond! And slim! Damn him to hell, that's Elias Wade! There's no way he made it down there so quickly." She turned back again, bumping into Kara. "So who in Hades locked us in?"

But Kara had sunk down on her knees. The shadows were advancing from the corners.

"No. No." Shouts were *not* coming from the dark. There were no harsh, denigrating words. No sudden slaps or cuffs to the head. No scarpering feet or sharp bites waking her from fitful sleep. "They are not there."

Covering her head, she curled up, making herself small. "I can't," she whispered. "I can't. I can't." She closed her eyes against the advancing walls, the encroaching shadows, and the memories she could not keep out of her head.

⋙✦⋘

NIALL MANEUVERED THROUGH the backstage area, avoiding ladders and ropes and gas pipes, while he searched for Kara and Gyda. He even went down to make a round through the dressing rooms, eliciting yelps of surprise, winks, and several invitations, but they were nowhere to be found. Standing still, staring up at the men moving nimbly across the pipes on the fly gallery, he was trying to decide where to go next when he saw the wall open up and disgorge a trio of dancers dressing in flowing evening gowns.

He stepped in front of them. "Does that go all the way up?" he asked, nodding toward the stairwell, hidden once more.

"To the top," one of them chirped in answer.

"Like you'd know, Kat." Another rolled her eyes. "You ain't never gone any higher than Mr. West's office."

"Shut it, Alice."

They moved on, bickering, but Niall was already exploring the wall, trying to gain access. He depressed the right spot and felt something give way—and he was in. Up he went.

He'd just come back to the first landing after cruising a floor of offices when he heard banging from above. Loud, frantic banging.

He pelted up the stairs. The noise led him upward still. When he climbed high enough, he could hear someone shouting between thumps.

"Let us out! We're locked in here! Someone, help!"

"Gyda?" he called.

"Niall?" she answered, and the relief was clear in her voice. "Thank all the old gods. Open the door! Get us out! There's something wrong with Kara!"

His heart stopped. "What's wrong? Is she hurt?"

"No. Yes. I don't know, exactly. I think she's scared, Niall. Horribly frightened."

He frowned. He'd seen Kara face down threats from indignant family, Society gossips, aggressive constables, bullies, even murderers. Not once had she shown even a hint of fear. She was always confident, self-assured… He stopped, took a look around, and realized.

"Yes. Fine. Stand away from the door, Gyda." He waited a moment, braced himself with a hand on the wall, and kicked hard at the latch. With no discernible effect. "Damn dress shoes," he muttered. He wished fleetingly for his sturdy boots, or for his forge hammer. He tried again.

Nothing.

"What is all the racket up there?" someone shouted irritably from below.

Relief flooded him. "Keys!" he shouted down the stairs. "We need the keys to the attic. *Now!* Someone is trapped up here!"

"All right, all right," the voice grumbled. "Just stop the noise! We can hear it all way down at backstage."

"Hurry, Niall!" Gyda called. "I don't like the look of her."

"*Now!*" Niall roared.

"Coming, coming," the voice said. "I'll fetch them. Keep your britches buttoned."

After an agonizing wait, Niall heard footsteps climbing the stairs. "Hurry, man!"

"Yes, yes." A backstage crewman in an apron at last appeared below. Niall ran down, snatched the keys from him, and raced back up. He had the door flung open in a moment. Striding in, he froze as he took in the scene.

Kara lay slumped on the floor in a pool of moonlight, curled tightly. Gyda had her head in her lap. She stroked her hair and whispered soothing words.

"What is it?" his assistant asked, her eyes filled with sorrow and fear. "Niall, I've never seen her like this. I could not even have imagined it. Something bad has got a hold of her."

Moving forward, he knelt beside them. "It's the attics," he said roughly. "When she was kidnapped as a girl, she was locked alone, tied up tight in an attic. They treated her badly—when they didn't abandon her to the rats." Reaching down, he gently touched her shoulder. "It's all right, Kara."

She flinched at his touch. It nearly broke his heart.

"Kara, it's me. It's Niall. I am here."

She curled tighter into herself.

"The door is open, Kara," he said softly. "I'm taking you out of here."

Her head turned a little. "Open?" she whispered.

"Yes. It's time to go." Reaching under her, he scooped her up. She didn't fight him, thank all the saints.

"She needs warming up," Gyda said. "Her skin has gone ice cold."

Climbing carefully to his feet, he held her close and contemplated where to take her. His first thought was to go to the White Hart. It seemed to be the place where they went to restore and recover. But he recalled the bulbous-nosed watcher lingering in the taproom several evenings ago. Bluefield was too far. "Her rooms on Adams Road are closest. Will you run down and call for the carriage?"

He could feel her trembling in his arms.

"And send for Turner!" he yelled after Gyda as she set off.

Chapter Eleven

KARA WAS TOSSING and turning, trying to stay away from the darkness. It kept reaching for her, trying to pull her in. She eased a little when a hand tugged her blankets higher, smoothing them over her shoulder.

Niall, was her first thought, before she sleepily thought better of it. He would be far more likely to climb in and snuggle close, warming her with the heat of his body.

"Turner?" she asked, rolling over and only halfway succeeding in opening her eyes. If she could sleep a little longer…

"Holy mother of—" Gasping, she sat up straight and scooted back against the headboard. "What are you doing?" she rasped at the stranger standing by her bed.

"I heard you wished to speak with me," the man said quietly.

She stared. He wore impeccable morning dress, every seam straight and everything brushed and neat. He held his hat in his hand, turning it as he watched her carefully through thick lashes. His blond hair caught the morning light.

"Elias Wade?" she whispered.

He nodded. "I heard you were injured in some way, looking for me last night. I only came to say how sorry I was, and to make sure you were recovered."

It all came rushing back then. Horrified, she tugged the covers up and over her shoulders. Oh, she'd made a colossal fool of herself. Showed herself a weakling. She'd let Gyda down. And Niall, and Wooten and Josie... Now they would all know. Closing her eyes, she dropped her head in her hands and groaned.

"Are you in pain? Shall I call your gentleman back?"

Looking up, she saw a blanket and pillow on a chair pulled close to the bed. "Niall? Where is he?"

"He was called down to speak to a police inspector. The older man was with them as well. I was waiting for a chance to talk to you alone, so I came up."

They were in the Adams Road building, she realized belatedly. The older gentleman must be Turner. She had a vague recollection of hearing his voice last night. Suddenly, she pierced Wade with a frown. "Where were you waiting?"

"Out of the way, where I could see and hear and wait for my chance."

"You were hiding."

"Yes."

"Did you follow us here?"

"Yes."

"Why?"

He shifted. He didn't look directly at her, but watched his hat and stared at the bed. "I heard about you and your friend looking for me. I saw her when they were taking you out." He made a face. "I didn't wish to talk to her. I thought she might be...difficult. I would rather it was you, if I had to speak at all. What was it you wanted?"

She stared. "We need to speak with you about Frederick Cole's death."

"Why?" He sounded surprised—and reluctant.

Kara paused to watch him. She thought about all the disparaging remarks she'd heard about him. He didn't appear arrogant to her, merely forthright. She'd known others who could be quite literal in their interpretations and their conversations. Such directness could be interpreted as dismissal or defiance. She'd met more than a few such souls in the scientific fields—men who could focus intensely on the smallest details of their work, who could persistently chase their scientific goals but not understand a joke or grasp the importance of social rituals or expectations. She rather thought she shared a few of those traits herself.

"For many reasons," she began, but the door opened and Niall walked in. He stopped, surprised, then his brow darkened and he started for the other man.

"Niall," she said quietly, giving a small shake of her head. He halted. "I am glad you are here. Mr. Wade heard I was ill and came to check on me. Also, he wished to know why I was seeking him out." She looked back to Wade. "I feel better speaking with you while Niall is here, but if you are not comfortable with him, I can ask for Inspector Wooten instead."

He quickly shook his head. "I don't like the police."

It was a commonly held opinion. She knew many people distrusted the police. Still, she asked, "Why not?"

"I know there are good men among them, but many of them remind me of the watchmen who worked at my grandfather's factory. They enjoy the power and superiority that comes with the position, and they enjoy misusing it. I've seen them preying upon those whom they find weaker or just lower."

Niall had rapidly adjusted to the situation. Moving quietly, he went to the head of the bed and took her hand. "I know just the sort you mean. But I believe there are less and less of their kind in London's police, as the years go on."

Wade looked doubtful, but he merely sighed. "I don't really wish to talk about Frederick at all."

"We heard you were close to Mr. Cole," Kara said with sympathy. "His loss must be difficult for you to bear."

Wade was obviously struggling with emotion. "I was so content," he said, his tone low and sad. "So happy. I had at last found the exact place where I belonged. I hadn't felt that way in a very long time. Not since my mother died."

"I'm very sorry. You were lucky to find such a position. Josie said it came about because you worked with her?"

"Yes. I saw her on the stage when I first came to London. She was wonderful. Better than all the other actresses. I went backstage to tell her so, and I saw the chaos and the mess she was forced to endure back there." He shook his head. "It wasn't right. Someone of her talent, her gifts, she deserved better. I started to go back there, whenever I could get past the crew, to tidy up for her. I walked her home to keep her safe. She called me her pageboy, and said I made her feel like one of the grand ladies of old. I liked it, and when she offered to hire me, I was happy for the job." He looked up at Kara quickly and away again. "London is expensive."

"So it is. And you did well together?"

"We did. I quickly learned how to best serve her."

"And how did Frederick tempt you away?"

"Oh, he needed me even more than she did. He would come around Miss Lowe's rooms so often, I grew to understand him. I began to see to him, as well, and he enjoyed the attention. He liked that I could anticipate and be ready with whatever he required. He asked me to work for him, and I had to agree. He had so many needs that no one was seeing to. I became his personal servant and saw to his calendar, too."

"It sounds like a lot of responsibility."

"It was, but I like to be organized. Tidy. On time. On top of things. I was quite good at keeping Frederick on schedule." He sighed. "I was happy. We both were."

"If you saw to his personal needs and his appointments, then you would have known if Mr. Cole had been suffering from a physical ailment," said Niall.

Wade glanced away. "I am not supposed to discuss it."

Niall nodded. "A wise stance to hold to while Cole lived, but now that he's gone, surely you can see that you should share what you know."

"No. Why should I?" Wade seemed genuinely not to understand.

"Because Cole was killed by a large dose of medication. We need to understand how it happened."

Wade shook his head. "No. That cannot be right. I was the one who prepared his medication. No one else."

"You gave him digitalis?" asked Kara.

"How did you know that?" he whispered.

"Mr. Wade, what sort of condition was Frederick suffering from?" Kara watched him closely. "Was there something wrong with his heart?"

The man grew visibly agitated. "No. It's a secret. I'm not to tell." He drew a deep breath. "I cannot discuss it, but I can tell you that I prepared his medicine."

"It was too much digitalis that killed him," Niall said firmly.

Wade shook his head. "No. That's not possible. He took it in his nightly tonic. I had strict instructions from his physician. I know how to prepare the mixture correctly."

"How could you fix him a nightly tonic if you no longer lived in his household?" Kara asked sharply.

Wade paled.

"You need to tell us," she insisted. "Or I will have to ask Mrs. Cole and her staff."

"No!" he exclaimed. "Don't talk to her. She'll find out."

"Find what?" demanded Niall.

The man's shoulders slumped. "That I am living in the room at the back of the old carriage house."

"On the grounds of her house?" asked Kara.

He nodded. "Please don't tell her. It's just an empty room. The whole place is just used for storage. If she discovers me, though, she will send me packing. I don't know yet where I am to go or what I am to do. I was hoping you would know when Miss Lowe will be released."

"She might not be released, if we don't find who truly killed Mr. Cole."

"His medicine did not kill him," he insisted. "I can show you the powder. The apothecary gives it to me in small vials, with just the right amount for a dose. If you come—"

He stopped as movement sounded in the other room. Likely it was just Turner, but Wade was already sidling toward the door.

"You can come. Just you two. I'll show you. But please don't tell anyone I'm there. Not yet."

"We won't tell Mrs. Cole," Kara assured him.

"And we will come," Niall said.

Wade nodded. When the door opened, he slipped out, startling Turner. His gaze flew to Kara, but she nodded and beckoned him in. "I'm all right. Come in."

"Was that…?" Turner was watching the man flee.

"Yes. Elias Wade," Niall answered.

Kara let thoughts of the young man and his peculiarities fade as Turner entered. She felt her color rise as memories of last night came rushing back. Sinking down in the bed a bit, she covered her eyes with a hand. "I'm so sorry," she whispered.

"Don't be ridiculous," Niall chided. "You've nothing to feel sorry for."

Turner perched on the foot of the bed. "It's been a long time since you've had one of these spells."

"Yes, well, I've been extraordinarily proficient at avoiding attics. Until last night," she said on a sigh. "Thank you for coming. I don't recall much, but I knew you were here, and you know that always helps." She shook her head cautiously. "And I don't feel fuzzy headed from laudanum. I know that must be thanks to you."

"He stopped us from dosing you," Niall admitted.

"It always makes the nightmares worse. It traps me so that matter hard I fight, I cannot escape them."

"Once we had you safe and warm in familiar surroundings, you calmed down." Turner gave her a tender smile. "I gave you your favorite chocolate to drink, and you dropped off naturally."

"Thank you, Turner. For always being there."

"I always will," he vowed.

She looked up at Niall. "I'm so sorry for disrupting the evening and the investigation. And for becoming such a burden."

"You were not a burden, nor could you be. How many times have you cared for me, in a thousand different ways?"

"But what must Gyda think of me?" She grimaced and ducked her head again.

"She thinks she was happy to be there when you needed her." Gyda stood in the doorway, holding a nosegay of violets. She continued as she came into the room. "Come, Kara, don't be tiresome. You've bandaged and comforted me plenty of times. It's what friends do."

"It's what family does," Niall said quietly.

"I'm just glad I could return the favor in one of your rare moments of fragility." Gyda laughed. "Actually, I'm just glad to know you have them, occasionally."

"Fragility. How nicely you put it." Kara made a face. "I should call it dissolving into a blubbering mess."

"Eh." Gyda shrugged. "Everyone fears something."

"True," Niall agreed. "Water, insects, heights. At least attics are easily avoided."

"I suspect it wasn't just the attic," Turner said. "Being locked in, as well? It likely made it worse."

"Yes." Kara shuddered. "And when Gyda mentioned rats? That was the last I truly remember."

"My own aversion is far more difficult to avoid." Gyda stuck out her tongue. "Radishes. I ate so many as a child when there was naught else to be had. Now I flee the table at the mere sight of them."

Kara laughed. "Thank you. All of you. You are very gracious." She smiled at the clutch of violets in her friend's hand. "Are those for me? Thank you. Violets are so cheerful, aren't they?"

"They are indeed for you, but they didn't come from me."

"From whom, then?" She took them and breathed in the fresh scent.

"They were delivered downstairs, to Rachel, in the coffee

shop. The gentleman who left them said they were for you."

"Did Rachel get his name?"

"No, he did not leave it. She said only that he was swathed in a dark coat and had a nose like a spring bulb."

Kara exchanged a startled look with Niall. Without a word, he leapt up and charged out of the room.

Chapter Twelve

"**D**AMN IT ALL to hell and back," Niall cursed as he started back upstairs to Kara's rooms. The bulbous-nosed watcher was long gone. Rachel had not even seen which way he went when he left. The man had lingered, examining a display case of pastries, then ducked out when she was busy with a customer.

"He's gone," Niall said as he came back to the bedroom. "And, of course, he's left no clue."

Kara had donned a wrapper and sat at a table, where she'd convinced Turner to sit with them and take toast and tea. "Come and eat something." She beckoned to Niall. "You'll feel better."

"No, I won't," he grumbled.

"Well, I will," she said, handing him a plate of toast and a dish of preserves.

Gyda set down her cup of tea and stood. "If you mean to stop in to see Josie this morning, then I will return to Bluefield. I have an impatient customer waiting on a customized shield." She raised a brow at Niall. "And it seems as if the forge will be free."

"For now." He nodded. "I'll stay in Town, at least for the day. We have too many questions and next to no answers."

"Very well, then." She gave Kara a quick embrace, waved, and departed.

"Well, at least we did get the chance to speak to Elias Wade," despite my bumbling things last night," Kara said, settling back into her chair. "What did you think of him?"

Niall thought a moment. "I think there is more he is not telling us. More than just the specifics of Cole's medical condition."

"I thought the same. We'll have to go and visit him, as we told him." She cocked her head. "Were you able to get any answers from West last night?"

He guffawed. "No, he was too far gone in drink, even before we arrived. I don't know if he was putting on a performance or if it was heartfelt, but he was being very maudlin over Cole's loss." He accepted a cup of tea from Turner. "What of Abbott? Did you learn anything useful?"

"He was largely reminiscing over the old days, when he claims he helped Cole start his business. I was briefly excited when he mentioned his conservatory, but he only grows foreign and exotic plants, and foxglove is as common as you get." She raised a brow. "But I did hear something interesting. About Mr. Carver."

"Ah, yes." Niall recalled. "He was perhaps the only one not mourning the dearly departed Cole."

"Abbott said that Cole and Carver got into some sort of argument shortly before Cole died."

"Did he? Someone should speak to him, then. Do you think Wooten has questioned him already? Perhaps we should find the inspector and compare notes before we move any further ahead."

"I rather expect that he's at Mrs. Cole's this morning."

"Oh, yes. Damn it all!" Niall's frustration came surging back. "There is nothing but questions and more questions in this mess. And are we dealing with two messes, instead of one? That bounder with his ropes and nosegays! Who the hell is he? If he's watching us for malevolent reasons, as Stayme suspects, then why did he help me out of that cellar? And send you posies? We spotted him before we received Josie's call for help, so he surely must be related to my background and not the murder enquiry."

"Unless someone anticipated our involvement?" Kara wondered aloud. "And also, who locked us in that attic last night? It couldn't have been Wade. Is it the same person who has tried to warn us off helping find Cole's killer?"

With a growl, Niall shoved in the last bite of his toast and washed it down with a long drink of tea. "I think I'll check in with Stayme again. He might have discovered something."

"Perhaps you should change first," Kara said with a raised brow. "Although, I must confess, you rather do justice to the 'rumpled formal' look."

"I brought you both a change of clothes," Turner said calmly. "You'll find yours in the next room."

"You are a wonder, Turner."

"So I have heard," the older man said complacently.

Niall laughed, letting his irritation go. "Would you care to join me?" he asked Kara.

"No, I promised Gyda that I will stop in and see how Josie is holding up, then I will go home and check on Harold."

"Harold came into Town with me last night," Turner said. "I sent him on to Maisie." He gave Kara an apologetic glance. "I wasn't sure how bad it was, and I didn't want him to see you..."

"Yes. Thank you," she said, nodding. "That was wise."

"In any case, he plans to help out in the shop today."

"Very well. Still, I'd like to be at Bluefield if he returns tonight." She smiled at Niall. "But send Stayme my best."

"I will. I'll come back to Bluefield tonight and give you chance to rumple me again."

"You do that," she said, grinning.

"Not in front of the child, please," Turner said. "Or the staff."

Laughing, Niall strode out, and in less than an hour, he was in an omnibus, heading north. He was careful to make sure he wasn't followed, by Bulb Nose or anyone else. Cautiously, he watched the other riders and the streets around him.

He could detect no sign of anyone following, so he climbed

out to walk the last bit, happy for a chance to stretch out into a loping stride. His bruises had not appreciated the night in the chair. But the morning was bright, though chilly, and he felt better for the movement.

When he knocked at Berkeley Square, Watts answered and immediately looked relieved to see him.

"Is he sulking again?"

"No, sir. It's *worse*. He's gardening."

"Gardening? Has he left London?" The words *Stayme* and *gardening* just did not seem to go together.

"No. He's been reading books on the topic. Stacks of them. He talks of nothing but drainage and prime planting times."

"But it's still winter." Niall remained confused. "Where and how is he *gardening*?"

Watts opened the door wider and gestured. "Just look there, sir." He pointed to the fenced, circular garden in the midst of the square. "He's out there harassing the hired gardeners. He's gone out to lecture them on winter pruning and soil replenishing and bulb selections."

"Good heavens." Stayme was worse off than Niall had thought. "I'll go and talk to him."

He crossed the pavement and the wide street and entered through the gate. He could hear Stayme lecturing after taking just a few steps into the garden.

"Now, be sure and cut far enough away from the mature wood," the viscount was telling a man holding a set of long-handled shears. "You only wish to cut out the new growth where it is too crowded or where it is rubbing—" He stopped when he saw Niall. "There you are," he said. "It's taken you long enough to visit again."

Niall blinked. Stayme was far gone if he was clamoring for visitors. "Come on, old man. Come and walk with me, so we can talk."

The gardener shot him a grateful look.

"Fine, fine," Stayme grumbled. "Mind what I said about the

mature wood," he warned before he turned away to join Niall. "So, what's happened?"

"What hasn't?" Niall said sourly.

He started explaining. Stayme stopped him occasionally for questions and clarifications. "Hmph," he snorted. "Well, that trio didn't mean to press-gang you. If they worked for someone like me, they never would have left you at the bottom of that hole. They would have yanked you out, shuffled you off to the docks, and got the job done."

"That's what I thought, as well. But why else chase me like that?"

"To scare you off," the viscount said with certainty. "Someone doesn't want you mucking around in Cole's death."

Niall continued on, but it wasn't until he got to the events of this morning that Stayme began to perk up. "Violets, you say? A nosegay of violets?"

"Yes. Does that mean something to you?"

"Perhaps. And you say the man who left them was the same one who threw you the rope?"

"Yes."

"The same man whom you caught watching you?"

"Yes."

"A nose like a bulb, you say." He grinned up at Niall. "You may finally have given me something I can work with, boy!"

"Have I?"

"Yes, indeed." Stayme rubbed his hands together. "I can do something with this. Just you wait and see." He turned abruptly and headed back toward the house. "Come and see me in a day or two. I should have something by then."

"I…" It seemed that the viscount was coming back to himself. "Very well, then."

Stayme, thankfully, didn't even look at the gardeners as they passed by. The viscount left Niall on the pavement, bidding him farewell and then practically skipping up the walkway.

Bemused, Niall watched him go in. Well. This had gone more

quickly than he'd anticipated. Running down a mental list of tasks needing attention, he decided to head toward the park and Cole's house. He doubted West was likely to be coherent yet this morning, so perhaps he could catch Wooten after his interview with Cole's widow.

TURNER OFFERED TO accompany her to Lambeth, and for a moment, Kara was tempted to accept. Her nerves were still a little shaky after last night. But Mrs. Cole's words about her wasting her life and ruining her chances at happiness with her unconventional behavior kept coming back to her and rankling her very soul.

Kara's choices *were* unconventional, but so had her life been, since the day her kidnappers shot her attendants and took her for a chance at a ransom. Her father had seen to it that she learned things no other young girl in the peerage would have considered. She'd learned to survive, and she'd learned the skills that would help her if it happened again. She was different, there was no denying it, and she'd finally learned to live according to her own dictates, to satisfy her creative needs and find her own way to happiness. She had no desire to bend to Society's rules and try to fit herself in their small box of acceptability. It only appeared to apply to women, in any case. None of them seemed especially happy with their confinement there, either.

Kara was going to live her own way and follow the dictates of her conscience and her heart. She had cast off the constraints of other people's opinions. She was not going to take them up again after a scolding from a bitter widow.

And so she thanked Turner, bade him return to Bluefield, had her carriage brought around, and set off on her own.

London traffic moved briskly this morning, perhaps spurred on by the cold air. She pulled her cloak tightly around her as she climbed down before the police court building. The vast crowd had at last dispersed, leaving just a few people gathered, stamping their feet and blowing on their hands as they watched the comings and goings.

"Do give Miss Lowe our best wishes and tell her of our support," a man shouted as Kara went in.

"So I will!" she called back.

There was far less bustle in the front of the building compared to the other day. A constable greeted her respectfully. He was posted at the start of the corridor that held Josie's room, but he did not try to stop her. "Just a short visit, miss," he said with a nod for her to continue.

Well, that was an improvement.

Opening the door to Josie's room, Kara found more pleasant changes. There was a thick blanket and a pillow on the cot, a brightly colored rug on the floor, and stacks of books and papers on the table. Josie sat in the chair, quietly strumming on a guitar. She was entirely caught up in her work, playing a few bars over and over and humming quietly along.

Kara waited a moment, then cleared her throat.

"Oh, Kara!" Josie looked up, surprised, and smiled in welcome. "I'm so glad you are here." Jumping up, she took Kara's hands and pulled her in, insisting that she take the chair. As Kara tried to protest, the door opened and the constable came in with an extra chair and a shy smile in Josie's direction.

"Well," Kara said cheerfully as they settled in. "You are managing far more comfortably than I imagined."

"It is rather surprising, isn't it? Who knew that being held over for an inquest would be so...relaxing! I've had nothing to do but look after myself and work on my music. I've been writing so much and losing myself in the creation of it. It's just been so heartening."

"And clearly the constables have changed their attitudes toward you."

"Oh, yes! A few of them know that I have agreed to stay to

help their case, and they have been so lovely about showing their appreciation."

"You are helping their reputations as well, perhaps at some cost to your own," Kara reminded her.

"Yes. They are indeed happy not to have the public panicking or watching over their shoulders and bemoaning a lack of suspects, and I think they appreciate that nearly as much. Sergeant Landover has promised to shout my innocence for all to hear and to praise my cooperation. He says he'll leave no doubt in the public's mind that I was cooperative and an asset to the enquiry."

"He'll do that as soon as they have a true suspect, I presume."

"Yes, of course." Josie looked around with a sigh. "Still, I am happy to spend a little more time here, hiding away from the world. Mr. Barrett has been by several times, and we've made quite a good lot of progress. We are creating a catalogue of songs and recitations set to music that will help me to stand out."

"So you don't mean to return to the Adelphi?" Kara asked gently. "I know it was Cole who was enthusiastic about your career at the Rogue's Hideaway."

"I believe I will return to the traditional theater, at some point. At least, I hope to." Josie sighed. "But it would be far more satisfying to return as a successful music hall star than as a former bit player whose patron has passed."

"I can see the wisdom of that," Kara agreed.

Josie looked down at her hands. "Did you go to the tribute?" she asked in a quiet voice.

"We did."

Her shoulders hunched a little. "And?"

"And everyone who spoke of you lamented that you were not there, and expressed their support of you."

She looked up. "Truly?"

"No one of any differing opinion was so foolish as to express it to me," Kara said fiercely.

"And how was it?"

"It was about what you would expect."

"West had the direction of it all to himself. Mr. Barrett wasn't involved in the new acts at all. He was a little worried about it, but I haven't seen him today or heard his opinions."

"The place was full to the gills. The stage acts were…interesting." Kara described those she'd seen, and Josie swung between laughter and cringing dismay.

"How Frederick would have hated it," she whispered.

"Jimmy Gibbs was of the opinion that Mr. Cole would have enjoyed it." Kara shrugged. "But that was before the acts began."

"He would have enjoyed the attention at one time, but Frederick had begun to change these last few months."

"Do you know why?"

"All I know is that he was having some difficulties with his business. But he didn't really discuss that with me."

"You really didn't know he was ill?"

"No. It was a shock to hear that it was a sort of medication that was in the wine." She paused. "I'm not sure he ever would have told me about suffering any illness. He was terrified of becoming sick as he grew older. He hated the thought of anything that made him look weak."

"West said that they did argue, as you told us, but that they made up and that his father's investment group did pledge money for the new club."

Josie's eyebrows rose. "Well, that is a surprise. I thought Frederick was set against it."

"Do you know if Frederick had any trouble with any of the other members of his group?"

"He and Randall Abbott were always spitting at each other like cats. It's not a new development, by any means, though. They've been skirmishing for years."

"What about Mr. Carver?" Kara watched her closely. "I can tell you, he did not seem to be mourning Frederick like the others last night."

Josie frowned. "Carver. He's the youngest one, yes?"

"Yes."

"I don't think it was real trouble between them, but there was something. I don't know the entire story. I recently had a strange exchange with Frederick."

"About Carver?"

Josie nodded.

"Tell me."

"I only met the man once. He came to the club one night. He was at Frederick's table when I came out after my performance."

"Just him?"

"No, there were a few of the others from Sock and Buskin. But I noticed that Carver didn't seem comfortable. Still, he complimented me very kindly. He left soon after, and I thought nothing further of it until Frederick brought him up a week or so later."

"What did he say?"

"He asked me what I thought of Carver. It was an easy answer." Josie laughed a little. "Carver told me I was the best singer at the club, so of course I liked him very well, indeed."

"Did Frederick not like that?"

"He didn't have any visible reaction. He just asked if Carver mentioned him when we spoke, or anything about the partnership. I told him we exchanged almost no other words than the ones I'd told him about. I did ask him why he wished to know. I'd heard only a little about the man before that. He hadn't been with the partnership long, but Frederick had seemed very keen on him when he was invited in. I mentioned it."

"What was Frederick's response?"

"He said the man had exceptional skill with numbers. Give him an hour with the books and he could analyze what a company's potential was, how fast they would grow, that sort of thing. He had a real gift for knowing which investments were likely to bring a profit. But Frederick said that sometimes knowing a man's values and motivations were as important as the numbers."

"Was he speaking generally, or did he mean Mr. Carver specifically?" Kara asked.

"I don't know. I did ask Frederick if perhaps Mr. Carver had religious objections to the performances or the drinking at the club, as I'd noticed he seemed uneasy. He seemed quite eager to get away, and left long before the others."

"What was his answer?"

"He didn't know of any such objections, but admitted he did not know much about the man's personal life," Josie replied. "I asked him if he was having some sort of trouble with Carver."

"What was his answer?"

"He said he had wondered, but now he was not inclined to think so. I let the subject drop, but he must have been still mulling it over, for I later heard him mutter that he was not so old and feeble as to be led into Othello's role."

"Othello?" Kara straightened, thinking of the play and how the Moor was manipulated into a jealous rage, believing that his wife was unfaithful. "That would imply that someone was playing the role of Iago." The envious, plotting subordinate who set forth a rolling stone of jealousy, manipulation, murder, and suicide.

"Yes, but who?" Josie asked.

"I think we'd better find out."

The door opened, and they both started. A man paused on the threshold, looking surprised.

"Oh!" Josie stood. "Mr. Barrett, how kind of you to come. Do come in and meet my friend. Miss Levett, may I present Mr. Barrett? He is the musical director at the Rogue's Hideaway."

Kara stood to greet him as well. "How lovely to meet you, Mr. Barrett. I must thank you for making Josie's stay here more bearable." The man was older than Niall, but nowhere near Frederick Cole's age. He looked very distinguished, with just a sprinkling of gray hair at his temples.

"As I must thank you for trying so hard to see her exonerated." He smiled over at her friend, and Josie brightened. "I can't imagine a truer demonstration of friendship."

"Well, Josie has certainly done as much for me and for Niall." Kara gathered up her cloak. "And speaking of which, I should get back to it. That will leave the extra chair for you, sir." She hugged Josie and shook his hand. "I look forward to hearing the music you are both working on." She denied the man's offer to stay instead of him. "I will keep you updated, Josie, dear. And if you think of anything else, ask Sergeant Landover to send word."

She bade them farewell and headed outside. Her carriage, waiting down the street, began to move toward her, just as a small boy ran up. It was the same small boy that had intercepted her the other morning, before they went into the club the first time to speak to West.

"Miss Levett," he called, breathing heavily. "You must come to Red Lion Street! Mrs. Moseman needs you, right away!"

Chapter Thirteen

W HEN CREECH OPENED the door at Red Lion Street, he unbent enough to look relieved at the sight of her. "Please come in, Miss Levett. Mrs. Moseman is upstairs."

A spate of sobs came echoing down from higher up. "Oh, dear."

"Go straight up," Creech said, taking her cloak. He gave her an encouraging motion. "She will be happy to have reinforcements."

Kara paused with her hand on the stair rail. "It's not Harriet?"

"No. Heavens, no." Creech's look indicated his belief that Miss Moseman would never exhibit such a breach of decorum. "It is Miss Cole."

"Oh!" That put a different spin on things. She hurried upstairs and followed the sound of weeping to Harriet's room. Opening the door, she encountered what could only be called a *scene*.

Harriet sat in a stuffed chair near the window. Her mother stood, wringing her hands by the hearth. Miss Cole, it must be presumed, had collapsed in a puddle of expensive black silk onto the floor, with her head resting in Harriet's lap. A fine black bonnet festooned with raven's wings had been cast upon the bed.

Kara went to Mrs. Moseman just as their guest gave a low moan.

"You don't understand, Harriet. You could never understand, no matter how hard you tried. *Your* mother is apparently completely and utterly sane. Even of temper. Kind of heart. Grounded in reality. My own mother is none of those things!"

"Oh, dear. I'm sure Mrs. Cole is just overset at the loss of your father," Harriet said kindly.

"Ha!" Miss Cole's head came up. "If only it were so! I might even suspect her—indeed, I think she would be glad of his death, were it not for—"

She stopped herself and pinched her lips closed. Climbing to her feet, she began to pace.

"It is a very different thing for me. My mother knows only how to be critical. Nothing satisfies her. She quarreled with my father without ceasing, always trying her best—her worst!—to wound him. It's no wonder he found solace elsewhere."

Mrs. Moseman gasped, and the girl had the grace to blush.

"I'm sorry! I know I shouldn't speak of such things. It's just… My mother is a monster! She always finds fault with me. She falls out with her friends. She torments the servants. We cannot keep a decent housekeeper or cook, because she will only condemn and reprimand, and never finds anything to praise."

Miss Cole stopped at the window and leaned her head against it. "It's been my burden to bear, but I had Papa to lighten the load. I had a future, an escape to look forward to. A Season. A husband. A family of my own, where calm and encouragement would reign." She started to cry again. "All this is gone now."

"My dear," Mrs. Moseman said gingerly. "I know it seems dark now. The loss of your father is dreadful and will be felt in repercussions throughout your life, but there will be light again, one day. There will be love and family and peace."

"No, there will not." Miss Cole sounded bleak. "My mother wants to *pretend*. To live in denial and falsehood. To try to fool the world and fake our way. But it will not work. She will only make things worse. I must face the truth. The terrible, awful truth that I will be left alone with her forever. There will be no escape. I am trapped."

Turning, the girl rushed over to Harriet and clasped her hands. "Oh, promise to help me, Harriet, my dear friend." Tears ran over her cheeks. "Someday I will reach my limit. I know it. I will have to break away. Promise me, when that day comes, that I may come to you? You will take me in, give me a place? I will not ask for charity. I will be your companion, your governess, your housekeeper, whatever you need! I will do what I must, but I will feel so much better knowing I can count on you!"

"Of course. Of course you may come to me at any time, darling Charlotte," Harriet told her.

"My dear Miss Cole, calm yourself," Joanna Moseman said. "You may always count us your friends, no matter what comes, but I do believe you are seeing things as bleaker than they need be."

"Will you remember your promise?" Miss Cole asked Harriet in a whisper.

"Always," Harriet said fiercely.

Kara spoke up. "You have been given your promise, Miss Cole. That leaves us with the important question. Does your mother know you are here?"

Miss Cole breathed deeply. "She does not. I sneaked out when she closeted herself with the police inspector."

"Well, she will certainly not be pleased to find you gone," Kara said. "She will be afraid and angry, not to mention upset that you went out unaccompanied. You do not wish for her anger and chagrin to fall upon the Mosemans, I know."

Charlotte Cole shook her head.

"They will scarcely be able to stand by your side if your mother forbids the friendship."

"That is true enough. I will return home. But Harriet, I thank you, most deeply. I do not know when the day will come, but it eases me, knowing I will able to count on you."

Harriet's smile trembled as she hugged her friend close. Kara knew there must be more going on here than a mother and a daughter at odds. She wanted to know what it was.

"Miss Cole, we have not had the opportunity to be introduced. I am Miss Levett."

Charlotte looked surprised. "Oh! Well, I am pleased, indeed, to meet you. I heard about your visit with my mother. I don't know how you got the upper hand on her, but I've never known another, besides my father, who has done so."

"I have reached an understanding with Mrs. Cole, which makes me the ideal person to return you home. The Mosemans need not be involved." Kara let a warning creep into her tone. "Or mentioned."

Wiping her eyes, Miss Cole nodded. "Yes, of course. A wise suggestion." She kissed Harriet's cheek. "Thank you—you are a true friend." She gave Mrs. Moseman a nod. "I do apologize for disturbing you, ma'am." Taking up her bonnet, she strode out.

Kara exchanged a startled glance with the other two.

"Thank you," Mrs. Moseman whispered quietly.

Throwing her a nod and a grin, Kara set off in Miss Cole's wake.

A THEORY WAS building in Kara's head, built on small, scattered comments made by several of the people they'd met in this enquiry. Apart, they hadn't meant much, but sorting them together, they were giving her an idea—one she hoped a visit to the Coles' house might confirm.

She had plenty of time to consider it, as Miss Cole, looking pale and wan, spent the short trip merely staring out the carriage window. Fortunately, traffic was still moving at a good pace, even down the crowded Strand.

It was obvious when they hit the rushes before the girl's home. Kara leaned forward to look out and was the first to descend from the coach. She was surprised to see a cluster of street children on the corner, huddling about and hanging on the fence.

"Do you usually have street urchins in this neighborhood?" she asked, surprised, as Miss Cole stepped down beside her. "Or are they attracted by the notoriety of your father's death?"

The girl glanced in their direction. They must have seen her, for all at once they scattered, running in different directions.

"No. We do see them about, although in greater numbers this last year, I believe."

She made no other comment, merely waited for the gate to be opened, then walked briskly to the front door. She didn't knock, just opened the door and strode in, with Kara at her heels.

The eerie silence she'd noticed at her last visit was not to be found. It had been shattered with servants rushing about, upstairs and down, calling out to each other. An angry tirade sounded from somewhere off to the left of the grand staircase.

"That wicked girl! She's done this particularly to overset my nerves, I know it!"

Miss Cole sighed. "I've been discovered, it seems."

Kara started to drift toward the commotion when a footman emerged from the corridor. The inept footman she'd encountered before, to be precise. He took a look at the pair of them and stopped in surprise. "Miss Cole! You're back!" He drew a deep breath. "She's back!" he called. "Miss Cole, that is! Here she is!"

The young lady shot him a look of dislike as she strolled past him. "Do shut up, Charles."

Biting back a smile, Kara followed as she headed down the wide passage. A parlor door stood open. Inspector Wooten stood outside of it, speaking in low tones to the butler. He broke off as he spotted them. "Miss Levett." He raised a brow at her in question before he turned to bow at Charlotte. "Miss Cole, I presume. Your mother will be glad to see you safely returned."

The girl gave him a nod, heaved a sigh, and entered the parlor.

"I want to speak with you afterward," Kara told him as she

followed. "But I do not want to miss this."

In high color, clutching a long, lacy handkerchief, Mrs. Cole was already berating her daughter. "Wretched girl! You purposefully vex me at every turn! Where did you go? What have you been up to?"

"I just went out for some air, Mother," the girl said, casting a glance back at Kara.

"Indeed, and I found her and took her up in my carriage," Kara said, sweeping in.

"Miss Levett," Mrs. Cole greeted her with a suspicious frown. "I wasn't aware that you are acquainted with my daughter."

"We've only just met this morning, but when I saw a girl in mourning silks, I surmised her identity." Not a lie. Not exactly. "I came this way hoping to speak with Inspector Wooten." Also true, if not comprehensive.

"Thank you for returning Miss Cole," Wooten said soberly. "We only discovered her absence because I wished to verify a few things with her directly."

"What things?" Miss Cole looked interested and also oddly defiant.

"There's no need for you to talk with the police, Charlotte," her mother said, glaring at Wooten. "I agreed to do so. You were not part of the bargain."

"I don't mind, Mama."

Wooten gave her a nod of gratitude. "I've heard a few rumblings as I've headed up the enquiry into your father's death. There is some quiet suspicion that he was facing trouble on the business front. Your mother says that neither you nor she would know anything about that."

"I know about it," the girl said stiffly.

"Nonsense! No, she does not!" Her mother pointed a finger at her. "Do not speak of that which you do not understand, girl!"

"I do understand, and I will not be quiet! I will not lie about our situation. There is no money, Mama! You cannot pretend that there is."

"She doesn't know what she says," Mrs. Cole said desperately. "Frederick never talked to either of us about anything like that—or about anything important."

"He talked to me," her daughter countered with an arch look at her mother. "He always had done. He asked after my studies, my interests. He gave me advice and care, instead of just orders. He loved me, and now he is gone." She paused and swallowed several times before she continued. "He spoke to me on the day he died. About our financial circumstances."

Inspector Wooten approached the girl. With a soft touch, he led her to a seat. Pulling out a notebook, he took the chair opposite her. "We very much wish to find your father's killer, Miss Cole, and bring them to justice."

Tears fell, and the girl roughly wiped them away. "Yes. And I want it known how he was treated by his supposed friends and partners."

"What did he tell you?" the inspector asked.

Miss Cole heaved a great sigh. "He said things were going to change."

Her mother sank into a chair and covered her eyes.

The girl refused to look her way. "He said he'd been made to look a fool and that his partners at Sock and Buskin had abandoned him. He'd been left bearing the responsibility for several investments on his own, instead of with the combined backing of the group. It apparently took nearly all our money."

Her mother perked up. "Investments? Not lost to gambling or ruin? If he made investments then we should see a profit from them!"

"Yes. He said he had hope that the projects would prosper. He could not go back on his word to support them. But he said it would take years before we saw any substantial money from them. And, of course, there was always the chance we would see nothing."

Mrs. Cole sank back again.

"Papa said we would always have the bank. That the simple

people who trusted him enough to bank with him would never desert us. But our income would be much, much smaller. It would not be enough to maintain our lives here, in this house, or in London. Our home, our status, our expectations—everything would have to change. He apologized for the timing of it all."

"Right before your debut," her mother mourned.

The girl's head dropped. "And he apologized, as he'd been forced to take my dowry."

"What?" Her mother snapped straight up again. "That is ridiculous. He couldn't touch your dowry. That was set out in our marriage settlements."

"Set out, but apparently not protected, Mama," the girl said sharply. "It would appear his solicitors were more skilled, or at least wilier, than yours. He had some way, some backdoor clause or some such, that allowed him to get the money. And he had already done so."

Mrs. Cole wore a look of horror—and of incredible anger.

Wooten cleared his throat. "You said he'd been made to look a fool, Miss Cole? Did your father give any indication who might have done that?"

Tears began to flow again. "He told me very bitterly never to trust old friends or relations." Miss Cole choked back a sob. "I told him he was giving me a fine example of just such a lesson." Her face crumpled. "I was so shocked and angry and hurt! I left him then. We parted on such hostile terms. And then he died! They were my last words to him!" The girl fell against the back of the sofa, crying as if her heart would break.

Kara waited for her mother to go to her, but Mrs. Cole just sat very still, staring bitterly ahead. So Kara went to the girl and eased down beside her. Charlotte fell upon her shoulder, weeping.

"You heard her," her mother said to Wooten. "Words from Frederick's own mouth. Never trust old friends or family. Abbott or West? Take your pick!"

Wooten nodded. "I have noted it, but we cannot jump to

conclusions. We must have evidence."

"Then find it! It is your job, is it not? One of those men ruined him. And if that was not enough, they had to finish the job with his murder!"

"We cannot know yet if one person did both," Wooten replied.

"Then find proof," Mrs. Cole ordered him coldly.

The inspector closed his notebook and stood. He looked from the widow to her daughter, still sobbing and now enfolded in Kara's arms. "Shall I send for someone? Your butler, perhaps?"

"Have him send the girl's maid." Mrs. Cole stood. "I'll be waiting to hear from you, sir." Without a further glance at any of them, she strode from the room.

Kara and Wooten exchanged glances. "Please do not leave, Inspector," she said. "I need to have a word with you."

He inclined his head. "I believe I'll wait outside for you, then, Miss Levett."

She nodded in understanding, even as she embraced poor Charlotte. For she was also more than ready to leave behind the uncomfortable atmosphere of this house.

Chapter Fourteen

NIALL HAD A hunch that Wooten was going to be questioning Mrs. Cole for far longer than he had talked with Stayme. From what Kara had said of the woman, he suspected the inspector was going to have a difficult time obtaining any useful information.

By his calculations, he had plenty of time to take a turn around the impressive girth of Frederick Cole's house and scout out the carriage house where Wade said he'd been living. He would wait for Kara to make their visit, but a bit of reconnaissance couldn't hurt.

The house sat on a street corner, its front and far side facing the streets. Niall approached from the other side and ducked down an open lane between the place and its neighbor, following the fence that defined the perimeter of the house and the narrow plot of ground surrounding it. About three-quarters of the way down, the grounds gave way to a wide, well-kept stairway, no doubt leading down to a delivery entrance for the kitchens. It widened into a landing below, where several crates of vegetables were stacked, waiting to be taken inside. A young footman, likely tasked with the job, sat on the steps, idly smoking. The boy stared openly, but Niall merely nodded and went on.

After another section of well-tended grounds, Niall found a

tall wooden fence intersecting the iron perimeter. It helped to enclose a functional space in the back corner of the property. Within, there was a kitchen garden with a few wintergreens still alive, another stairway down to the below-stairs area, a row of privies, and a chicken shed. Beyond it lay a wide lane and then the mews.

A stable block took up most of the space there. It looked like there were stalls for four horses, at the least, as well as storage for tack and rooms above. Two groomsmen sat outside, playing cards over a barrel. Past the stables, there stood a wide sliding door. It sat open, and Niall could see another groom polishing the lamps on the carriage stored there. Another, narrower sliding door came next. This one was closed tight, and an old lock hung upon the latch. A regular-sized door stood just to the side of it, also closed. The doorstep was dusty, and that whole end of the building looked unused. It must be the old carriage house.

The grooms were eyeing him, so Niall walked on, keeping to the house side of the lane. Past the kitchen garden, the fancy grounds started up again. He reached the corner of the house, where the mews lane intersected the street on the side of the house. He was just about to make the turn when he saw two men approaching, coming his way down the lane that continued on behind the houses on the other side of the street.

Pulling up, he looked again. Yes. They were two of the men who had chased him through Lambeth the other day. They paused on the opposite corner, and one of the men must have sensed his attention. He looked up and spotted Niall.

The man recognized him right away. Niall saw they both wore workmen's clothes. They had looked relaxed and at ease as they walked, but now the man who had spotted him grabbed the shoulder of his friend. They all stared at each other—then, in unison, the two men turned and fled.

Niall's first instinct was to give chase. He leapt out into the street, then had to jump back as a dray rumbled by, the driver shouting at him. He dodged traffic to reach the other corner, then paused.

Already the men had gone. He could find no sign of them in the mews lane. They could be hiding in any of the stables, or they could have cut through the yards or lanes of any of the houses ahead.

Niall curled his fists in frustration. He didn't know this area of Town. He was alone. He was unlikely to find them, or to force them to talk even if he did catch them.

With a sigh, he decided to let it go. But his mind whirled as he crossed back to the pavement running beside the Coles' house. Who the devil were those men? Why were they here, acting so comfortably, so near to Frederick Cole's house?

Rounding the corner to the front of the stately home, he was surprised to see Wooten exiting the gate. He hurried, wanting to catch the inspector, but Wooten paused next to the fence, pulled out a notebook, and scribbled something in it. As Niall grew close enough to hail him, the gate opened again and Kara came out onto the pavement.

"Kara?" Niall waved as he approached. "Wooten! Kara!" He came to a halt before her. "What in Odin's eye are you doing here?"

She looked lovely, as always, in blue-gray skirts, buttoned over with a cloak of camel-colored wool. The embroidery on the cloak was wide and finely scrolled in the same color as her skirts.

Niall bent low over her hand and caught the solemn look on her face. "Is everything all right?"

"Yes. Well, mostly." She explained how she'd been summoned from Lambeth. Afterward, Wooten relayed what they had learned from Charlotte Cole.

"I'm assuming you have a theory on who might have conspired against Cole to separate him from the investment group?" Wooten asked Kara. "At least, that's why I thought you wanted me to wait."

"I do, yes, and I'm sure it's the same name you have settled on," she answered.

"It would be Abbott, I presume?" Niall interjected. "I remember what he said to you. You thought he resented Cole's lack of recognition of his efforts in the partnership."

"It's a reasonable assumption," Wooten said, but he hesitated. "The pair of them are known to have engaged in a longstanding feud about their respective contributions. I hesitate because of it, though. If they've been having the same argument for years, what could have made it escalate to murder?"

"I don't know the motivation, but I believe Abbott has changed his game recently," Kara said.

"That's exactly what Carver said about Abbott," Niall recalled. "He called him a player of games. A director of theatricals, even within the business."

"That's exactly what I suspect," Kara agreed, excited. "I spoke with Josie this morning." Niall and Wooten both listened closely as she told them about Cole's questions about Carver. "It sounds as if Cole was feeling manipulated. If he felt someone was trying to get him to act the role of Othello, then that implies that someone was playing Iago, trying to discredit him and perhaps trying to make him think Carver had an interest in Josie."

"Except Cole was wily enough not to fall into a jealous rage. Instead he went to Josie and calmly asked questions." Wooten sounded impressed. "And he might have begun to ask other questions as well."

"Questions that might have led to his murder," Kara said quietly.

"Questions we will need to ask as well, if we are to prove it was Abbott pulling the strings." Wooten still didn't sound convinced.

"Start with Carver," suggested Niall. "Gyda and Kara saw him in a shouting match with Abbott behind the club last night."

"I barely saw him," Kara said.

"I spoke with him a little," he reminded her. "And he left me with the impression that he is clearly not a fan of either Cole or Abbott. Why is that, I wonder?"

"I tried to speak with Mr. Carver last night," Wooten said. "He made it clear he has no interest in answering questions regarding Cole's death or their business relationship."

"We need to find out what happened in that partnership," Kara said.

"The other members appeared more willing to cooperate. I will begin interviewing them today."

"If you can get a clear picture of what happened between them all, then I'm willing to bet you'll be able to use it to force Carver to talk to you," Niall mused. He shook his head. "If what we suspect is true, you'll want the full story before you confront Abbott. He used to be on the stage, as he told Kara. He'll know how to dissemble. And he'll enjoy playing against you. You'll want plenty of ammunition."

"I also still want to know what changed. Why go so hard against Cole now, after years of butting heads?" Wooten was frowning over that thought.

Niall shrugged. "Check his financial status, perhaps?"

"Yes. I'll set Sergeant Landover to looking into it. He was upset at missing this interview, but he was summoned by his superiors in the coroner's office." Wooten sighed. "I'm afraid I'm going to have to go to the commissioners with all of this. These are prominent men of business with connections everywhere. I'll need backing if I am to push them." He sounded both grim and determined. "Miss Levett, I may call upon you and Miss Winther when I am ready to question Mr. Carver. He will be a reluctant witness, I suspect. He will wish to deny any connections to the case. Men sometimes find it easy to lie to the police, but it's harder to deny your actions when faced with an eyewitness."

"I am sure we will both be happy to help, Inspector," Niall replied. "In any way we can, as always."

"Thank you. I must go. I have much to do." Wooten gazed between them. "I know I asked you to step back, but you've both been helpful with this enquiry. Thank you."

Smiling, Kara reached out and touched his arm. "Your skills

and patience saved me when I needed it. We are always ready to return the favor." She lifted a shoulder. "I've only just been reminded that that is what friends do."

"I do appreciate it. And I'll be in touch soon."

Niall shook his hand and watched the inspector walk away. Kara tucked her arm into his and smiled up at him. "That's Wooten sorted! He'll speak to the major players, in his official capacity. I think we should seek out some of the less obvious parties. There are those that are not directly involved, but might know something useful. We might find something to support Wooten."

"Or something entirely new," Niall predicted. "And since we are here, I think we should begin by talking to Elias Wade again."

Her eyes widened. "Oh, yes! In all of the fuss, it slipped my mind."

"It did not slip mine. I tried to scope out the old carriage house earlier. There were too many grooms about to learn much, but I did have a curious encounter." He leaned in to tell her about his sighting.

KARA ABRUPTLY STOPPED walking to stare up at Niall in disbelief. "You mean two of those men who chased you into that pit? They were walking, quite at their ease, right here?"

"Right there." Niall pointed.

"But...but...what does it *mean*? Surely it means something? You don't think...?" She covered her mouth with a hand. "Could they have been coming to see Mrs. Cole? Or a confederate? A subordinate acting on her orders?"

"It was my first thought, but after you spoke to her, you felt strongly that she had nothing to do with her husband's death."

"Indeed, I did feel that way." She glanced back at the house. "But after today, seeing how unfeeling she was with her daughter… Now I wonder if I was wrong? Oh, saints!" Looking back again, she scanned the street. "We should tell Wooten."

"He will only comment on her lack of motive. There certainly seems to be no profit for her from his death."

"That's true. Abbott will have at least got a final revenge on his longtime rival." She pursed her lips. "But Mrs. Cole did say that money was all she got from the marriage, and if that was gone… But did she know about the loss of the partnership? She certainly sounded surprised at Charlotte's news."

"Perhaps Wade can tell us more about their relationship? And also about who might have known about Cole's financial troubles."

"Yes, he might. Let's go see what he knows."

Niall took her arm and nodded ahead. "That is the mews lane. When I scouted it, I noticed the doors to the old carriage house were locked and looked as if they had not been used in a good, long while. Even the stoop to the door lay thick with dust."

"Another entrance, then?"

"Probably around back. Let's head back there and see what we can find."

It was a narrow alley behind the Coles' mews, separating it from a mirrored image of the next home's stable block. Further down the cramped space, it was cluttered, strewn with cracked and discarded oat casks and other garbage. Closer to the street, it had been swept clean. A door of small proportions waited there, a few steps down. Exchanging glances, they slid into the alley, and Niall knocked smartly upon it.

He had to knock again, but eventually the door opened a crack, just enough for a pale blue eye to peer out. "Oh! You did come." Elias Wade swung the door wide.

"As we promised we would," Niall replied. "May we come in?"

The young man frowned slightly, but moved aside. "Of course."

They stepped into a small antechamber lined in old wood—

completely bare save for a built-in bench. As soon as they were in, Wade shut and locked the outer door.

"If you'll just… Excuse me." The young man moved past Kara and opened another door. "Please, do come in."

She stepped through and her mouth dropped. The young man had said he'd moved into an old storage room. She'd imagined something dark and dusty, perhaps filled with old tack or equipment. Or, in the other direction, something stark and bare.

This space was neither of those things. It was light, clean, and furnished. It had been made into a home.

A very cozy home, indeed.

The walls looked freshly painted. The wooden floors shone. Upholstered furniture sat around a pot-bellied stove. An old, but only slightly worn, Turkish carpet covered part of the floor. Cupboards hung in one corner and shelves lined another. Print copies of famous paintings hung on the walls.

"Mr. Wade," she said breathlessly. "When you said… I can scarcely believe…" She gave up. "Well. What a lovely job you've done in here."

"Elias, please," he said bashfully. "Everyone calls me Elias."

While she'd been gawking at the décor, Niall had been standing in one spot, staring up at long, square column cut through to the roof. A skylight window had been set at the top, far above. It was clean and let a considerable amount of light into the room.

"Ah, yes. It's nice, isn't it?" Elias asked him. "I think it was added so that the grooms could see to oil the harness and polish the tack, but I quite enjoy it."

"Don't you lose all of your heat to it?" Niall asked, ever practical.

"I did at first." Elias went to the spot, reached up, and uncoiled a short rope on a hook. He pulled, and it tugged down a hinged piece of wood that blocked the shaft. "I had this installed for when the bitter cold or damp hits and I want to keep the heat more than I want the light."

"That would fix it, handily," Niall said in approval as the young man returned the wood and rope to their former positions.

"It's all delightfully cozy," Kara said in appreciation. She eyed a door that she presumed led to a bedroom.

"Thank you. I do enjoy a comfortable space." Elias's gaze darted around, and he wore a look of satisfaction and pride. "So many people do not realize what can be accomplished with trading, bartering, and bargaining."

"*Trading?*" Niall sounded incredulous. "You *traded* for all of this?"

"Most of it. Although a few small things were gifts."

"What do you trade?" Niall asked, and Kara wondered if he'd had the same thought she had—was Elias trading Frederick Cole's secrets? Either personal or business related?

"Oh, any number of things," Elias said. "It's never the same, is it?"

"Isn't it?" Kara asked.

"No, of course not. It all depends on the person you are trading with. You have to understand them if you really wish to get a good bargain. You must know what they wish and long for the most. As an example..." He crossed to a shelf where a small Jasperware bowl sat in a place of honor. "I got this in trade from a merchant gentleman. He grew up in Wales, but lives in London now. He doesn't get back to his home due to an unfortunate condition of his spine. We spoke of some of the things he misses terribly, and one of them was the taste of real, sweet salt-marsh lamb." He shrugged. "It's one of those things you cannot get anywhere else. I happened to know of a quality butcher, and I convinced him to send a shipment. The gentleman was thrilled to get it. He said it took him straight back to his youth. You see, it meant something wonderful to him, but wouldn't be the same to most others."

"That's right. Josie mentioned that you come from Wales," Kara said lightly. "I thought I heard a faint accent come through occasionally, but I scarcely notice it at all."

Elias blushed. "My grandda would not be happy to hear you say I let it slip at all. He tried everything to rid me of any accent. He said I'd never make anything of myself, out in the wide world, sounding of Swansea." He stopped and blinked in surprise, as if he'd revealed more than he meant to.

Niall glanced back to the skylight. "Did you trade for the installation of that wooden piece?"

Elias shifted and looked away. "Yes."

"What do you trade for that sort of thing? A skilled service from a craftsman is completely different from a bit of porcelain. Even famous, valued porcelain."

Elias swallowed. "I found the craftsman a new position."

"Using your connections," Niall mused. "At the Rogue's Hideaway, perhaps?"

The young man nodded. "Yes. They always need carpenters for set pieces and keeping the backstage in working order."

Elias was looking more and more skittish. Kara wanted to put him at ease again. "You know, I'm very interested in what you said about knowing whom you are trading with. Not everyone would understand that. It's a way of thinking that you use in your work, surely. Perhaps it's what makes you so good at it? Where did you learn such a skill?"

She'd succeeded, at least a bit—Elias's expression softened. "I learned it from my mother. She loved people, and she loved making them feel comfortable."

"What a lovely quality to be known for. Was she a recognized hostess, then?"

"Oh, no." The young man shook his head. "Not in the way you mean. She was not out in Society. Not even in Swansea. She ran the company store that was part of my grandfather's factory."

"Oh." Kara was surprised he'd revealed even more, but it was almost as if he could not let her incorrect supposition stand.

"She hated the whole idea of it, forcing the workers to spend their wages back with the factory, so she took over the running of it. She made sure the employees and their families had quality choices, at good prices. She always said it was extra money. The store didn't need to make a great profit as much as the factory needed happy, satisfied workers."

"She sounds like a wise woman."

"Oh, yes. So kind, too, to everyone. She sang like a bird while she worked. She would make up little songs, and I always sang back to her."

"You worked with her?"

"From the time I toddled at her knee," he said with a faraway look. "It was best that I stay with her. For everyone. I learned everything, too, working in the storeroom and behind the counter. I learned how to make things neat and organized. How to ensure that everything ran smoothly. I saw how important it was to her, to make the workers feel satisfied and valued. But then I learned the trick, and I surpassed even her success."

"The trick?" asked Niall.

"Yes, as I said before, the trick of knowing and truly understanding your subject."

"Your subject?" Kara asked. "You make it sound quite scientific."

"It could be considered so, I suppose, when you make someone an object of study. That is how you learn what tickles their fancy, what makes them feel welcome, understood, and at home. My mother, you see, made shopping at the factory store palatable, but I made them *want* to shop there. When I was done, they happily gave their money back into my grandfather's pocket."

"Oh, my. I'm sure he must have been proud."

"He deplored my methods, but he could not argue with the results."

Kara felt a tinge of unease. "Your methods?"

"It is a matter of delicacy and degree." Elias grew more earnest as he continued. "A factory worker's wife is still a woman, though she might even be employed herself. She wants a taste of luxury, a bit of a feeling of being pampered."

"Who doesn't?" Kara asked with a grin.

"True enough, but you cannot offer a woman like that a fancy tea service like you might get in a London shop. She will recoil. No. A small table or two, just slightly worn. That is what you want. Clean, neat linen, nothing crested or heavily embroidered. Offer a small, inexpensive pot of strong tea, and include a plate of plain biscuits with the price. She will be comfortable with that. A worn, harried woman gets a few minutes to herself, or with a friend. It is simple, but to her, it feels rich."

It made sense. But why did it also make Kara want to cringe?

"My grandfather thought it was coddling them, but the trick is knowing what is acceptable and feels good. No fancy handkerchiefs. But a soft and pretty flannel face cloth can be both decorative and functional. No leather-bound books, but chapbooks or serials are perfect. They foster community. People get caught up in the story, and they will gather to talk and pass copies around, but soon enough, a family owning its own copy is a small luxury that feels larger."

"It doesn't sound like something your grandfather could object to," said Niall.

Elias's expression went still. "He wasn't inclined to approve of anything I did or said," he said quietly.

"Oh, dear. Well, clearly he did not share his daughter's wisdom." Kara kept her tone gentle.

"No, he honestly did not, for all of his success," Elias agreed.

"I noticed you speak of her in the past tense."

"Oh, yes. She died. Influenza. It went through all of the factories. My grandda sent me away then. He died, too, not long after I left. It's why I was so glad to find Josie."

"And then Frederick Cole," Niall said.

The young man heaved a long sigh. "Yes. I was so happy working with him. It was satisfying in every way. We were both happy, and I thought my future was set, my fate decided. It was why I felt steady enough to make improvements in here." Elias almost visibly pulled himself out of the past. "But, of course,

Frederick is why you have come. Let me show you his medicine." He went to a corner where a small counter and coordinating cupboards had been built. Reaching up, he pulled down a wooden box.

Kara and Niall followed. The box contained a drawer below and a top that had been divided up into square compartments. Most of the squares held small glass vials filled with powder.

"I had just been to the apothecary on the day that Frederick died. Once a week he gave me seven vials, each with a single day's dose. He made it easy. I didn't have to measure or worry with anything—I just mixed it with fortified wine into a tonic that Frederick took before bed."

"Why are there only six in the box?" asked Niall.

"I took the first vial to the club that night. I knew it would be a late night. I wasn't sure if we would return here or if Mr. Cole would stay with Josie."

"What happened to the vial?" Kara tried to keep the sharpness out of her voice.

"It's here." Elias pulled a small, wrapped bundle from his pocket. Unrolling it, he showed them the still-full, stoppered vial. He blinked furiously. "I never got to mix it for him. I don't know why I'm still carrying it about with me. It just makes me feel as if..." His words trailed away.

Kara cleared her throat. "You said that Mr. Cole's illness was a secret. Are you sure that no one else knew of it?"

"No one. He was adamant that no one should know. He hated the very thought of it. He always wanted to be seen as strong, knowing, and vital."

"Not even his wife knew?"

"Especially not her. He would never have told her. She already suspected—" He stopped abruptly and pressed his lips together.

"She suspected...what?" Kara paused. "Had she guessed he was having financial troubles?"

"She wasn't supposed to know that either. I don't think she

did know—she was only guessing. Likely because Frederick warned her to curb her spending once too often."

"Elias," Kara said calmly. "Do you think it is possible that Mrs. Cole had her husband murdered?"

His shock at the question was real, if she was any judge. "What? No! I could not believe it to be so."

"Why not? From all accounts, they did not get along at all."

"No, they didn't."

"If his money was all that Mrs. Cole valued about her husband—"

"No," Elias said firmly. "She is not a nice woman. She has no regard for most people, and certainly not for anyone she considers below her on the social ladder. But she and Frederick, they possessed an odd sort of respect for each other. I don't pretend to understand it. At times I think they delighted in making each other miserable, but in a strange way, they also enjoyed it." The topic was making him uneasy again. He started to pace from one end of the room to the other.

"You do not believe she had anything to do with his death?" Niall repeated.

"No. Of course not." Elias sounded bitter now. "For then, whom would she torment? No one else stands toe to toe with her, giving as good as she tosses out. They were often at war, but they were equals in it, and I think they both found it exhilarating."

He walked away again, to the far side of the room where it was darker and he could hide his emotion. "At least she gave him that much, little though it was. Frederick was a man besieged, you know. Everyone wanted something from him. Money, contacts, opportunity. A word, a whisper of advice or a recommendation. His so-called friends?" He scoffed. "Abbott only ever wanted to outdo him. Every minute he doesn't spend in his precious conservatory, he is plotting to outperform Frederick, to steal his thunder, ride his coattails to riches." He snorted. "And the opposite, too, I suspect. The very few projects Frederick backed that didn't return profit? I would not doubt that Abbott had a hand in their failures. And Carver? All he craved was Frederick's praise. Always trying to prove himself. Like a puppy, he was."

Niall followed him down to that side of the room. "Why did you follow Abbott and Carver out into the yard of the club last night?"

"They were plotting against Frederick, interfering in his business."

"How do you know?" Kara asked quickly. "Do you have proof of it?"

"No. But it fits." He paused. "You know about the partnership? How Frederick was pushed out?" At Niall's nod, he continued. "It's exactly the sort of scheme Abbott might come up with. And Carver is gullible enough to have fallen in with him."

"Wait a moment." Niall frowned. "Do you know exactly how they accomplished it?"

"No. That's why I followed them. I saw them sniping at each other earlier in the evening. Abbott left the bar and headed backstage, and I saw Carver move to follow. I saw them from behind the chairman's desk. I wanted to hear what they would say to each other. To hear them admit their guilt, even if only to each other. And to see if they had plotted at anything worse."

Elias pressed a hand to his temple. "Frederick had scarcely anyone in his life who cared for *him*. Who would give back to him. They all just wanted to take and take from him." The young man broke into angry tears, an outburst that he quickly tried to get under control.

Kara came quickly to lay a light hand on his shoulder. "It sounds as if he had you, Elias."

He wiped at his face. "Yes. I only wanted what was best for him, always."

"I assume you must count Josie as one of the good people in Cole's life?" Niall asked him.

"Oh, yes. Yes, of course. She was very good to him." Elias

sighed. "Frederick often said his best evenings were spent in our company."

Niall had questions about how Frederick spent his evenings, but Kara was distracted when she noticed a shadowed alcove in this far end of the room. Curious, she moved toward it. Narrowing her eyes, she saw the walls were bare, but there was something on the floor. Crouching down, she ran her hand over a soft bundle and then another. "Elias," she called. "What are these?"

He turned to look, and his face grew still. "Pallets."

"Oh? Do you have pets? A dog?"

"No."

"Who are they for, then?"

He shrugged. "For whoever needs them. Unlike Mrs. Cole, I do not scorn or despise those less fortunate than me. I realize how easily circumstances can change. How people and things can just…slip away. I have friends who do not have a snug place like this to sleep. Sometimes I invite them to share my supper and sleep warm for the night." His shoulders dropped. "It's another reason why I don't wish for Mrs. Cole to discover I am here. I am still looking for another position and my next place to live." He turned a hopeful eye to her. "In fact, if you might know anyone who needs assistance or looking after…"

"You will be the first to know if we hear of anything," Niall said, clapping his shoulder. "Thank you, Mr. Wade. You've been very good to answer our questions."

"You won't tell Mrs. Cole?" Elias gestured around them.

"Absolutely not," Kara vowed.

"Thank you," Elias breathed.

"We appreciate your help," Niall told him.

"Please give Josie my best."

"We will." Kara pulled on her gloves as Niall urged her toward the door. "Good day to you!"

"Good day."

Kara looked back as Niall led her into the antechamber. Elias appeared forlorn and alone, even in the midst of the comfort he had collected. "Why are you in such a hurry?" she asked as Niall took her arm and set out briskly for the main road.

"Because sometimes when that boy speaks..." He gave a shake of his shoulders. "I did not want to hear about the trades he makes with his less fortunate friends."

"Oh, come now. He is odd, but just a touch, I think." Now she gave a shiver. "Although the way he thinks about things, talked of those factory workers, it did feel..." She made a face.

"Manipulative?"

"Yes."

"Enough of Elias Wade," Niall said firmly. "It's a good deal past noon already. Not even you can live on toast and drama."

She laughed. "Nor would I wish to."

"Did you send your carriage to the livery on North Row?"

"Yes."

"Good—let us fetch it and then we can go to Maisie's and share a pie. We shall see if Harold is ready to return to Bluefield. You need a night at home."

"That sounds lovely."

"When we finish, you and Harold can take the carriage home. I'll take the train."

She sighed. "Are we back to that again?"

"You heard Wade. He doesn't think Mrs. Cole hired out her husband's killing. He likely had a closer idea of their relationship than anyone else. Which leaves us again with those two men. Were they following me? Had they heard you were here?" He put a hand over hers and squeezed. "I love you, Kara Levett," he said gently. "It's been a long road for me to allow myself to embrace it, feel it. Longer to confess it to you and the world. I cannot risk you, nor Harold. I will do whatever it takes to keep you safe."

Alarm shot through her. "Except leave me behind."

He let his dark gaze roam over her. "Even that. But only if it is utterly necessary, I promise."

Kara gripped his arm tight. "I swear it, Niall Kier—if you

leave, I will follow. I will take every train, ship, coach, goat cart, or donkey back to find you. I will chase you down, and when I find you, I will beat you senseless right before I drag you to the nearest altar, marry you, and make you blissfully happy."

The line of his jaw tightened a moment before he laughed. Heat leapt up between them. "Stayme thinks he is onto something," he whispered. "Hopefully we will hear or learn something soon. Then we can skip the chase and go right to the bliss."

"Yes, please. I vote for that course." She frowned playfully at him. "But I will have the goat cart greased and readied, just in case."

Chapter Fifteen

"**O**H, LOOK AT that! What a fine job you've done." Kara sat in a chair near the forge and carefully examined the simple blade that Harold had made. Running her finger down the fuller and carefully twisting it about so that she could look at it from every angle, she grinned at the boy. "Oh, Harold, you must be so proud. I know I am full to bursting with it." She hefted the blade in both hands. "It has a lovely weight to it, and the proportions are elegant, but is it not a bit too long for you?"

Harold beamed. Bright-eyed, he stared at his handiwork as she held it. "Oh, it's not for me. I made it for Turner."

"For *Turner?*" Kara could not hide her surprise, or how touched she was at the thought of the boy giving his first creation to the older man.

"He told me once that he thought of getting a *sgian-dubh*, like the one Niall keeps in his boot. He said life comes fast and sometimes threats do too, so it's best to be prepared. Especially when you are around."

Kara choked back a laugh, but Niall, behind the boy, let loose a long chortle. "True enough, lad. And you've done well."

"I'm going to make you one next," Harold told her with a shy grin. "And one for me. Then we'll all be ready."

"Indeed, we will be," she replied. "I would be honored to

carry a blade you crafted, but make mine small so I can tuck it away."

"I will, but first I must learn to make a handle for this one. Niall is going to teach me this evening."

Her betrothed gave her an apologetic look. "Gyda has gone to Town to deliver her shield, leaving the forge open. I was going to let Harold choose his own material and set him to shaping it while I work on my fern piece." He gestured. "It's nearly finished."

"Oh, it's lovely," she said, moving over to inspect it. "I swear, I can almost see those fiddleheads unfurling. Your client will adore it."

"You won't mind if we spend a few hours in here?"

"Not at all. I have plenty of work to keep me occupied." She sent Harold an approving look. "And I have seen the work you've done on your clockwork figure. Very well done, sir. Your tiny gentleman's gait is perfect, and his boots are very realistic."

"Turner helped," the boy said bashfully.

"Oh, I know how Turner helps," she said with a laugh. "He hovered behind your shoulder while you did all the work. It's a good way to learn, though, isn't it?"

"Yes. It's the same way Maisie teaches me to make pies."

"Is Maisie teaching you as well? So many skills you are acquiring, young man!"

"Yes." He grew serious. "I want to learn them all."

Ruffling his hair, she leaned in to kiss his forehead. "And so you shall."

She left them to their work and went to hers. With the gait of her horse automaton sorted, she had to start molding and sculpting the skin of the creature, incorporating all of the musculature as well. For the movement's sake, it would have to be encased in sections. Neck and withers, shoulders and forelegs, hips, dock, and back legs all kept separate.

It was exacting work that took a while, though part of her mind was freed while her hands and eyes were busy. Her thoughts kept drifting back to Mrs. Cole's words about wasting her life. While she knew it wasn't true, she began to worry that she'd made a bad bargain with the widow. Perhaps there would not be enough High Society types attending her wedding to satisfy the woman. Kara had certainly drifted further from their inner circle. She knew her true friends would attend, but others might not.

Well. Mrs. Cole would have to be reconciled. She hadn't exactly been overly cooperative with Wooten, in any case. Perhaps they had both inadvertently entered into a bad-faith bargain.

Thoughts of the wedding inevitably led to thoughts of Niall. At first, she'd found his and Stayme's fears to be overblown, but it was worrisome that the viscount had been disconnected from his shadowy role in government circles.

Still, she felt an abduction was unlikely. They certainly couldn't expect her to sit quietly and allow such a thing. A sudden thought chilled her. Perhaps *she* was the problem?

She left the workbench for a bit, needing a break and the chance to stretch her back and fingers. It was a possibility, she conceded. She didn't conform to normal feminine roles. She never had. And though the queen's reign was held up as an example by those who advocated for more rights for women, it was privately known at court and amongst certain peers that Victoria firmly believed that other women were meant only for domestic pursuits.

With a sigh, she sat back down to her determinedly not-domestic work. She wound the master gear, watching her horse move in a gloriously complicated gallop. *Concentrate on the work in front of you.* It was what Turner had often told her as a child.

Perhaps she could animate the mane and tail, as if blown in the wind? She frowned. It would take significant articulation, but would it look natural? Grabbing a sheet of paper, she started to sketch.

Sometime later, the laboratory door opened. "You're still in here?" Niall called.

Kara looked up. "Oh. Yes. Are the pair of you finished, then?"

"For tonight. I sent Harold for a bath, but I thought I would look in on you. How is your work progressing?"

"Slowly. It is going to take some delicate work to make it look the way I want it to."

"You can do it," he said.

"Thank you." Leaning against him as he came to stand by her, she whispered her fear out loud. "Niall, I've had a terrible thought. What if *I* am what's troubling the royals and their people as they consider you? Perhaps I am too…irregular for them?"

"Well, we are one of us as bad as the other. Together we bring a good deal of unconventionality to the table." He gave a shrug. "They are going to have to learn to trust us."

"But what if they don't?" She blinked and reared back, then stood and gripped his shoulders. "Niall! What if we took the decision out of their hands?"

"How we accomplish that?"

"We could go abroad! Travel together! We said we would someday. We could look for a place to settle."

He frowned. "You wouldn't wish to leave Bluefield."

"I would rather have you than Bluefield." She moved her hands to cup his face. "I would rather have you than anything."

He gathered her into his embrace. "You know I feel the same. But what of our friends? Our family?"

"We'll take Turner and Gyda and Harold with us," she said with enthusiasm. "Everyone else, we will visit, or they can travel to visit us." She brightened. "Maybe we can convince Towland to allow us to establish another branch of the Druidic Bards? How lovely would that be? Think of it. Italy. Austria. Switzerland. We could go anywhere!"

"I can think of several places that would make the Foreign Office very nervous indeed, if I were to take up residence."

"Anywhere represented by the League of Dissolution, you

mean," she said sourly. "But we defeated them. The League has disbanded."

"And I do not wish anyone to think I am trying to rekindle it."

"No, you don't." She sighed. "But that still leaves us many places to consider." She pressed closer. "Do you remember that morning at the mirrored lake? Just the two of us?"

He ran a hand over her hair. "Of course. How could I forget?"

"We said then that we would make our own world, do you recall?"

"Yes." His finger traced her jaw. "It is my fondest dream, Kara."

"Oh!" She looked up at him. "I've had a thought. America! Surely we wouldn't be considered so unconventional there?"

"Only in the best ways," he admitted. "It is not a bad idea," he said slowly. "None of it is out of the realm of possibility. But, Kara, this is your home. My home. We both have connections here that I do not think you are considering."

"You want to stay," she said, deflating.

"I want to build our world here, among the people we love, if we can. I want to take you to my home in Scotland and show you my forge on the cliffs over the sea. I want our children to run wild there, with Rob's kin. I want them to pick huge bouquets of bluebells here. And make tarts with Cook and terrorize Turner and creep in delicious fear through secret tunnels. I want to spend our lives amongst art and science and all the love we can gather. And we have already made a decent start, here."

Tears sprang to her eyes. "You make it sound so lovely and perfect."

"It will be. We will make it so."

She sighed. "If they will let us."

He kissed her. "If we have to convince them, then we will."

She breathed deeply and burrowed into him. "Yes. We will."

Chapter Sixteen

THE NEXT MORNING, Kara was savoring Cook's famous egg dish baked with vegetables and watching Niall devour one apricot-glazed breakfast bun after another.

"Slow down, Niall, or you'll choke."

"Can't," he said, his mouth full. "They are best while they are still warm, before the glaze hardens." He chewed and swallowed with a blissful expression on his face.

She exchanged glances with Turner, who was delivering a full rack of toast. They both looked up when Tom, the underbutler, entered with a silver salver in hand. "A message for you, miss. It's from Inspector Wooten, so I knew you'd wish to see it straight away."

"Thank you, Tom." She read it over before she looked between Niall and Turner. "It's bad news, I'm afraid."

"What?" Niall asked.

"Somebody is going to need to wake Gyda."

"Not me!" Niall said at once.

"Gracious, but I am afraid I must return this to Cook," Turner said, taking up the empty toast rack and moving the new one into place.

"Hold!" Kara commanded. "Cowards, the both of you! I woke her the last time, and I paid the price. It's time for one of you to take a turn."

They stared at each other for long moments before Niall broke. "Oh, very well. But if she bites me, I will insist you both tend to the wound."

Turner hid a grin as he turned away.

"Finish eating, then," Kara urged. "Wooten has made an appointment to interview Mr. Carver in Lambeth this morning, and we are to be there."

"I'll go now." Niall pushed back his chair. "Fear has robbed me of my appetite."

"Here, sir." Turner held out a long-handled serving spoon. "Nudge her with this and keep your limbs out of harm's way."

Niall snatched it up. "You say it as a joke, I know, but I need all of my fingers."

They left the room together. Laughing, Kara went back to her eggs.

>>><<<

"THANK HEAVENS YOU are here." Sergeant Landover met them in the entry hall of the police court building once again.

"When are we *not* here?" barked Gyda.

"We do apologize for the delay," Kara told him. "Some of us were out very late last night."

"She means me." Gyda snapped her fingers at the sergeant. "Coffee. If you expect me to be of any use, I'll need some very strong coffee."

Landover gaped at her, then nodded to a constable. "This way, if you please, ladies." He looked at Niall. "The inspector wishes only for the ladies to come into the interview room, as they were the ones who witnessed the argument between Carver and Abbott."

Niall nodded. "I'll go and visit Josie. Come and fetch me when you are done."

Landover led them into the opposite wing. "The inspector

was obliged to begin the interview, as Mr. Carver was very impatient. He's as sullen a witness as I've ever seen. Like a child caught smeared with jam, with his fingers wedged in the jar, swearing he never touched it." He shook his head. "He's already denied going out behind the club with Abbott."

"The hell he says," Gyda grumbled. "We saw him with our own eyes. Let *me* talk to him."

"Yes, I'm to bring you in, straight away." Pausing, Landover stared at Gyda as if he'd been sent to fetch a ball and pulled back an explosive instead. "Inspector Wooten would prefer if you follow his lead." He stopped at the door, his hand hovering over the latch. "Please, just file in quietly. There are seats for you on the inspector's side of the table." He gazed at them questioningly, and Kara nodded.

He opened the door. Kara took Gyda's arm, and they walked in together.

Carver's expression did not change, but Kara thought he paled a little.

Wooten stood to greet them. "Ladies, I thank you for coming." He helped them remove their outer garments, then saw them seated on either side of him. Kara settled in with a passive expression on her face, but Gyda glared at Carver, and he stared back in fascination.

"Now," Wooten said, settling back into his position across from the man. "We need you to help us understand what was happening in Frederick Cole's business, and in his life, right before his murder."

"You cannot think I murdered him," the man insisted.

"We do not. Not at the moment. But your resistance is making me question that opinion."

Carver snorted.

"I asked you about your argument with Randall Abbott out behind the club, the night before last."

Carver looked bored. "As I said, I did not go out behind the club."

"Liar." Gyda sounded both annoyed and disgusted. "We saw

you with our own eyes."

"Impossible." Carver shook his head. "You cannot have."

A knock sounded on the door, and a constable came in with a mug of coffee. He set it down before Gyda, then jumped when she gripped his forearm. "Thank you," she breathed. "May Freya make you brave in your undertakings."

The tall young man blushed. "Ah, thank you, miss."

Letting him go, Gyda drained half the mug in one swallow. For a moment, her eyes closed in bliss. They popped open and she fixed Carver with a black stare. "Like every other man at the club that night, you wore a top hat and tails, but your trousers boasted a silk stripe down the side. A small but fashionable detail. You stood at the back gate and had a shouting match with Abbott, where you wore a dark brown coat with fur around the collar and partway down the front placket. Thick black fur. Probably bear."

"I assume you wore a coat on this chilly morning, Mr. Carver." Wooten spoke in a bland and polite tone. "Shall I have the constable fetch it from the cloakroom?"

Carver let his gaze roam over the garments that Kara and Gyda had draped over their chairs. They obviously had not stopped in the cloakroom. He frowned, and Kara thought he would deny it again.

"We were not the only ones to see you, sir," she said clearly. "We spotted someone else watching the pair of you, hidden behind a stack of empty casks."

Carver pinched the bridge of his nose and surrendered to the inevitable. "Where were you?"

"Hanging out the attic window," Gyda said icily. "Which afforded us a perfect view."

"Who was spying on us?"

"Elias Wade," Kara said.

He rolled his eyes. "I should have guessed. You don't understand. I am just a businessman. I do not want to be caught up in any of this."

"You are caught up in it already," Wooten told him. "Lying

to us only serves to make you look guilty."

"I'm not guilty!" Carver insisted.

"Nor did we think so, until you began to lie," Wooten said flatly.

The gentleman heaved a sigh. "Very well."

"Thank you. Now tell us, please. Why were you arguing with Mr. Abbott?" asked Wooten. "We know the two of you conspired to have Cole ejected from the Sock and Buskin investment partnership."

"The business he started himself and nurtured for years," Kara interjected.

"That's not what happened," Carver said irritably.

"I've spoken to several of the other partners," Wooten told him. "That is what they all believe."

"They are wrong."

"Separately, they all recounted the same events. Each of them described Cole as declining, fading, or waning. They said he'd been making mistakes and that you confronted him about them."

"Blackguard," Gyda said with a sneer.

"Listen, you don't understand," Carver said. "That's not what happened. I did confront him about investing in West's second club. I visited the Rogue's Hideaway. He showed me the books. I don't begin to understand the appeal, but I cannot deny that it exists. West is making money hand over fist at that place. The concept is popular, and many believe it will only grow more so. We should have said yes to his request. But Cole was letting personal issues color his business decisions. He let his views about his son get in the way of the group making a significant amount of money."

Kara frowned. "Wait. You mean Sock and Buskin did *not* invest in West's new club?"

"Not at first."

"All of the partners report that you and Cole got into a heated disagreement over it, and that it happened during a business meeting, in front of all the board."

Cole looked away. "We did. I was right, and he knew it, but

the old man would never admit it."

"That wasn't the only altercation the pair of you had, though, was it?" Kara asked.

"No." Carver's frustration was clear. "Cole began to question every recommendation or adjustment I brought up. He was making the exact same mistake with me. He let his dislike of me affect his business decisions. I couldn't let him get away with it. I had to point it out. It erupted into another scene." His expression darkened. "And that is when I began to realize that Abbott was behind it all."

"Behind all of what?" Gyda scoffed.

Carver poked his finger into the table as he spoke. "That old manipulator was behind a great deal of the drama. He was the architect of our disagreements. He'd been speaking to me privately, and when I saw the satisfied smirk on his face when Cole exploded at me—I realized he'd been goading my anger and frustration, and he'd likely been doing the same to Cole."

"But business wasn't the only thing he was manipulating, was it?" asked Kara. "He was pushing you toward Josie Lowe, wasn't he? Trying to get you to take an interest in her. Befriend her, perhaps? Or more?"

"How did you—?" Carver's eyes narrowed. "Oh. Cole talked to Josie about it?"

"He asked some questions that aroused her suspicions."

"Well, thank goodness Cole was not so gullible as to fall for all of that nonsense. Perhaps, like me, he'd begun to see Abbott's maneuverings."

"So, how did Cole get pushed out of the partnership, if it wasn't by you?" asked Wooten.

"Abbott had been talking to the other partners about Cole as well. I think he intended Cole's eruption at me, accusing me of trying to steal Josie, to be the climax of his little drama. It never came, but it turned out that he didn't need it. Even without it, the others were easily persuaded to turn their backs on the old man." He sneered. "Driven by the prospect of one fewer division of the profits, no doubt. Or just out of pure dislike of Cole's high-handed ways."

"Did Sock and Buskin offer to fund West's club after they kicked Cole out?" asked Kara.

"Yes." Carver sat back. "And at first he accepted, but he recently recanted. He rejected their offer and flung their money back in their faces."

"But why?" asked Wooten, surprised.

"Because he found another investor," Kara said quietly, seeing the truth of it in Carver's face. "You."

"What? Why?" Gyda demanded. "Was it guilt?"

"It was the least I could do for the old man, to untangle his son from the nest of serpents who stole his father's company," Carver replied.

"Randall Abbott has been telling the other partners that you are likely the one who killed Cole," declared Wooten. "Because of your rivalry and because you wish to take over the partnership."

Carver's face darkened. "The wicked, lying old bounder." Abruptly, he laughed. "Well, they will soon see the absurdity of that."

"Why?"

"Because I *left* the partnership. And much luck to them. Without me and without Cole, they will need it. We were the major sources of growth."

Gyda ran a leisurely eye over him. "Well, then. Perhaps you are not such a scoundrel as I thought you to be."

Carver returned the look. Before he could respond, though, a knock sounded on the door. It was immediately opened by Landover.

"Inspector. You must come, quickly. Someone has tried to kill Randall Abbott."

Everyone stood. Wooten pointed at Carver. "You will stay here until I know more." He eyed Kara and hesitated.

"I'll get Niall," she said in a tone that brooked no dispute. "We are coming."

Chapter Seventeen

"It happened at the Rogue's Hideaway," Sergeant Landover said as Niall left Josie and strode quickly back to the main hall. "Abbott is alive, but injured. He's already been taken to his home."

Wooten nodded and glanced around at the group of them. "Perhaps we should split up."

"You go to Abbott, we'll go to the club," Niall said.

"Take Baker and Johnson with you." Wooten nodded toward a pair of constables. "Find out what happened. Talk with everyone who was in the theater this morning." He shot Kara and Niall a grateful look. "We'll speak after."

Wooten and Landover set off for Mayfair.

"I'll stay here and catch Josie up," Gyda said. She was eyeing Carver, who stood in the open doorway of the room they'd been questioning him in. "Send for me if you need me."

Niall handed Kara into her carriage and listened to her summary of the interview with Carver. It was only a short ride to the club. She'd just finished when they pulled up. "Well, then. Let's go see what West has to say."

The theater was eerily quiet when they entered. Not too surprising for midmorning, perhaps. Moving past the entry, he peered into the main hall, the constables following on his heel.

"There's West," he said, beckoning Kara. The man was slumped over a table near the bar. There was no one else about.

"Oh, dear," Kara said.

"He's quite upset," a voice said, seemingly from nowhere. Kara jumped, as did one of the constables. Niall spun on his heel, but it was just Elias Wade, leaning against one of the pillars.

"Elias!" Kara scolded. "I nearly jumped out of my skin."

"Apologies."

"What are you doing here?" asked Niall. The young man looked solemn.

"I've been going through the things in Frederick's office upstairs. West doesn't have the heart for it."

"Did you see what happened to Abbott?"

"Oh, yes. West and I were at the bar, having breakfast, when one of the seamstresses came running to report that they'd found Abbott downstairs, rummaging through dressing rooms and asking wild questions of the staff, cornering them as they arrived for work. Abbott came following behind her, but he didn't come down here. Once he reached the stage, he stayed up there."

"Why?" asked Niall. "Did he find something?"

Elias shrugged. "He just strode about up there, mumbling. He was still dressed in evening clothes. I think he might have still been drunk. West just watched him at first, but he grew irritable and shouted at Abbott to get off the stage and out of his club."

They waited expectantly, but Elias was staring up at the stage.

"Well?" Kara said in exasperation. "What happened?"

"I don't know, exactly," the young man answered. "Abbott came downstage, right up to the edge of the pit. He started ranting. Cackling about the perfidy of sons and daughters. Raging against Frederick, going on about how he'd gone too far, invading his home, about how he knew Frederick had a last secret and he was going to find it. So dramatic, he was, gesturing and grimacing, as if he was delivering a soliloquy. Frankly, we laughed a little. But suddenly, he pitched forward a step. I thought he'd tripped on something, but the stage was clear. Abbott straightened, reaching for his head, but then he stumbled forward again. He teetered on the edge for a moment. We rushed out from behind the bar, but he went over, crashing into the orchestra pit. I think he broke a leg. I know he broke several chairs and music stands."

"Good heavens," Kara breathed.

Niall looked around the empty hall. "Where is everyone now?"

"Downstairs," Elias replied. "The seamstress saw the whole thing. She went down to fetch help, and after we got Abbott onto a makeshift stretcher and sent home, they all went down to hear her story. They are likely all still there, gossiping."

Niall gestured to the constables. "Go down and question the girl. Talk to everyone who spoke to Abbott this morning. Find out what he was asking, what he was saying. Talk to each and every one." He turned back to Elias. "Will you show them the way? We want a word with West."

Elias nodded and gestured for the men to follow.

Niall gave Kara a serious look. She followed as he crossed to the table where West slumped.

"West?" Niall touched his shoulder.

The man peered up at him. "You are too late. They already took Abbott to his home, where his doctor can see to him." He slumped over again.

"We know. We came to talk to you."

"Sit. Sit." He waved a hand, but kept his head down.

"Mr. West? What are you doing, sitting here alone?"

He gave up and sat straight, leaning back in his chair. "Everyone is downstairs. They are likely huddled in one of the dressing rooms talking about the accident." He sighed. "Theater people. They are a superstitious lot. They are probably deciding the place is cursed."

"Accident?" Niall asked.

"Yes. Or perhaps divine intervention."

"He was alone on the stage, Elias says."

"Yes. Quite alone. Strutting about and waving his arms as if he was reciting Shakespeare. Taunting me with the age-old truth of sons disappointing their fathers."

"The police have gone to question Abbott," Niall told him. "What do you think he was about, searching downstairs and questioning your staff?"

"Oh, he had a rummage about upstairs, too. One of the clerks told me. He must have been here all night."

"What is the man up to?" Kara asked.

"He's still trying to ruin my life, no doubt," West said bitterly.

"Ruin your life?" Niall watched the man closely. "We heard that Randall Abbott convinced the Sock and Buskin partnership to fund your new club. After they removed your father." He arched a brow. "That is not ruining your life, surely? Nor is it exactly what you led us to believe, when we came to ask if you had been arguing with your father."

"Well, you came in talking of alternate theories, and I didn't wish to be one. It was all Abbott's fault that we were fighting, in any case. Horrible, nosy, interfering man."

"We've heard several descriptions of the man lately, and most have been in the same tone, if not the exact words."

"No surprise there. The old bounder did ruin my life. He deliberately destroyed my relationship with Frederick. After all of these years of squabbling over business, he had to make their quarrel personal, steer it into my life. Go digging into my past. Frederick knew nothing until he told him. Whenever someone spoke of my scandal, he assumed they alluded to my birth."

Niall saw Kara frown. West saw it too.

"Oh? You haven't heard of my scandalous beginnings? That's the part that everyone knows."

"You are not the only man ever born out of wedlock," she replied.

West smirked. "I wasn't born out of wedlock, my dear. No, no, it was far worse than that. My mother was married. Just not to Frederick."

"Oh, dear."

"Oh, yes. Frederick used to be quite the man about Town, did you know? An acknowledged royal bastard, rich by his own making? Society loved him. He was already married to his merchant's daughter by then, so he was no danger to their precious girls. He was accepted almost everywhere, but his first love was always the theater. He was famous for keeping a box in each one—a scandalous extravagance. And that's where he met my mother. She was in love with theater, too. He noticed her, coming often, always alone except for a female servant. He watched her as she shared his delight, throwing herself into the performance with laughter and tears. She was pretty and fragile, and he was enchanted. He discovered her name. Mrs. Felix Westfall, wife to the third son of the Earl of Dentham."

"I don't imagine the man was thrilled to hear of Cole's devotion," Niall said wryly.

"Oh, I don't believe he ever heard of it. He was a fiend for the races. A gambler who followed the turf, winning and losing fortunes. As he was never home, Frederick found it easy to arrange a chance meeting in the park, and perhaps easier to woo my mother into an affair. When word came that the earl's son had been kicked in the head by a nervous racehorse and died, she was already with child."

"Frederick's child."

"Yes. Me."

Niall leaned in. "What's the part Frederick didn't know, West?" He arched a brow. "*Not* Westfall, I notice. I assume that's part of it?"

"Yes." West's expression was bitter. "It was my own doing. I was weak."

Niall eyed Kara, and they both waited.

Finally, West sighed. "It will all be out soon enough. Abbott will make sure of it. I will be vilified. No one will come back to the club once the story makes its way around London."

"What is the story?" Kara asked in a whisper.

West lifted a shoulder. "It's an old one. The cuckoo in the nest. Dentham didn't abandon my mother—he folded her into the family and hid her away, tucked into the country. But he never let her forget what she had done, and none of them ever let me forget what I was. That I did not belong. Not truly. It was…cruel. Even the servants treated me with disdain and mockery. I was so grateful to be sent to school, but my cousins made sure the rumors followed me. It was just more of the same treatment. So, I began to rebel. I raised every sort of hell I could think of. Eventually, I was sacked for cheating. Sent home."

"Oh, dear," Kara said with sympathy.

"My mother was disappointed. She berated me. The earl raked me over the coals and threatened to turn me out."

Niall had an inkling, but he asked the question anyway. "What did you do?"

"I acted like the stupid, sulky boy I was," West admitted flatly. "The earl often left his safe unlocked, when the land steward needed funds or documents. I snuck in, stole all the banknotes out of it, and took the set of jewels my father—my real father—had given my mother. And I ran. I went to Paris. I had many adventures and even more misadventures, but I eventually grew up and discovered what it meant to be a man."

"How long before you decided to come back?"

"Years. But I did come home, just using a different name. West, instead of Westfall. I sent the earl the amount I'd taken and a bit more, but I had no more contact with them. I built this club." West threw out both arms. "It was quite a sensation, even as it went up. I worked hard, incredibly hard, to make sure it opened successfully. And once it was established, I went to introduce myself to Frederick."

"That could not have been easy." Niall understood complicated family relationships. It had been a brave step, he considered, but not one he could undertake himself.

"No. I had to gird my loins to do it, make no mistake. But Frederick was willing to accept me—on the same terms that his father had accepted him. As long as I didn't ask for anything, and as long as I stood on my own two feet. I think it helped, in fact, that I came to him already in possession of a successful career, that I was a self-made man, as the Americans call it. Just as he was."

"But he didn't know about the theft?" Niall suspected that it would have been a sticking point.

"No, nor the cheating. Not until Abbott went and dug it all up. Using business diligence as an excuse, of course. But it was truly so that he could gleefully fling it in Frederick's face and hold it over my head as long as we were in business together."

"Frederick didn't react well?"

West snorted. "You could say that. He was beyond furious. Disappointed in me, that a son of his could act so dishonorably. Angry that I hadn't told him."

Niall gave a huff. "You couldn't have. Not after that welcome."

West looked grateful that he understood. "Mostly he was horrified that Abbott was going to use it against him. He was going to be embarrassed. Not for a second did he consider that *I* was going to be embarrassed and *ruined* when my lost honor was exposed. As if I didn't exist other than as a reflection of him. So, I became furious as well. We engaged in a terrible fight."

He put his head down on the table again and sat silent. After a moment, he spoke again, his words muffled. "That wasn't the worst part."

It all sounded horrible enough. Niall wondered what could be worse.

"I should have given it to him." West sat up. "I had the chance to reconcile with him, or, at least, to make a start at it. But I refused."

"What did he want?" Niall leaned in.

"The money."

Kara understood first. "The money Sock and Buskin was going to invest in your new club?"

West nodded. "He wanted me to turn it over to him. To help him recover, after they took the partnership. He said I could find other investors." He sighed. "He was likely right. But I was still angry. Resentful. I told him I could give it to him, but then he wouldn't be standing on his own two feet."

Kara gave a little moan.

"I know," West whispered. "It was terrible. Petty. He turned so white. He said nothing, just turned and left. And the next night, he died. Before I could change my mind and do the right thing. Before I could reconcile with him. Someone killed him." He turned to Niall. "Do you think it was Abbott?"

"I think it's a possibility," Niall said grimly. "It's clear he's still fixed on Cole." Standing, he held out a hand to Kara. "Let's go see what the constables have learned. And then we'll go and see what Abbott has said to Wooten."

Chapter Eighteen

RANDALL ABBOTT'S HOME was lovely, but not nearly so large or grand as Frederick Cole's. Kara would be willing to bet that fact regularly rankled Abbott's soul.

Wooten met them upstairs, in the passage outside of Abbott's personal suite of rooms. "The surgeon is in with him now." They could hear moans and cursing behind the doors, along with a bit of harsh name calling.

"How badly was he hurt?" asked Niall.

"Several broken ribs and an injured leg. He's lucky he didn't land on his neck. But the leg was sliced open as well as severely strained. I believe they've finished sewing it. The shouting is over, at least," Wooten said wryly. "They are trying to immobilize the limb now. The gentleman is not cooperating."

"They couldn't dose him with laudanum and do it while he slept?"

"The surgeon could not allow it, as Abbott was still so intoxicated from last night."

"Good heavens," Kara said, her mouth set.

"He's still drinking brandy in there. And he is still claiming he was pushed off the stage at the club."

Niall shook his head. "Not according to the three witnesses we spoke to."

The door opened and the surgeon came out, Abbott's man-servant trailing him. "Keep him as still as you can," the surgeon told the harried servant as he wiped his brow. "And let's hope he passes out sooner, rather than later."

"What's that? I can hear you! Stop lurking in doorways, talking about me, damn you!"

The surgeon wished them luck, took up his bag, and set off.

"Send that police inspector back in here!" Abbott roared.

The rooms could have been attractive, Kara observed as they followed Wooten in. The walls were cream and beige, the furniture very fine. But someone had been given too much freedom with gold gilt for good taste. A sitting room gave way to a coordinated bedroom, with an enormous four-poster bed. Abbott reclined there, his face red and his pomaded hair poking in several directions.

"Well?" he demanded. "Have you lot found and arrested the blighter who pushed me off that stage?"

Niall stepped forward. "That's not the story being told at the club, sir."

"What would you know of it? You were not there." Kara met his gaze as he glared at her too. "Nor were you, young lady."

"No, but we spoke to three witnesses who all swear you were alone on that stage." Niall met the man's gaze directly. "No one pushed you."

Abbott's color heightened further. "Nonsense! Who told you such lies? West, I'm sure," he sneered. "I tell you, I was pushed. First something struck me." He reached a hand around to his neck. "Right here! Here, at the base of my skull. It came hard and swift and unexpected, and it knocked me off balance."

"He does have a lump there," his manservant said.

"And then I distinctly felt it. Hands, on the back of my legs. Someone pushed me, and over I went."

"Perhaps it was Frederick Cole's ghost," Kara said dryly. "For no one was seen up there with you."

The older man's eyes widened. "Do you really think so?" He

blinked several times.

"You are not helping," Wooten said with a twitch of his mouth.

"No, no," Abbott decided. "It could not have been a spirit. I felt them, distinctly. Those hands were very human."

"Inspector Wooten, did Mr. Abbott tell you that he spent most of the night at the Rogue's Hideaway?" Niall looked to the man in the bed. "What were you looking for, sir, searching the offices and questioning the staff? West said you were going on about Frederick Cole's 'last secret'?"

Abbott blinked again. He couldn't seem to stop. Was it an effect of the alcohol? "Well, I am not about to tell you, sir," he said grandly. "And allow you to steal my thunder? I think not! In any case, it was tit for tat! I may have had a rummage through Cole's things at the club, but he invaded my privacy first! Did he think I wouldn't know? That I wouldn't be able to tell when my desk has been rifled through?"

"Someone broke in here?" Niall said flatly.

"Yes, damn it! The bounder came in and went through my things when I wasn't home." Abbott gave a dramatic sniff and blinked again. "And if that doesn't strain the bounds of friendship, then I don't know what does."

"Murder, perhaps?" Kara suggested.

"I sent Landover downstairs to question the servants about a possible burglary, as it was apparently never reported to the police," Wooten said.

"Why bother when I knew Frederick was behind it?" Abbott scoffed. "He tried to deny it, of course. Said he knew nothing of it. But I knew it for a lie. I know his tricks, don't I? Who else would know them better?"

Wooten tried to step in and steer the conversation again. "Mr. Abbott, you and Frederick Cole have been rivals for a very long time," he began.

"*Friends* and rivals," the old man corrected him. "It is possible to be both, simultaneously."

"Friends do not act as you have done lately, sir." Wooten shook his head. "You plotted against Cole in business. You had him ejected from his own partnership."

"And you tried to turn him against Josie Lowe, who was one of the few supports in his personal life," Kara added.

"Psh." Abbott flicked his fingers.

"Why, Mr. Abbott?" Wooten asked. "After all of these years, why did you escalate your rivalry with Cole and move so harshly against him?"

Abbott looked mulish. "I had to."

"Did he insult you in some way?"

The blinking had returned. "He spent *years* insulting me!"

Niall tried. "Was it because you believed he sent someone here, into your house?"

"No, no."

"Then *why*?" Wooten sounded exasperated.

Abbott lay back against his pillows. "Well, because he was ill, wasn't he?"

"You knew he was ill?" Kara asked, surprised. "Cole didn't think anyone knew. He didn't wish for anyone to know."

"Ha! I knew everything Cole didn't want me to know." The old man's tone had turned lofty. "It wasn't so hard to see something was bothering him, and when I discovered what it was, it made sense. It was his greatest fear, you know."

"Appearing weak, you mean?" she asked.

"No, girl! Getting the dropsy!" As they all gave him a blank look, he laughed. "No one really did know that was it, did they? Even now?" He sobered. "It killed Frederick's father, you know. He'd always been dreadfully afraid it would get him, too."

"How did you discover it?" Niall asked.

Abbott rolled his head on his pillows. "I had someone follow that manservant of his. He was going to the apothecary on the regular. Not hard to overhear conversations like that."

"But...but...why, sir? Why would you not go easier on your friend, knowing he was ill and afraid?" Kara could not begin to understand such behavior.

"Well, I couldn't just let him *die*, could I? Not before I evened the score between us. He had to pay for all the belittling, the criticisms, the slights. I made a good start at it. Had him on the rocks. Then he had to go and get himself murdered before I could loose all of my weapons."

Kara's jaw dropped. Her eyes filled with tears. Niall reached for her as she turned away from the old man.

Wooten sighed. "Mr. Abbott, do you mean to say that you did not kill Frederick Cole?"

"What? Me?" Abbott gaped. "No! Decidedly no! Whoever did it robbed me of the last weights of justice I meant to throw on the scales."

"I cannot stay," Kara whispered.

"Come." Niall started to lead her out.

"Where are you going?" Abbott called. He reached out. "Inspector. Inspector! Let them go, but you must stay. You must send out your men and find the villain who pushed me. Look for someone with small hands, I tell you!"

Niall stopped. "Small hands?"

"Yes. Small, warm hands on the back of my calves. They pushed me, I know it. I felt it!" He gestured at Wooten. "And find the cracksman who came in here at Cole's behest, too, Inspector! He nearly killed my bougainvillea, not to mention my pineapples!"

Kara turned. "Your bougainvillea?"

"Yes, a beautiful little vine from South America—"

"Your conservatory," she interrupted, meeting Niall's eyes. "They came in through the conservatory?"

"Yes, damn him! He put all of my exotics at risk! He knew how I felt about them…"

He continued on in that vein, but Kara ignored him. "Shall we?" she asked Niall.

"It's worth a look," he said.

They left, heading downstairs to search out a footman. "The

conservatory," she said to the first servant to show himself. "We'd like to see it."

"Yes, miss. I can show you. If you'll step this way?" He led her through a lovely room with a round settee in the center, crowned with lush ferns.

"Do you think Abbott is lying about killing Cole?" Niall said low in her ear. "I thought you said he only grows exotic plants from foreign locales?"

"Well, we'd be remiss in not checking it out, wouldn't we? I wouldn't put anything past him, especially lying to save his own skin."

They followed the servant, who stopped before a pair of thick, brocaded curtains. Pulling them back, he revealed a set of glass doors. "Through here, if you will."

They entered a lush green world. Large palms, camellias, and banksias towered over exotic, lush shrubs, yuccas, and caladiums. A table and chairs and a chaise sat surrounded by green fronds and colorful blossoms. Narrow walkways led away from the center, tempting one to explore.

"It's beautiful," Kara said softly.

"It is Mr. Abbott's pride and joy," the footman declared. "He takes a great interest in his foreign specimens. You'll find plants here from every corner in the world."

"And they are lovely, but does he not grow any British native plants at all?"

"Not really. If a plant hasn't traveled a long way on a ship, then the master is not interested," the servant said with a grin. "But one of the gardeners keeps a tiny corner of domestic varieties." His tone grew conspiratorial. "It's all down to Mrs. Becker, our housekeeper. The downstairs can be so dark and dreary, you see. The rest of the house is bright and filled with all sorts of greenery. There's not much to be done about the lack of windows downstairs, but she does insist that we get a few bouquets to brighten the place up. Mr. Abbott does not wish to waste his exotic beauties on us, though. So, there's a few common British varieties tucked away in the back."

Kara looked at Niall. "I should love to see them."

"Of course. This way." The footman led them from the lush jungle of the main areas of the conservatory to a section that looked more functional than decorative.

"Oh, those are the pineapples?" she asked.

"Yes, indeed, miss. And they are devilishly hard to grow here, if the gardener's grumblings are any indication." He pointed. "And there are the common British specimens."

Kara stood still. "Niall."

"I see it."

Roses, poppies, daisies, and primroses filled the back corner, all in different stages of forced growth. And behind them stood several tall plants with spikes decorated with purple and white bell-shaped blossoms. "Foxglove."

"Those are Mrs. Becker's favorites," the footman confided. "She says they remind her of home."

Moving closer, Kara saw that several of the plants looked poorly. More than one of them had been stripped of all the lower green leaves at the bottom. She turned to be sure Niall saw it, but he was staring toward another section of the outer glass wall.

"What happened there?" He gestured toward a low panel on the outer wall, which had been boarded up.

"Oh, we had a break-in here, not so far back. They have yet to fix the glass pane."

"A break-in? In this section of town?" Niall acted as if he knew nothing of it.

"Yes, it was odd enough, it was. There were a few clues left of their passing, but they never tried to get at the silver or the safe. They didn't seem to take anything of great value. A few pieces of bric-a-brac, a fancy candy dish, some food from the kitchen, and the kitchen maid's scarf, if she's to be believed."

"Perhaps they broke in for something else altogether," Kara said significantly, gesturing to bring Niall's attention to the stripped foxglove.

He nodded, but turned back. "And you think they came in through that pane?"

"Must have done." The footman shrugged. "Everything else was locked up tight. But they must have picked their smallest cracksman, though, eh? Look at the size of that pane. They'd have to squeeze through, to be sure."

"Small hands," Niall said suddenly. He grabbed hers. "Come, we must go."

"We need to go back upstairs and tell Wooten about the foxglove," she protested as he pulled her along, back toward the house.

"We'll come back if we must. But I don't think it was Abbott!"

"What are you talking about, Niall?"

"Small hands!" he said, forging on. "Come on!"

Chapter Nineteen

"**B**ACK TO THE Rogue's Hideaway," Niall told her driver, opening the door and waiting for her.

"I do apologize," she told John Coachman before she climbed in. "I know it feels as if we are traipsing back and forth…"

"No worries, miss," he answered cheerfully. "I know how it is when the pair of you get mixed up in one of your adventures."

"Well, that's all to the good, for we might be heading right back this way before long."

She climbed in and sat back as Niall followed and settled across from her. Waiting expectantly, she raised a brow at him. "Small hands?"

"I am formulating a theory." He sounded distracted. His gaze was locked on the wide Mayfair street outside, but she was fairly sure he wasn't seeing it. "May I have a moment?"

"Of course."

She watched the streets go by as well, but she was thinking of those foxglove plants. Randall Abbott had made no bones about his wish to hurt Frederick Cole. She absolutely believed that he would lie to protect himself. And those foxglove plants were there, denuded of the leaves that could be dried and ground to produce digitalis, growing in his greenhouse.

Surely he must be the poisoner? What was the alternative?

That someone had broken into his conservatory just to get those leaves? Well, they couldn't go out into a field and pick them, to be sure. Not at this time of year. Had someone wanted to make Abbott look like the killer? But who?

She leaned back, breathed deeply, and let her mind cast back through all the conversations and events they'd engaged in these last days. Her breathing slowed. Voices and images moved in and out of her mind.

Suddenly her eyes popped open wide. "Oh! I begin to understand what you are thinking."

Niall glanced over at her, approval and affection alive in his gaze. "We need to get a look at that stage."

They climbed down eagerly when the carriage pulled to a stop. Striding inside, they found more people about than there had been this morning. It was midafternoon, and preparation for the evening's entertainment had begun.

Hurrying up the short stairs at the side of the stage, they scanned the area. "Excuse me!" Niall hailed a leather-apron-clad stagehand. "Were you here this morning, by chance, when Randall Abbott took his fall?"

"Aye, sir, but I were downstairs. Just arrived."

"So you don't know where Abbott went over?"

"I didn't see it myself, sir, but Lizzie—she's the seamstress that saw the whole thing—showed us just where he was."

"What's your name?" asked Niall.

"It's Siddons, sir."

"Like the famous actress of old."

"Aye, sir. My mam likes to claim the connection, but I think it's all a humbug."

Niall laughed and offered his hand. "I'm Niall Kier. Could you show us the spot Lizzie pointed out?"

"Just over here." The stagehand led the way and gestured.

Niall immediately stepped back and began to examine the stage. Just a step behind the designated spot was an outline of a square made by four seams in the floor. "Siddons?" He indicated the spot. "What is that?"

"Trapdoor, sir. Though this is a wee one, mostly good for passing props up to the stage, or sometimes holding smudge pots for smoke."

"Can you open it for us?"

Siddons scratched his head. "Now, I think I know what ye're about. Some of us had the very same thought, especially after hearing that Abbott fellow shoutin' that he'd been pushed. But we counted it out, all of us who were in the building this morning, and none of us were unaccounted for. 'Twasn't one of us who pushed the gentleman."

"Would you let us see it, in any case?" Kara asked with a smile for the man. "It truly would be a help."

Siddons flushed a little. "Sure, then. Of course. Be a moment, though, as I got to go down into hell to get the door open."

"Into hell?" Niall asked, startled.

"That's what the under-stage area is called," Kara told him.

"True enough, miss. I'll be but a moment."

"Thank you. We'll wait here."

The stagehand set off, and Kara tugged Niall over to the edge. The mess of broken and fallen chairs and stands had been cleaned up. All sat ready for the members of the orchestra.

"If Abbott was gesticulating and overacting, then perhaps everyone's attention was focused high, not low," Niall speculated.

A whisper of a sound drew their attention to the trap. Together, they went to peer down at Siddons, visible through a roughly square chute only several feet wide. "There's a ladder down here we use to pass a prop up, but it were locked away," he called up. "Still locked away, it is. And as you can see, it takes a smallish one to deliver it."

"Small hands." Kara looked to Niall. "I didn't want to think you might be right... It was a child, Niall?"

"Chimney sweeps crawl up through narrower spaces than this."

"But could even a sweep have braced themselves to reach out

and push Abbott?"

Niall considered. "Sweeps mostly brace their knees against one side of the chimney and shove their backs against the other side to move upward. Their hands are usually full of a bag or something to catch the soot as they climb. Even with free hands, that position wouldn't work. But if they braced their feet against two walls and used their hands, too, someone could hoist themselves up pretty easily. Especially if they were light and nimble."

"And strong enough."

"Yes. Just climb up like a monkey, brace your feet, reach out, push, and drop down. No one in the audience area could see if the trapdoor was open or shut." He peered down again. "Is that a mattress under your feet, Siddons?"

"Aye! Of a sort. It's so there's no clatter if a prop is dropped down."

"I have another thought," Niall said suddenly. "Hold a moment."

He ran to the side of the stage and made his way down into the orchestra pit.

"What are you looking for?" Kara asked as he weaved through, peering under chairs and stands.

He gave a whoop and dived down, close to the stage. "This!" he said triumphantly. He held something up, and she went to peer at the small, smooth object in his hand.

"Is that a…river rock?" She gave a gasp, clapping both hands over her mouth as the image came to focus in her head. An angry, defiant little boy with a slingshot hanging from his waist. "Oh, Niall! That boy! Those children!"

"Abbott said something struck his head, knocking him off balance," Niall called as he came back up on the stage. "And here it is." He stopped before her. "A blow to the back of his head makes him stumble, then hands push the back of his legs. And over he goes."

"The pane in the conservatory was only a bit bigger than

this," she said, her mind racing.

"There is one more thing I'd like to check," he said. He looked down. "Siddons, can you get your hands on the keys to the attics?"

A few minutes later, they were climbing the narrow stair.

"From the bottom to the top, eh?" Siddons said with a chuckle.

Kara's heart was pounding as they came closer to the attics. At least this time, Siddons had brought a lantern. But still, the shadows swirled outside the glow of his light.

"I've been mulling and mulling in my head," Niall said. "Who was it who locked you in up there, when Elias was outside?"

"You think it was those children? Those same children?"

"Kara, think back to that night. I know you were frightened. But Gyda told me something while we were bringing you home. She said your instincts were right. When you were searching the offices, the pair of you saw a shadow slip into this narrow stairwell. But you said you didn't think it was Elias."

"Oh, yes! But I was so nervous about climbing higher, I quite forgot. I thought the figure looked too small!" She was still nervous. It infuriated her. Panic began to darken the corners of her mind as they climbed higher. She would not give in. She would not. But her chest tightened as they reached the landing outside the attic door.

"Door's already unlocked," Siddons said suddenly. He frowned. "It's supposed to stay locked."

"You don't have to go in." Niall gave her a squeeze. "Stay here."

She clung to the doorframe as the two men ventured in. Siddons set the lantern down, as sunlight streamed in through the large windows at this hour. The stagehand helped move objects as Niall began to rummage behind racks of costumes and large props.

Kara tried to distract herself by concentrating on their discoveries. There was something nagging at her mind. It was so hard to think up here!

That trapdoor chute. Square and narrow.

"Niall!" she gasped. It had come to her, sliding past the fear that tried to steal her thoughts. "We've seen a shaft like that before! Long and narrow, with a window at the top. An utterly clean window, inside and out."

Niall was pushing through the collection of fake greenery. "You are right," he called out. "And so am I." He tossed something out into the middle of the floor.

"Is that...a pallet?"

"Just like the ones at Elias Wade's rooms. There are two more back here."

"Somebody's sleeping up here?" Siddons shook his head. "West won't like it. We aren't supposed to be mucking about up here, let alone sleeping here."

"A place to stay," Kara said. "Safe and warm. That's what he traded with them. But what he asked of them..." Her words trailed away.

"Who knows how long they've been here?" Niall said. "Months, perhaps."

"But where are they now?"

Alarm showed on Niall's face. "Siddons, do you know of a man who works here? A carpenter? He would have been recommended for the job by Elias Wade."

"Oh, aye. Burrows. He does a good enough job."

"Can you bring us to him? We have some questions for him."

"I would, sir, sure enough, but Burrows lit out early today. Not long after the police constables finished up here."

Niall waded out of the greenery. "Fine, then. Do you happen to know if Elias is still working in Cole's office?"

"Oh, no. He left, too. Took a stack of boxes out of the office this morning. Hasn't been back. Not that I know of."

"Send a note to Wooten, Kara." Niall was striding past her, aiming for the stairs. "I'll make sure John Coachman is still outside. We have to get to that carriage house."

Chapter Twenty

"We're in a hurry, John," Niall called. "Get us to Frederick Cole's house as quickly as you can."

"Yes, sir!" The coachman sprang onto his box.

Niall practically tossed Kara into the carriage. It set off immediately, and she braced herself as they went around a corner at a clip.

"Those men you saw in the mews lane outside Cole's house," Kara said. "They must have been going to see him? Not Mrs. Cole or a confederate, but Elias."

"One of them might be Burrows. Or other bartering associates, perhaps?"

"We'd been to see Jimmy Gibbs that morning, to ask how the foxglove leaves might have got into that goblet. They chased you after we left. Sent by Elias to warn you off looking into Cole's death?"

"Just as the children tried to frighten you away from the case."

"He sent those children after the foxglove leaves in Abbott's conservatory?" Kara shook her head in disbelief.

"He couldn't use the vials to give Frederick an overdose. It would have been too easy to track down when and how many he took home. Too easy to know he used more than the recommended dose. But why did he not just go to another apothecary?" Niall wondered aloud.

"He couldn't. That's not how it works. You recall my friend Dr. Balgate?"

"The one who works with amputees."

"Yes. He started out as a surgeon. *Mr.* Balgate. On the low end of the medical ladder. Surgeons *touch* their patients. They deal directly with bodies and blood and other fluids. They are paid directly by the patients they treat."

"Ah. They suffer the indignity of being in trade."

"Yes. But now *Dr.* Balgate is a physician. He's at the top of the medical chain. Technically, he shouldn't still be pursuing some of the work he does, fitting new limbs. A doctor talks to his patients, but he doesn't touch them. He discusses their symptoms. When it is required, they recommend medicines, which are supplied by a chemist or apothecary, with whom he has set up a financial arrangement."

"Or, in Balgate's case, artificial limbs?"

"Yes. That's how his money comes to him, through a second-ary source, not by direct payments."

"And thus preserving his social respectability?"

"Exactly, but the point is, the apothecary would not give just anyone something like digitalis. He'd have to have instructions from the doctor, for a specific dose for a specific patient."

Niall frowned. "And yet I can go into almost any apothecary and buy arsenic?"

"Arsenic is a household item, not a drug. And many places do keep track of who buys arsenic and how much."

"But *why* did Elias do it? Obtaining and using those leaves took planning. Careful maneuvering. It was not an act of passion, unless it was a sustained, cultivated feeling. But what would motivate such feelings? I don't think he was pretending to miss Frederick. He seemed to genuinely mourn the man. And he definitely mourned the loss of his position. What could have driven him to do it?"

"We're missing something," Kara said.

They were quiet as the carriage swayed on. John Coachman was indeed hurrying. Niall silently urged him on while he tried to understand.

On the bench across from him, Kara straightened. "You don't think..."

"What?" he asked.

"When we spoke to Elias at the club this morning, he said Abbott was ranting on stage about the perfidy of sons and daughters. And West said he taunted him about sons disappointing their father."

"Yes. Abbott still has West's secret to spill. He means to broadcast his youthful dishonor."

"He also said Cole still had one last secret and he meant to uncover it. What if that was the clue to what Abbott was looking for? *Sons* disappointing a father?"

"Sons?" It took Niall a moment to understand what she meant, but then understanding dawned. "As in plural? You think Cole's secret was that he had another son?" Her eyebrows were raised, and he took the thought further. "*Elias?* You think Elias is his son?"

"I don't know! Does it even make sense? Let me think about it."

"Elias said he was from Wales, the grandson of a factory owner."

Kara pointed at him in triumph. "Mother, grandfather—but he never mentioned a father when he told us about growing up in the factory store."

"Swansea is an industrial town, full of copper-melting factories."

"But what of fire clay manufactories?"

"It would make sense. I think I heard somebody in the Great Exhibition say that there are at least six hundred furnaces in Swansea alone. That would require a lot of fire clay."

Kara nodded. "If Cole owned a factory there, he might have

traveled there and had the chance to meet another industrialist's daughter."

"It's possible, but we have no way to know for sure."

"Only Elias would know."

"Hold on. We are approaching Cole's house." Niall rapped on the ceiling. "Stop here, please!"

They clambered out, and Niall stepped close to the coachman's box. "Roll up just before the mews lane. Stay there, if you can. Just stay put until you hear from one of us."

"Yes, sir!"

Niall took Kara's arm. "Let's just walk on as if we are out for a stroll. But keep your eyes peeled. I'll watch for those men."

"And I'll keep an eye out for lethal children," she said heavily.

They made it past the house without incident. There was no activity in the mews lane. Continuing on, Niall pulled her to a halt. "When we reach that narrow alley, you stay back a moment. Let me go around the corner and make sure all is clear."

She nodded, and Niall sighed in relief. He went on the last few steps, but as he got closer, he could hear a commotion. Pressing himself up against the building, he peered around the corner.

Odin's arse.

He whipped his head back. "Kara," he said in a harsh whisper. "Go back and tell John Coachman to go around the block. Tell him to stop and block the other end of the alley. Just pull in and put on the brake and don't move. Block anyone from coming out."

She turned to run, and he peered around again. His erstwhile pursuers were there, all three of them. Where in seven hells had they found a mule cart narrow enough to fit in this lane? Nearly full, it sat beyond the door leading to Elias's rooms. Two of the men were loading the pot-bellied stove into the cart, while the other sat in the driver's seat.

Damnation. Niall drew in several deep breaths, then walked casually around the corner. The stove had just been loaded in.

The two men turned back, wiping their hands and breathing their relief. They both spotted Niall at the same time.

"Need a hand?" he asked casually.

They exploded into motion. One jumped forward and up next to the driver. "Go!" he shouted. "Drive! Now!"

The mule was startled into motion. The cart started moving, and the second man leapt into the bed next to the stove. Niall started after it.

The garbage littering the alley quickly slowed their progress. Niall gained fast, and the man in the back decided to take matters into his own hands. He crouched and leapt, tackling Niall to the ground. Rolling, they parted, and each came up swinging.

KARA DELIVERED HER message and raced back, clawing in her skirt pocket for the small, rolled bundle she carried everywhere. She had not left the house this morning prepared for anything but an interview at the police court. But at least she had her roll of lockpicks.

She rounded the corner to find Niall well past Elias's door. He was trading blows with a large man, and they both looked like they'd taken damage. She started to unroll her bundle as she moved forward. She'd never stabbed anyone with her slender tools, but there was a first time for everything.

Oof!

The fastening of her cloak nearly choked her as she was jerked backward. Her feet went flying out from beneath her and her tools flew out of her hand as she went down.

Frantic, she pulled at the collar that still cut into her windpipe. She was jerked and dragged backward toward Elias's door. Looking up, she met Niall's gaze just as she went into the antechamber with a last, sharp tug.

Her throat eased as she was released. She started to cough as the door was slammed shut. She heard the lock turn. "Elias?" she choked out. "Is that you?"

The interior door opened. Elias stepped over her. "Get in here," he ordered her. When she continued to cough, he reached in, hauled her up, and pulled her inside. He shut and locked the second door.

She looked around. The rug, the prints, the furniture—it was all gone. Only the shelves and cabinets remained. Several boxes on the floor were half filled with the bric-a-brac that had filled them.

"Sit down. There. Be still. I won't hurt you unless you try to get away. I may need you to get past Mr. Kier out there."

She scooted back against the wall, still coughing a little. Quietly, she watched as he went back to methodically wrapping and carefully packing away his treasures.

"Elias," she said, her voice gone rough. "Are you quite well?"

He bent his head, then shot her a look full of anger. "Of course not! I am not well at all. I've lost everything, once again. I'll have to start all over, once again."

She sat silent as he went on packing. Finally, she whispered, "How did he find out? Did you tell him?"

He stilled. Looking over at her, he heaved a sigh. "You figured that out, too?" His eyes closed. "Does Abbott know?"

"I don't think so."

"The old bastard was spouting off about Frederick's sons. Asking the staff if he ever mentioned them. *Them.*"

"He suspects another son, but I doubt he has considered it is you. You would certainly know if he did."

"Well, there is that, at least."

"Frederick didn't know, did he?"

Elias shook his head.

"Did you tell him?"

"No, not really. Not on purpose. The timing wasn't right. After so many happy months, Frederick grew irritable. He had so much weighing on him. The illness. Abbott. Carver. He was very angry one night. So upset. He raged that everyone in his life just wanted something from him. Drained him. No one had anything to give. No solace. No succor. No consideration."

The young man sighed, holding a piece of his collection without moving. "Except for me, Frederick said. He told me that I always knew what he needed or wanted, and I never hesitated to give what it was in my power to give. Only me, he said. And Josie."

She saw the irritation in his face at having to share the spotlight. "They did truly care for each other, I believe," she said quietly.

Elias shrugged. "I know most men are built that way. They have soft feelings for the women they are bedding."

A thought occurred to her. "Elias, when you began working for Josie, it wasn't an accident, was it?"

"No."

"You didn't discover her at the theater by chance?"

"No."

"You knew about her connection to Frederick?"

He sighed. "When my mother died, my grandfather ordered me out of Swansea. Not just out of the factory—he wanted me gone from the town. He wanted no chance of seeing or hearing of me. Ever."

"That seems...harsh."

"He blamed me for ruining her life. But it wasn't ruined. She was happy. We were happy. Just not in the way he wanted."

Kara gave a sigh.

"I didn't know where to go, at first."

"You knew Frederick Cole was your father?"

"Oh, yes. My mother would speak of him sometimes. Usually late at night, after she'd had a bit too much wine. She never held any bitterness toward him. She enjoyed her time with him, she said. He treated her well. He made her laugh and feel cared for. And she couldn't regret coming to know him, she said, for he left her with a gift. Me."

"I'm very glad you had each other," Kara whispered.

"But then she was gone. My work, my purpose, was gone. It frightened me. I felt so...lost. But I thought about what she would want me to do. And so, I thought I would go to him. I made my way to London and began to ask about him. It was easy enough to hear tales of him. People like to talk about him."

"You heard about his relationship with Josie."

"Yes. Everyone liked to talk about that."

"So you targeted her."

"It wasn't difficult. She's a performer. I knew what she wanted to hear. I provided the little services that meant something to her. And she was kind. I didn't mind working for her at all. She grew to trust me. And eventually, she introduced me to Frederick. It was the chance I needed."

"And you made the most of it," Kara said wryly.

"I did. I dedicated myself to him. I became indispensable to him. And he appreciated it. I was thrilled. Frederick needed me. And I needed him to need me. At last, he was realizing how much I was worth, how much I understood him. How I could make his life easier, better." He put the wrapped piece in his box. "We grew closer as time moved on. And then he said he was happiest in my company. I was elated. I remember I was putting away the pieces of Frederick's wardrobe that had come from the laundress. I was folding stockings and singing in Welsh. A song that my mother had sung to me. She was always making up little songs. *Tunelings*, she called them."

She could see the happiness of the memory on his face. But it didn't last.

"Suddenly, Frederick was there, behind me. His face had gone dark with fury. He gripped my shoulder, spun me around. He almost screamed at me, wanting to know where I'd heard that song."

Kara waited.

"I gave a nervous little laugh and told him it was just a little lullaby that my mother would sing to me. I saw his face and knew I'd made a mistake. He called me a liar. 'Your mother? No!

Susannah wrote that song—she made it up—for me.'"

Kara held her breath.

"And, I decided, perhaps it was time. I straightened my shoulders and told him that Susannah sang it to me—her son. His son."

"He didn't take it well?"

"He was furious. He called me a liar, a betrayer. I told him he was wrong. I cared for him. I only wished to make his life easier, happier. And his face changed. He looked so cold. So cruel. He asked if I thought that was the sort of son he would welcome. The sort of son any man would be proud to claim. A toady. A sniveler. Someone who was happy folding a rich man's stockings."

"Oh, Elias."

"Those words, they stabbed me, straight to the heart. He had just told me how happy I made him, but then he rejected me. After all I had done for him. Just like before, with my grandfather. I gave everything, and it was not enough."

"Elias, I am so sorry," Kara said. "I can't imagine how painful it must have been for you. But even your pain was not enough cause to kill him."

He looked at her, exasperated. "I know that. I was angry. Horribly hurt and angry. I sent the children to get the foxglove leaves from Abbott's greenhouse, but I tucked them away. I kept my head down, and Frederick's anger cooled. He spoke to me civilly again. But then disaster struck. The partners ejected him from Sock and Buskin. He was...lost. He tried to recover. He took the girl's dowry. West was his real hope, though. When he refused to cooperate... I think something broke in Frederick. He acted *vacant*. A shell of a man. The dropsy had finally caught up with him. His partners deserted him. His oldest friend betrayed him. His daughter and son were both angry and disappointed in him. I know he dreaded his wife finding out about the loss of his fortune. He just...had no hope."

"Elias," Kara said with both dread and warning, "if you think his devastation gave you any more right than your anger—"

"Did you not listen to me when I spoke to you of my gift? I *knew* Frederick Cole. I knew his thoughts, his heart. He lived like a lion. A beast of prey. A man of leadership who was looked upon with awe, respect, and, yes, fear. He lived for the hunt, the success, the adulation."

"Elias, you cannot know—"

"But I did. I do!"

"You were with him a matter of months."

"And yet I understood him in a way that no one else in his life did. They didn't even try."

"You don't know that," Kara said. "Abbott is a lost cause, not worth mentioning. But Frederick had his daughter. Josie. Even his wife, in their twisted way. And he had you! He would have rallied."

"He would not even want to," Elias said with a sneer. "Frederick would have been miserable. I *know*. I understood his foibles, his pride, his ferociousness. He wasn't meant for a small life, for mediocrity or defeat. He would have bowed, bent, wilted."

"It was not your decision—"

They both started as a sharp bang sounded, close by. Elias, though, seemed to know what it was. He turned, looking up.

And Kara's eyes widened when a girl shimmied down into view, moving down the shaft that led to the skylight and the window. Jumping down, she landed lightly on her feet.

"Ye done yet, guv?" she asked Elias. It was the same girl that had helped waylay Kara in the street. Kara stiffened as she turned to her and gave a jaunty salute. "Missus. I see ye're still failin' to take my advice." She shook her head. "I thought ye was a smart'un." Not waiting for a reply, she went to one of the boxes and closed it up. "Time ter go, guv."

"Has Stewart dispatched Mr. Kier?" Elias asked.

"They are still battling it out, but I wouldn't lay odds on Stewart. He just got his bell rung. We'd best go out the back way."

He began to protest, but they all grew still as a noise sounded from the antechamber. A rattling noise, with nothing following, but they knew what it meant.

"That's it, then, guv. He'll be through before you can shake a cat. Time ter go." The girl picked up her box and went to the darkened alcove at the end of the room. Kara saw her fiddling with the wainscoting, then suddenly a panel below swung open, into a dark space beyond. The girl pushed her box through into what must be part of the unused carriage house beyond. Looking back, she said to Elias, "Leave the rest. It's sure they've sent for the peelers, aye?"

Elias started to speak, but a scraping noise sounded from the antechamber, slight but sure. "Damn him!" the young man cursed, and headed for the door.

Chapter Twenty-One

T HAT DAMNED HENCHMAN of Wade's had been harder to dispatch than Niall expected. They'd been fairly evenly matched for bulk and strength, but the bounder had not hesitated to fight dirty. Fortunately, Niall had a bit of experience there himself.

After a mostly even few minutes of thrashing each other, Niall had shoved the man's head into an empty cask and struck it hard with a stray stick of wood, effectively ringing the man's bell. He used the same stick to sweep the man's feet out from under him. The blighter's head struck the filthy floor of the alley, and he didn't stir afterward.

Breathing heavily, Niall stumbled to Elias's door, where he'd seen the nasty stripling drag Kara inside. The outer door was locked. It was also solidly built. He shook it uselessly for a second, then turned to try to find something to help him break through.

What he found was an eminently useful surprise. Kara's small bundle of lockpicks lay scattered in the dirt. He gathered them up and knelt before the door. He didn't possess the same skill as Kara, who had started learning young and devoted herself to practice in the last months. But she'd given him a few lessons, and he knew the basics. It took him longer than it would have her, but he got in.

Now he leaned against the interior door in the antechamber, trying to listen. Nothing, but perhaps a murmur of voices? He knelt again to apply himself to this lock. He would gain the element of surprise if he could burst in unexpectedly, but the light in here was worse, and—

The door opened quickly and he was caught off balance. He fell into the room. A tinkle of laughter greeted him.

"Stand up, Mr. Kier, and move into the corner. There. Away from the door." Elias Wade's tone was calm, but Niall's blood boiled as he saw Kara standing stiffly in the middle of the nearly empty room. A dirty girl stood grinning next to her, with a filthy blade pressed to her kidney.

Elias stood far back, out of his reach. "No trouble, sir, or your betrothed will pay the price."

"Are those lockpicks?" the girl called. "Get them off him. We can put them to use."

"Into the corner," Elias ordered him.

Niall slowly obeyed. The young man gathered up the tools, then went to pick up a box. Niall had to crane his head to see as he carried it to a panel open in the shadowed back alcove. Elias shoved it through, then came back to close the door. Watching Niall carefully, he shoved the key in the lock, then broke it off with one, two quick blows. He headed quickly back to the open panel and ducked through.

The girl followed, pulling Kara and keeping the knife to her lower back. "There's a bar and a latch on the other side, so ye won't be coming after us." She pushed Kara away and ducked through. The panel swung shut.

Niall was up and off the floor in a flash. He met Kara in the middle of the room, sweeping her up and into his arms. "Are you all right? When I saw that little weasel dragging you..." He set her down and examined the reddened welts on her neck. "I'll thrash him."

"I'm so glad you are all right. I was so worried for you." She pulled back. "Elias did it. He killed Cole. He said as much."

A noise sounded, and the panel creaked open again. The girl's dirty, thin face poked from the shadows, wearing a feral grin. "So, the guv says he's gone and told ye all. Well, that was a mistake. Seems like I keep busy, fixin' his mistakes."

"Well, she's a charmer, isn't she?" Niall asked with utter irony.

The girl pulled back, and suddenly something was tossed into the room. It was a travel lantern, the oil-filled sort that sometimes hung on the outside of carriages when they traveled at night. It was lit, and she swung it in an arc, smashing it into a corner, where the oil splashed over two walls and began to spill along the floor. Flames quickly followed where the oil led.

"Hell and damnation." Niall pushed away from Kara and tried to dive for the open portal, but the girl closed it quickly, and he heard the bar drop. Switching directions, he raced for the door. The latch would not shift with the broken-off key inside. "Kara, quick, look to see if he missed any of the lockpicks." He dropped before the door to see if he could reach the end of the key.

She searched. "He got them all, I'm afraid."

"Is there anything left that I can use to pry this key out?" He coughed as the smoke began to fill the room.

She went to rummage through the cabinets and shelves. "Nothing. But hold on." She lifted up a thin-edged plate and smashed it to the floor. Picking through the pieces, she chose one and used another shard to chip away at it. "Try this," she said in a moment, handing over a thin slice of porcelain, only slightly curved.

"Well done. I'll give it a go."

Niall could feel the heat rising as he worked. He spent several minutes trying to move the broken key.

Kara coughed. "Hurry, Niall."

"It's truly stuck," he said at last. "I'm not going to get it in time." He turned to see the flames engulfing two of the walls in the back. The smoke was thickening. "Stand back."

He took a few steps back, feeling the heat on his back. He

rushed the door, throwing his shoulder into it. It barely rattled, let alone budged. "Damn. It's solid. It's going to take me a while to break through."

Kara was coughing. "Niall, the girl came down the shaft, through the window. Should we try it?"

He hesitated, staring from the column and back at her a moment before nodding emphatically. "Yes! Hurry. Let's go." He went to stand beneath the shaft. "Come here. Let me lift you up."

"What about you? How will you reach up there?"

"I'll drag a cabinet over, but let's get you started first."

He lifted her until she could brace herself on the walls of the chute and climb onto his shoulders. "That's it, Kara. Now, just press your hands tight and pull up your feet to brace them against the wall."

"I'll have to turn diagonal to fit my shoulders."

"Yes. Perfect. Do that. Now, take it in turns. Hands. Feet. Hands. Feet." She started to move up. "Excellent job."

She was several scoots up when she paused and looked down. "You're not going to fit, Niall," she said, her voice stricken.

"No, my love," he said, rasping from the thickening smoke.

"Niall!" She started to creep down.

"No! Go on! All the way up and out, Kara! You can climb down off the roof and open the door to let me out."

She was panicked. "But what if there is no way down?"

"Then you'll figure it out." He coughed and could barely stop. Smoke was rising with her into the shaft, too. "Wooten and his men will be here any minute. Go!"

"But—"

"Kara! Go! The quicker you go, the better chance you have of getting to the door in time!"

Tears coursed down her cheeks, but she set her face and started up again, moving quickly. "The window is unlatched!" She shimmied out, a sight that Niall would have enjoyed in any other circumstance. Turning, she peered down. "I'm out! I'll be right there!

"I love you, Kara Levett," he called, trying valiantly not to cough.

"No!" she shouted. "Damn you, Niall Kier! Don't you dare say goodbye. I'm coming to get you!"

She disappeared, and Niall went to the corner near the door, furthest away from the fire. But the flames were creeping across the ceiling, as well as spreading along the walls. He lay down on the floor, where the smoke was thinnest.

Kara wouldn't make it down to the door in time, but she was free. She could run along the roof of the building. There was plenty of room for her to be safe. The fire would attract attention. Someone would fetch her down. She would be free and un-harmed. That was all he needed to think about.

The heat was growing. He turned his face toward the wall and covered his mouth and nose with the ends of his shirt. That was slightly better. His back grew warmer, and his hands and cheeks did too. All of his exposed skin let him know the fire was growing nearer. Abruptly, he pulled the shirt away from his face. It would be better if the smoke choked him before the fire reached him.

Suddenly, the wall shook. A great boom sounded. Was that shouting? Another shudder and a loud noise, and the door shattered inward.

The fire rushed to meet it, but men filed in, their faces covered with kerchiefs. They hauled him to his feet and out the door. Niall stumbled, and they half carried him out of the alley and partway down the wall of the next building.

Chaos filled the street. The fire brigade had arrived. Horses and grooms from the mews came pouring out onto the street. Spectators gathered.

Niall coughed and coughed. "Kara?" he croaked out at last.

"She's fine." One of the men knelt next to him. "Cole's grooms fetched her down with a ladder."

Niall stared at him. He knew. But still, he reached out to pull the kerchief down.

The man's dark eyes crinkled at him over a bulbous nose. "It would surely make my job easier if you would stop getting yourself into such trouble."

"Who?" Niall croaked. "Who the hell are you?"

"Soon," the man answered. "In fact, please tell Miss Levett that I would like to call upon the both of you at her estate, if I may?"

Niall nodded.

Whistles blew and shouting sounded as a police van pulled up. Constables poured out.

"Ah, here is your friend Wooten, I believe. I will let him handle the clearing of all of this." The man stood and touched his hat. "Good day, Mr. Kier." He melted into the crowd.

Niall leaned his head back and tried to cough up a lung. At least, that was what it felt like. At last, he stopped long enough to climb to his feet. By Odin's eye, he was tired.

He heard his name.

"Niall? Niall?"

It was Kara. She sounded frantic. He tried to call, but it only started him coughing again.

And then she was there. She was still crying. Or crying again? It didn't matter. She threw herself at him, and he held on. She gripped him tight, like she'd never let him go. His legs gave out. Slowly, he slid down the wall, pulling her with him until he was on the ground and she was in his lap. He buried his face in her hair and ignored the rest of the world. Let it all burn, as long as he had her.

Chapter Twenty-Two

I T TOOK ALL evening and into the night to tell all their tales and answer the many questions aimed at them. Once the fire was out, the police had set up a temporary shelter and gathering spot inside the Coles' stable block. Kara cooperated, of course, but she also turned imperious, giving orders and sending out for cold ale and hot soup. She forced them down Niall, trying to ease his irritated throat. Between interviews, she bathed his swollen eyes and kissed his cheeks where the fire had reddened his skin.

Wooten finally found them, and he bore good news. Choate, the Coles' butler, had caught Elias Wade in Frederick Cole's bedroom. He had insisted he was just there to fetch something that his mother had given Cole long ago. Choate did not understand. He might have just driven the young man off, but the commotion on the streets made him suspicious.

"If you want to rob a bank, start a fire," Niall said, his voice still rough.

"I doubt Choate has read *The Art of War*," Wooten said dryly.

"Probably not, but I'm impressed that you have."

"The strategy didn't work, in any case, as Choate locked Wade into the boot room downstairs and sent for the constable."

"Did you see any sign of the children?" Kara asked, and was disappointed when Wooten said that no one had reported seeing them.

"The fact that Elias is Cole's son will come out in the trial," Niall said.

"Exactly the opposite of what Elias wished," Kara said.

"I wonder why Elias wanted to keep it quiet? So much so that he was willing to harm Abbott to keep him from searching out the truth."

"Perhaps he just wanted revenge on Abbott for all of the harm he'd already done to Cole?" Wooten guessed.

"No. Elias wanted to preserve and protect Frederick's memory so far as was possible," she told them. "Frederick convinced Elias that he would be ashamed to claim him as a son."

Niall made a sound of protest.

"It's ugly and awful, but it is true. How many times did we hear that Cole valued spirit and brash independence? Elias was the opposite of that. He was utterly content to stay in the shadows and serve his chosen master. Even more so when he finally wiggled his way into Cole's orbit. He was so convinced that he knew Cole and his true desires that he killed the man rather than allow him to appear weak or defeated in the eyes of the world. He remains convinced that he did the right thing for his father. Having committed such a sin, how much easier would it be to hide his own identity as Cole's son? Or to get a measure of revenge against the man who played such a large part in bringing Frederick Cole low?"

"So, since Cole didn't want it known, he did all he could to protect that secret?" Niall asked. "I suppose he especially wouldn't wish to see Abbott spin it out into a scandal and embarrassment to lay against Frederick's memory."

"He did what he could to prevent it." Kara hardened her tone. "It's not how I would have gone about it, but Elias was right about one thing. Abbott does deserve some punishment for his part in wrecking Frederick's life."

"Well, if Carver is right, Abbott will shortly receive a bit of comeuppance," Wooten reminded them. "According to him, the partnership of Sock and Buskin is strained already and might not last out the month."

"I'm sure that will comfort Elias in his cell at Newgate." Niall rolled his eyes. "And what of West and his part?"

"I think West is suffering," Kara said quietly. "And there is still a scandal to come for him."

After that, she insisted that she be allowed to get Niall back to Bluefield and into a bath. "The steam may help clear his lungs of smoke," she ventured.

John Coachman arrived quickly when summoned. The hour had grown late by now. He'd changed horses, but tried valiantly to stay awake as he waited, dozing off up on his box. Niall tried to praise him for blocking the alley. One of the men in the mule cart had taken off, but the others hadn't wanted to abandon their goods. Wooten's constables had taken them in for questioning. But Niall succumbed to a bout of coughing before he finished thanking the coachman, and Kara hustled him into the carriage.

She had brought along a covered jar of tea laced liberally with honey. She made him sip at it, and he eventually recovered. After his chest had eased, they discussed his rescuer.

"Well, whoever he is, at least he appears to be on your side," Kara said with relief.

"Perhaps now I can give up the dread of being press-ganged." He joked, but she could hear the relief in his voice.

"Did he say when he would come to Bluefield?"

"No. Only that he wanted to call upon both of us." Suddenly, he stiffened at her side. "Stayme! He'll hear about all of this soon enough. Before the papers break the story, of course. I should have gone to let him know I am well."

"He'll know already," Kara said with conviction. "The fact that he didn't show up at Cole's stables demanding to see you is indication that he knew you are fine."

In fact, Stayme was waiting for them at Bluefield. Kara stared at the old man in shock as they made their way inside, supporting each other, and found him waiting in the entry hall.

"Well, you took your time about it," the viscount said irritably. His foot tapped as he looked them over. "Go on, then. You both look a fright. My news will wait until morning." He raised a brow at Kara. "Turner has put me in the plum bedroom overlooking the gardens. I'm too old now to go traipsing back and forth just to see the pair of you. I think you should consider assigning those rooms to me on a more permanent basis, for when I am visiting."

She laughed. "Consider them yours, my lord."

"Thank you, I will."

Still chuckling, she pulled Niall upstairs and turned him over to Turner. She took her own bath and had Elsie, her maid, put her in a worn, comfortable gown instead of a night rail. Then she went to lie in wait for Niall.

"I'm not letting him sleep in the loft tonight," she told Turner. "He needs watching. I almost lost him." Her eyes filled with tears, but she refused to let them fall. "I want him close, where I can see to him, at least for tonight."

Turner, a stickler for the usual proprieties, looked like he might object.

"Open all of the doors leading to my mother's drawing room," she said, forestalling him. "We'll spend the night in there. Anyone can see us from three different accesses, should they care to watch us both sleep."

Niall was too tired to object, so she brought him downstairs and into the room. "I've always loved this wide sofa," she said, pushing him onto it. "Now, scoot over and make room for me."

They slept, wrapped together, all through what was left of the night and deep into the next morning. They were awakened when Harold pushed a cart into the room. "Lord Stayme says you must wake up, for you will have visitors and you need to rise and greet the day," he recited dutifully.

"Do you have hot tea?" Kara asked. "Ah, come here, you darling boy."

"Cook and I made you hand pies for breakfast. Apple and

berry."

Niall stretched and sat up, only coughing a little. "Does Maisie know you are baking pies with Cook?"

Harold grinned. "Yes, but she says if I tell Cook how she makes her crusts, she will beat me with her rolling pin."

After they ate, Kara went upstairs to dress for the day, pleased that Niall's voice had improved and he reported less irritation in his throat. Elsie was just finishing her hair when her bedroom door opened.

"Josie!" she cried, seeing her friend in the mirror. "Gyda!"

Josie rushed to fall all over her. "Oh, Kara! I heard everything! I had to come straight away. Are you well? And dear Niall?"

"We are all well. And you are set free."

"And she came out of it smelling of roses," Gyda said with a grin.

"You will never guess." Josie clapped her hands. "Sergeant Landover did an interview with the *Times*. He told them how helpful I was and how valuable my information was in solving Frederick's murder."

"Well, I am sure that such publicity will do both you and Sergeant Landover a deal of good," Kara said.

"West is thrilled. He says people will flock to the club to see me."

"And they will come again and again, once they hear you." Kara stood. "Come. Let's go down and share your news."

Josie exclaimed over Niall, crying a little as she saw the damage the smoke had done. "Oh, Mr. Kier. I am so sorry. I had no idea the situation would become so fraught with danger."

"You risked quite as much for me," he reminded her.

"That's what I said," Gyda said. "But Stayme shushed me."

Despite the levity, Niall tired quickly. When Josie left, he napped while Kara cornered Stayme. "What do you know that we don't?" she asked as they took a stroll in the quiet of the winter gardens.

"Nothing very concrete, but I have suspicions." Stayme

watched her with a twinkle in his eye. "I think we will hear something soon, so I do not think I will ruin the surprise."

She relented. "But only because you and Niall both seem to have lost all the dread that was making him so anxious."

"He was anxious over you, my dear, more than himself."

She thought of what he'd done yesterday. "I know," she whispered.

They spent the rest of the day resting, eating, and filling everyone in on what they had missed. After dinner, Stayme retired with a shrug. "Your mysterious friend will show up when he is ready, I suppose."

As dark settled in, Niall came to Kara carrying two thick blankets. "I'd like to sit on the terrace, if you'll come with me."

"Of course."

"I want to breathe in the cold night air, though it makes my chest ache a little. And look at the stars."

They huddled together, just enjoying the night sky and the quiet peace of the dark. After a while, Niall gave her a nudge. "Kara."

"Yes?"

He nodded toward the edge of the terrace where a figure stood in the shadows.

"Please," Niall said politely. "Will you come and have a seat?"

"I was hoping the pair of you would come for a walk, perhaps to your forge?" It was indeed the gentleman with the bulbous nose. "I would prefer to speak to the two of you privately."

Exchanging a glance, they rose to step out into the grounds. Kara kept her blanket and carried Niall's. When they reached the forge, Niall unlocked it and set about lighting lanterns, while she moved seats together. Draping the blanket over Niall's shoulders, she sat, and the men took their seats as well.

The gentleman cleared his throat. "I am an...assistant, of sorts, to the royal family."

Kara raised a brow.

"They have received reports, from several sources, about

what happened between you and Petra Scot and her disastrous League of Dissolution. The family were all happy to find that most of the reports were very complimentary of you."

"Most?" Kara said indignantly. "*Most?*"

"Your defense of your betrothed is heartening, Miss Levett. I can tell you that your apparent devotion to Mr. Kier has helped reconcile certain parties to your involvement in his life."

Annoyance burned in her chest. She would bet that "certain parties" wore black every day and a crown to the necessary occasions.

"Maria Fitzherbert, your grandmother, endured a great deal in her lifetime. It didn't go unnoticed. Not everyone in the family disapproved of her as a person."

"Just as a Catholic," Niall said.

"And as a person entering into a royal marriage without the king's consent," the gentleman reminded him. "Still, she had sympathizers among the royals. King William IV was one of them. He wanted to make some sort of amends to her. In 1830, he invited her to the Royal Pavilion in Brighton. He offered her the title of duchess."

Kara gaped.

"She declined," Niall said.

"You knew of it?" the gentleman asked.

"Yes. I also knew that after that meeting, her servants all wore royal livery."

"So they did." The gentleman hesitated. "How did you know?"

"King William gave her copies of the papers, certificates—everything she needed to claim the title of Duchess of Sedwick. I have them, along with the lockets that you also surely know of, after all of those reports."

"Ah, we wondered if you were in possession of the papers." The gentleman sat back. "And yet you never claimed the title."

"No."

"Why not?"

Niall laughed. "It has been pressed upon me since I was a raw lad that I must keep the secret of my birth at all costs. Proclaiming myself as a duke of the realm would hardly have accomplished that."

"Yet most men would have made the gamble and reached for the title."

"Niall Kier is not 'most men,'" Kara said acidly.

"I know that now. It was part of my assignment to discover that, actually. To uncover what sort of man you really are. I am happy to say that I've been able to give a glowing report. Her Majesty is very pleased with you, sir." He leaned forward. "She invites you to take up your title at this time."

"What?" Kara gasped in horror. "No!"

She turned to find an expression of satisfaction and pleasure fading from Niall's face. "What is it, Kara?"

She grasped blindly for something to say. "The scandal! You know how they hate any hint of it touching the royal family. You might quickly lose favor after your history is spread through the papers. Where would you be then?"

The gentleman spoke carefully. "Her Majesty knows there will be talk and excitement. She believes the story can be told, emphasizing all the favorable themes. Love abandoned for duty. Enduring affection. And, of course, Mr. Kier's heroism."

Kara scoffed. "It sounds to me like something is coming down the pipeline at them. They likely want to cover their own scandal by dragging out yours. And how generous they will look, won't they, gifting you something you apparently already possess?"

Niall stood and shrugged off the blanket. Coming over, he knelt before her. "What is bothering you, my love?"

Tears welled. "A duke? How could you have known all this time and not told me?"

"I never meant to pursue it. Honestly, I've never let myself think of it, or allowed it to matter to me. Kara," he said gently. "Why does it matter so to you?"

She bit her lip, but it all spilled out anyway. "You'll be expected to become a part of Society. You've never been in their world, Niall. It's dull, dry, dusty, and confining. Many of their rules are ridiculous, but they are all absolute. I found my way out. I set myself free. I don't want to go back."

He nodded. "I see." He heaved a sigh. "I never worried about that title. It has always been just a few papers in a box. But now that the opportunity is in front of me, all I can think of is that there are benefits to such a status. Safety, Kara. I would never have to worry about leaving you bereft. I could keep our makeshift family safe. It would be so much easier to protect you from Petra Scot, were she to show up again."

"No, you would be occupied and worried about being embarrassed by your wife." She hung her head. "I do not think like them or behave like them. I don't fit in. I never did. It will be worse now that I've tasted freedom." She blinked back tears again. "I'm not suitable to be a duchess."

"You are perfectly, wonderfully suited to be *my* duchess," Niall insisted. "They've been investigating us. They must surely have considered my connection to you before they made the offer."

He glanced over at the gentleman, who gave a nod.

"There. You see? They have given their approval. If we turn out to be unconventional sorts of peers, they will have to adjust to us."

"Turning down such a mark of favor will not be well received." The gentleman made a face. "It would not go well for you."

"You truly wish this?" she asked Niall. "What of your art?"

"No doubt a duke's income will leave room for a forge to be built, wherever he spends his time."

"You will have duties. Estate business. Tenants."

"You have all that now, and your family businesses, yet you make time for your art."

"Political obligations."

Niall grinned. "They may have to adjust to me in that arena

as well." He took her hands. "When we pledged ourselves to one another, we said we would build our own world. And we've made such a beginning. All this means is that our world will be slightly bigger than we anticipated."

She stared at him, unable to dispel the deep misgivings inside her. But he'd saved her yesterday. He'd been willing to die while she lived. She loved him, so deeply. She could never give him up, not even if he dragged her to court and she had to act like a weak, insipid lady with no skills or opinions.

Swallowing, she nodded. "Very well, then."

"Thank you," he whispered.

"I love you," she whispered back, and tried to ignore the foreboding that hovered over her.

AUTHOR'S NOTE

The British music hall was a cultural phenomenon. A blend of social changes made it possible, including the emergence of a new working class after the Industrial Revolution and their desire for affordable entertainment.

Interestingly, the roots of the music halls started back in the coffee houses that were so popular across London and Europe, places where gentlemen could have a beverage or a meal while they talked business. Some coffee houses began to add entertainment to the mix, sometimes dedicating a room to musical performances.

The taverns picked up the idea. By the 1830s, many taverns had rooms devoted to "free and easies," or nights where both amateur and professional entertainers put on performances. They started as a weekend entertainment, but grew so popular that many pubs added musical nights two or three times a week. Also during this time, song and supper rooms emerged, where hot food and entertainment through the evening and into the late night served a more middle-class clientele.

By the 1850s, the music hall theaters began to appear. These were larger, grander places dedicated to providing a larger variety of acts to be enjoyed while the audience enjoyed eating, drinking, and smoking at tables and in galleries.

It was a very different experience from the formal theater evenings that had come before. It was more affordable entertainment in a more relaxed atmosphere. The acts included singing, dancing, comedy singers, mentalists, and acrobats. The experience was rowdy, often fun, but could also be chaotic. If the audience didn't like the act, they could get unruly. There was heckling, booing, and sometimes throwing objects at the stage.

Unlike in the older coffee houses and supper clubs, women were allowed to join in. They sometimes brought their babies with them, for lack of childcare, or sometimes just because it was warm inside the theater, as a ticket to the music hall could be cheaper than an evening's scuttle of coal. Some owners encouraged women to attend because they felt they had a calming influence on the men.

Stars were indeed born on those stages. The audiences had favorites, and they would learn a singer's repertoire and sing along. In the early days of the halls, popular performers could book three or four theaters a night, performing at one spot, then racing back and forth across the city all night to reach the others.

I based my Rogue's Hideaway on descriptions of a combination of several of the most popular music halls, including the Eagle in the East End and the Canterbury Hall in Lambeth. I had a grand time researching some of the famous acts of the time to inspire the entertainments at Frederick Cole's memorial.

ACKNOWLEDGMENTS

I am incredibly grateful to Kathryn Le Veque for giving Kara and Niall a publishing home. The support that Dragonblade has given the series is so appreciated. Many thanks to Arran McNicol for his wisdom, as well as to Shawn Morrison, Evelyn Adams, and Natalie Sowa for their cheerful help and support. Enormous thanks to Kim Killion for such lovely covers that capture Kara's spirit so well. Much appreciation to Tantor Audio for taking the Kier and Levett Mysteries to audio, and to Henrietta Meire for her wonderful narrations.

There are not enough thanks in the world for my Valiant Husband and the support he gives me. I'm sorry you have to endure the "end of book" phase, but I love that you can tell when it hits. Much love to my boys for believing that having an author for a mom is cool and enduring the teasing from their friends with wit and panache. Vast amounts of appreciation to my new Darling Daughter for sharing her amazing artistic skills and vision. Apologies to my mom for preferring writing to shopping!

Here I am once again, being grateful to all of my friends for being there. Thanks to Sabrina Jeffries, for being a great critique partner, finding all of those typos and for many research discussions. To Ava Stone and Tammy Falkner and Caren Crane for reading and encouraging, for sharing lives and books and for so much laughter. To Becky Fox Timblin for being the World's Greatest Assistant and Listening Ear. To Jerrica Knight-Catania and Jane Charles for enduring my snark and sharing their own.

To Nicole Locke and Annabelle Anders for being travel buddies and for write-in-silence days. To the Hermits for accepting me as one of their own.

Special thanks to Ava Stone and her Pilot for being friends who are family and for a million jokes that no one else would find funny.

Daily appreciation to the Debutantes, my VIP Reader Group, for being there every day and enduring my silliness.

And endless thanks to the readers who take the time to tell me of their enjoyment of the series and their connection to the characters. You make it easy to keep writing!

ABOUT THE AUTHOR

USA Today Bestselling author Deb Marlowe grew up with her nose in a book. Luckily, she'd read enough romances to recognize the hero she met at a college Halloween party – even though he wore a tuxedo t-shirt instead of breeches and boots. They married, settled in North Carolina and raised two handsome, funny and genuinely intelligent boys.

The author of over twenty-five historical romances, Deb is a Golden Heart Winner, a Rita Finalist and her books have won or been a finalist in the Golden Quill, the Holt Medallion, the Maggie, the Write Touch Reader Awards and the Daphne du Maurier Award.

A proud geek, history buff and story addict, she loves to talk with readers! Find her discussing books, period dramas and her infamous Men in Boots on Facebook, Twitter and Instagram. Watch her making historical recipes in her modern kitchen at Deb Marlowe's Regency Kitchen, a set of completely amateur videos on her website. While there, find out Behind the Book details and interesting Historical Tidbits and enter her monthly contest at deb@debmarlowe.com.

Milton Keynes UK
Ingram Content Group UK Ltd.
UKHW050430280324
440101UK00016B/1017